Amazing Grayson

M.E. CARTER

First Edition: July 2018
Library of Congress Cataloging-in-Publication Data
Amazing Grayson – 1st ed
ISBN-13: 978-1-948852-10-4

To my "Oli".
The teenage years are hard on everyone. These will probably be the hardest you'll ever have in your life. But we'll get through it, without actually killing each other. Because I believe in you. And you can do amazing things.

Amazing Grayson

THE BEGINNING

Chapter One

Greer

Inhaling a deep breath through my nose, I recognize the smell of those organic cleaning products I order online, fresh paint—which probably offsets the organic cleaners, but I'll get over it—and faintly of cardboard boxes. It smells like home.

Never, in my wildest dreams, did I think I was going to move to Flinton, Texas. I've resisted for years, mostly because the entire process sounded daunting. But life changes. Circumstances change. Now here I am, standing in my new house, everything already moved in, thanks to my brother, Jack, and his new girlfriend, Joie.

I'd never admit it to Jack because he worries enough as it is, but I feel a sense of peace I haven't had in a really long time. The last several years have been rough.

When the kids were still little, I filed for divorce from my ex-husband after I found out he was stealing money from our son's medical account. A few weeks later, the feds showed up at our door to arrest him. Over the next few months, he was tried and convicted of misuse of funds at his job where he was in line to be the next chief financial officer. Something about skimming funds off the top of people's accounts. I didn't really understand all of it, being that there were pages upon pages of mathematical data as proof. Basically, it boiled down to a whole lot of theft. Luckily for the company, it was caught before Neil could take over as CFO and do more damage.

*Un*luckily for me, however, part of the investigation looked into all of our tax returns. Turns out, he was falsifying those as well.

At first, fingers were pointed at me too, which was incredibly stressful. Very quickly they realized I had no idea this was going on behind my back. It wasn't that I didn't pay attention; I'm just not a numbers girl. I'm a word girl. Upper level math makes no sense to me, taxes practically making me itch, and he had a master's degree in business and accounting. I never thought twice about him taking on that task during our ten-year marriage. Until he was arrested, that is.

Because of his crimes, everything was confiscated—our home, all the bank accounts, his 401K. Everything. Fortunately for me, my parents left a sizeable inheritance when they died a few years before the whole fiasco started. It legally couldn't be touched in the seize, and that's the only reason the kids and I were able to start fresh without worrying where we would live.

I'm not happy about how I got the money. I would give it all back for my parents to be here with us, but I am grateful they had a good financial planner who knew exactly what to do when they died.

I still need to work to make ends meet. There are still utilities and medications and other life necessities, but at least I was able to pay for our home outright. That takes a lot of the pressure off. And having a special needs teenager, it's not like I can get a regular eight-to-five job. He has to be supervised at all times, and at seventeen years old, no daycare in the world will take him in.

Oliver is a great kid, don't get me wrong. He's kind and loving and funny. But there were issues when he was born. His umbilical cord was wrapped around his neck twice, forcing an emergency C-section. After we brought him home, everything seemed normal. He was a happy baby, and I loved being a mom. We trudged through the toddler years like everyone else and believed our sweet boy had come through his traumatic birth unscathed. But at about six years old, things started to change. He stopped maturing emotionally and became more defiant. Things stopped "clicking" for him, when they continued to click for the other kids.

We've done multiple batteries of tests, all of which have been inconclusive, with the exception of confirmation he suffered a certain level of brain damage, likely linked back to oxygen deprivation at birth.

All that being said, every day is a struggle when your child has the emotional maturity of an eight-year-old, with the impulse control to match, while living in the body of a hormonal seventeen-year-old. It can get rough. That's one of the reasons I'm glad we're finally in Flinton near family.

Julie, on the other hand, my fifteen-year-old daughter, is a stereotypical teenager in every sense of the word. Well, maybe not totally stereotypical. She has a special needs brother and a dad in prison. She's not normal at all.

But what she is, is relatively easy. Compliant. Mild-mannered. She doesn't like going to parties. She has a very small social circle, just a couple close friends. She loves trying new activities and being involved, but she doesn't strive to be the best at them, just enjoys the participation and knowing lots of things about lots of things. It's one of the characteristics I love about her. She has a thirst for knowledge.

I know I shouldn't rely on how steady she is because she's my child and I'm the mother, but with all the other chaos that goes on around us, it's nice having a low maintenance child. We can sit in the same room together and just *be*, without worrying about the other one having some sort of outburst.

Don't get me wrong. I don't consider myself her friend at this stage in our lives. I'm her mother. My job is to guide her, even when she hates me for it. But in a situation like ours, I imagine it's more of a unique kind of bond than in homes with greater stability. We rely on each other differently than most. It's either going to help us get through the tumultuous years, or I'll never see her again after she leaves for college. It remains to be seen which direction she goes. Especially now that we've moved.

We haven't had the opportunity to rest much lately. Between packing up our lives in Kansas, driving a moving truck down here while towing my car, which was an adventure in and of itself, and getting everyone enrolled in school, it's been a whirlwind. At this point, at least, everyone seems to be adjusting well.

In fact, while both kids are at school and things are calm, I better check in with my client.

Sitting at my new desk in the open dining-room-turned-office, I grab my cell and get comfortable. I've always dreamed of having a home office with custom bookshelves around the room, and this area was perfect. Because it's technically a formal dining room, I can see right into the living areas and keep an eye on things while I work. As soon as I claimed it for my office, I had bookshelves installed. Every time I sit in my chair and see the finished product, it makes me smile. As a freelance book editor, sometimes my clients will send me the finished product in paperback form, all pretty and usually signed. They finally, *finally* have a place to be displayed proudly, and it gives me a sense of accomplishment whenever I look up. I need that. It reminds me my hard work is worth it.

I always wanted to work in a publishing house, and I did for a while when I first got married. But once Oli's issues began to surface, there was no way for me to work. It's impossible to hold down a job when you have to be on-call and available to go to your child's school on a moment's notice if he's having a meltdown. It happens more frequently than any job would accommodate for. Not to mention summer break when there is no reprieve at all.

Thankfully, that was around the time the self-publishing world took off and many of my financial issues were solved. Or at least helped. I got a few jobs with indie authors who didn't want to spend years trying to get a publishing deal. They did it themselves, and I helped. Slowly but surely, I built a good reputation and gained new clients. And here I am, several years later, with a fairly successful business and clients who book several months out.

My first client, Aggie, known to the world as Adeline Snow, was one of the first indie authors to hit the New York Times Best Seller list. She was almost immediately picked up by a publisher and technically doesn't need me to do most of her editing anymore. But she's a perfectionist and wants each manuscript to be as clean as possible before sending to her official editor. Enter me. A super beta, a content editor, her biggest supporter. However you want to spin it, I'm still part of her team and get to work on her books first.

Plus, we've had a relationship for so long, we've become friends.

It only takes a couple of rings before she picks up the phone. "How did you know I was suffering from a horrific case of writer's block? Do you have super powers?"

I chuckle under my breath. "Are you at the bookstore?"

"How did you know that?"

"Are you staring at a cardboard cut-out of Spencer?"

"No, really, are you stalking me? Where are you? You're hiding behind one of the bookshelves, aren't you?"

This time I laugh out loud. "What if I told you I was standing right behind Spencer's cardboard body, staring at you though the holes in his eyes?"

"I'd tell you that was the creepiest thing you've ever said, and I may have to end this friendship."

I gasp. "You wouldn't dare."

"No, I wouldn't dare. But I really hope you're not here because that would be weird, and I refuse to be involved if you get arrested for loitering."

"Well, you can relax, my friend. I am not stalking you. I'm sitting in my new office chair in my new office in my new house." I swivel the chair, punctuating my point, even though she can't see it.

"Oooh! That sounds amazing! Did you get all your books unpacked?" I knew that was coming. Getting the bookshelf set up is every author's priority in a move.

"Sadly, I think I may not have enough shelving. I might

need to get another custom one made."

"Those are the single greatest words you have ever said to me."

"I knew you'd appreciate it." And I do. She might be a best-selling author, but she's a reader first and foremost.

"Seriously. I think I may have just had a Big O right in this bookstore."

Now the red flags go up. "You are making inappropriate comments in public. Exactly how bad is this block? If you drop the F-bomb, I'm flying out there to put you on a 5150-Hold at the local psych ward."

"Please don't," she groans. "I hear Courtney Love might be back in there, and she frightens me. I don't want to be her bitch."

My eyes widen. "Oh my. This is bad."

"I don't know what to do, Greer. I'm really stuck this time."

Shifting out of friend mode and into work mode, I put on my encourager cap. "First of all, it's a psych ward, not a prison. No one will make you their bitch."

"You've never been there. You don't know that for sure."

"Second," I interrupt, ignoring her theatrics, "you say that every time, Adeline, and you're never actually stuck. You only need a little bit of motivation."

"Which is why I'm here. I'm getting my motivation."

"Why don't you buy your own cardboard cut-out of Spencer for your house?"

"Because that would be creepy."

I quirk an eyebrow she can't see. "No creepier than sitting in a public store staring at it from across the room."

What sounds like a thump, vibrates through the speaker. I

assume it's her head hitting the table in defeat. "I don't know what to do, Greer."

"Well, let's sort this out," I say as I spin my favorite gel pen around my fingers. Which reminds me, I need to find the nearest office supply store. Pens, Post-it Notes, corkboards—they're my weakness. It's the one thing I miss about working in an actual office. It was like Christmas every time there was a delivery. "What do you have so far?"

"He's a surfer."

"Ooooh, surfing this time. I like it. You haven't done that one yet. What else?"

"That's it. It's all I have. He's a surfer."

The pen freezes in my hand. "Adeline."

"Yes," she says sheepishly.

"Honey, you do know you're supposed to have thirty thousand words to me in the next month."

"I know." Another thud. "I've never been blocked this badly before. I don't know what's going on. I'm looking at my muse—right at him. Oh crap. I just got caught looking at my muse."

A laugh bursts out of me.

"This isn't funny. I can't seem to get any inspiration, and I certainly can't do it when I keep getting caught trying to find it."

"Maybe you need to find a new muse."

The sound of a shrill gasp crosses the line. "You take that back," she whispers harshly, making me laugh.

"Okay, okay, fine," I respond, still chuckling. "Spencer is your muse. He will always be your muse. Why not take it a step further?"

She gasps again. "I can't write about what he actually

does!"

This is what I love about Adeline Snow. She's quirky, odd, and a bit socially awkward. Known for creating heroes who are extreme sports gurus, she has cornered the market of Sports Romance. Yet, she refuses to touch skateboarding simply because she never wants anyone to find out all her books are inspired by Spencer Garrison, professional skateboarder, unknown muse and author of a new autobiography, which is why his cardboard form is sitting in a book store.

I don't know how she does it. How she makes different stories about different sports all because of one guy. It's a talent. Spencer is a super hero in her eyes, and she can make him be anything she wants him to be.

Hopefully, their paths will never cross. I'm not sure she'd ever recover if she found out he's actually human.

"Well, what about making the heroine a single mom?" I toss out, beginning our back and forth brainstorming.

"Ugh. It's been done."

"What if she's older?"

"Like a cougar story?"

"Yeah. Why not?"

"I'm just not feeling it."

"How about a secret baby?"

"Wait." I can practically hear the gears turning in her head. "Like he left town to pursue his dream of being a pro surfer, and on his way across country, he has a one-night stand and doesn't know he has a child until she finally tracks him down?"

"Oh, Adeline that sounds great."

"Eh. Too cliché."

I smack my hand to my forehead. "You really are

blocked."

"I am, Greer. I so am," she says with a heavy sigh. "Maybe I need to go on this promotional tour and meet some people to inspire me. You know how much wandering around new cities and taking pictures helps open up my brain to creativity."

"That'll probably help."

We chat for a few more minutes about her work-not-actually-in-progress as well as a few more administrative things before I hear the front door open. Julie walks around the corner and waves at me, knowing better than to interrupt a phone call while her brother isn't home. Uninterrupted time is a commodity around here.

"Hey, Adi, I need to let you go. Kids are getting out of school, and I need to get into mom mode. They've only been in school for a week so we're trying to get this new routine down."

Poor Adeline. She knows my home life situation and is always accommodating. She doesn't know how much it makes things easier on me, but really does.

"All right, well, wish me luck." I know she really means it.

"Good luck. But, Adi, you've got this. I know you do."

"Thanks. And hey, Greer?" She stops me right before I hang up.

"Yeah?"

"You got this too. This move is the best thing for you."

My whole body relaxes at her words.

"Thanks, Adeline. I think we're finally where we're supposed to be."

And I do. Something in my gut is telling me this is it. This is the last place I'm going to live, and I'm perfectly okay with that.

We get off the phone right as the bus pulls up. Time to take over afternoon duties. That means switching from career woman mode into mom mode. Not that Adeline and I are all that professional when she's in a mood like today's. Still, the kids come first.

Opening the door, Oli ambles up the walkway and into the house.

"Hey, buddy. How was school?"

"Good," he says vaguely. Oli has a hard time coming up with intricate answers to questions. There's no asking how his day was and getting an explanation of an assignment he didn't like or a funny conversation. His standard answers are either "good" or "bad," which still isn't all that accurate. But I'll take this one to mean nothing overly upsetting happened. It's a small win, but I'll take it.

Unsurprisingly, he heads straight for the pantry. Oli may have his own issues, but his appetite is right on track for a seventeen-year-old boy.

"What was good about it?" I try to pull more information out of him. It's good practice for his social skills.

"Nothing."

Okay. It wasn't as good as I'd hoped, but I'm actually not surprised. We do this conversation song and dance almost every day. Then we argue over peanut butter, like we're about to again. I brace myself and hope he's in a good enough mood that we can practice some sandwich-making skills this afternoon.

"Oli, that's too much peanut butter. Remember we talked about how to spread it across the bread?" I ask gently, trying to sound encouraging and not nagging.

He grabs a jar of honey and begins squeezing it on the other slice of bread, completely ignoring me.

"And that's too much honey."

I snatch it out of his hands so he'll stop making a pool of liquid sugar, and he yells, "Hey! I was using that!"

"Oliver," I say sternly, "you are ignoring me. You need to spread the peanut butter and not use that much honey. That much sugar isn't good for you."

"Yes, it is," he says, smashing the two pieces of bread together and taking a giant bite. I'm almost positive he didn't get a hint of protein in that morsel since the peanut butter is still a lump in the center of the sandwich.

"No, it's not. And I'm not going to argue with you about it. If you won't use the right portions, you won't be allowed to make your own sandwiches."

He rolls his eyes, another normal teenage thing to do. "Why do I have to learn that anyway? That's stupid."

"It's part of being an adult. Knowing how to eat good portion sizes will help keep you healthy."

"I don't want to be healthy."

Our conversation is beginning to spiral, and I know if I don't change topics, it could be leading to a meltdown. So, I close the jar and the bread bag and hope to transition to something less volatile.

Who knew Jiffy could cause so much drama?

"Are you excited to work at the farm tomorrow?"

"No."

His answer surprises me. It's all he's been talking about all week. His new school offers a co-op opportunity for the special education kids where they go out to a local farm and work. It's a great opportunity, and we were lucky to get him in. Not everyone is accepted into the program. I hope this attitude doesn't transcend over to tomorrow. I'd hate for it to ruin his first day.

"How come?"

He takes a giant bite of his food before answering, "I don't like riding the bus."

Putting the food back in my new giant pantry, which may be my favorite part of the house, I purse my lips at him. "Since when? You love riding the bus."

"Huh uh," he argues. "I don't like when the other kids sneeze."

I lean my forearms against the counter, trying to figure out what he's talking about. "People sneeze all the time. Why does it bother you now?"

"Cause this girl sits behind me, and she sneezes and gets germs all on the back of my head."

A lightbulb goes off in my brain. Oli isn't usually obsessed with germs, but I can see why he would be grossed out by someone sneezing on him. I would be too.

"Have you told your bus driver about it?"

"No. Can I have my tablet?" The subject change is immediate, but not exactly surprising.

"You know you can't have it until seven o'clock."

Hands clenched together, he stomps his foot on the floor and yells. "That's not fair! It's my tablet, not yours!"

Aaaaannnnnd, here we go.

"It *is* fair. The rule is you have to do your chores first, and at seven, we'll talk about how much tablet time you've earned."

Pressing his lips in a hard line, he squeezes his eyes shut

and brings his fists to his forehead. If I wasn't used to it, the mood change would be jarring. It's almost sad that, because this is our normal now, it doesn't faze me.

Finally, after taking a few seconds to try and calm down, Oli tries a different tactic. "Mom, I had a hard day. I'm tired. I want my tablet time now."

"No, Oliver, don't ask me again."

Out of the corner of my eye, I see Julie walk in the room just as Oli gets more enraged. He bellows out in frustration, making Julie turn on her heel and head to her room. I hate that she doesn't even flinch when these outbursts happen. And I hate that I have to go talk to our new neighbors and let them know they don't need to call the cops.

No domestic violence here. Just a boy stuck in a man's body and all the frustrations that go with it.

"I hate you!" he screams at me. "You're the worst mom ever!"

I blow out a breath as he stomps off, grateful when his bedroom door slams shut. At least he didn't break anything on his way out of the room this time.

Deep breath in.

It still smells like cleaning products and paint and cardboard boxes. It's the smell of a new beginning to our lives. I'll take all the baby steps I can get.

Chapter Two

Ace

"Whew!" Pedro exclaims next to me, as we watch the black mare unload off the trailer in front of us. "She is a beaut, isn't she?"

I cock my eyebrow at him like he's insane, which quite possibly he is. The horse I see in front of me is haggard, has scars all over her body, probably from previous abuse, and she's still a little on the skinny side. Granted, she's a rescue, and we knew she wouldn't be in the best of shape, but somehow Pedro sees something I don't.

"Are we observing the same horse?"

"Aw, come on, Ace." He kicks up his leg, resting his boot on the wooden picket fence in front of us. "She just needs a chance. I'm telling you, she is gonna be a great riding horse once I build her trust. Maybe she'll even be good at rounding up the cattle."

The words no more than come out of his mouth before she rears up, causing the farmhand who's guiding her off the trailer to hang on to the rope for dear life, as he's lifted two feet off the ground.

I turn my head to watch Pedro, wondering if he's changed his mind.

"So, we've got some kinks to work out," he remarks before I can say anything. "But this is what we do here, right? Take the ones that have kinks, smooth them out, and help them find their best potential."

He knows I can't rebut that, because he's right.

All Hands Farm began as a dairy farm, and that's still our main function. With over three hundred Holstein cows, we provide milk not only to the local grocery stores in the area, but we're in the process of expanding to more states. It's a business that has been in my family for generations.

Shortly before my mom passed, though, she and I came up with a plan to expand even further. That includes the other side of the farm—the special needs co-op program.

For the last decade, we've been working with a couple local schools, specifically their special education department. The high school busses some of the higher functioning special needs students out here to give them some fresh air and a little bit of exercise. In the process, we teach them job skills varying from minor construction to lawn maintenance. Several work in the calf barn doing feedings and cleaning. I even had a couple kids learn how to use all of the equipment to milk the cows and were later hired on after graduation. It's turned into a win/win for everyone.

And I know from first-hand experience, having had a brother with disabilities, being around and interacting with the animals can make a huge difference. There's nothing like the nuzzle of a good horse to calm someone's impulsive behaviors.

The program has worked out great, to the point where at least a couple times a year, people from the Texas Education Agency come out to see how we operate and if there is a way to duplicate it in other parts of the state. As far as I know, they've never been able to, but at least we give them a good start.

It also means I don't have a good argument against Pedro bringing a wild mare into our midst. Especially since he purchased her with his own money, on his own time, and is going to be the one responsible for her care.

"I know I agreed to this," I say without so much as a glance at him, still watching the horse with a wary eye, "but you better make damn sure everyone on this farm knows no one is to get on her except you. You are it, my man. She's your horse. She's your responsibility. She's your liability. I'm not gonna have this place shut down because of your wild card."

He claps me on the back with a wide grin on his face. "No worries, man. I got this. You know me better than that."

I make a "hmfph" sound because I know full well if anyone can break her and get her under control, it's Pedro.

Pedro and I grew up together. This farm has been in my family for three generations. When my dad inherited from my grandfather, Pedro's dad was his number one farmhand. From the time we were practically toddlers, Juan was bringing Pedro to play with me and help out with basic chores. He and I, being the same age, of course became best friends, spending our mornings learning how to feed baby calves and muck stalls and the afternoons swimming in the lake, catching frogs.

We went to the same high school. Played in the same

sports. Admired the same pretty girls. He was more like a brother than a friend.

Even this many years later, that bond has never left. He's one of the people I trust most in the world. When my dad suddenly died of a massive heart attack in the west field, Pedro was the one who broke the news to me and picked me up at the airport when I flew home. And when I took over at the farm, Pedro was with me every step of the way—helping me get all the clients squared away, making sure we knew how to do the books, and hiring someone to run the office. It was a natural progression for him to move into the position of farm manager and my right-hand man when Juan retired. We've been a team for so long, there is no one I trust more. Not with my business nor with my life.

Except when it comes to this. This horse has a history of being unpredictable and potentially dangerous. Based on her skittish behavior, I have huge reservations about her ability to thrive around people, let alone be ridden safely. But there's no stopping Pedro from trying. That doesn't mean I don't think he's crazy for it.

I hear the bus pulling up behind us and turn to greet our co-op kids. Waving at the program coordinator, Mrs. Johnson, who doubles as the bus driver, I see mostly familiar faces getting off the bus.

"Hey, Mr. Ace."

"Hey, Donnie," I say to one of our regulars as he high-fives me on the way to the barn to start feeding our small collection of chickens and barn cats. I love working with these kids. It's nice to see them flourish and grow, and seeing the delight on their faces makes it all worth it.

Unfortunately, some of the delight is directed at Pedro's

new project, who is still whinnying and stomping in displeasure.

All of a sudden, a new face in the bunch takes off running away from the rest.

"Oli!" Mrs. Johnson yells after him. "Oliver Declan, stop!"

He doesn't listen, so I go immediately into "bouncer" mode. "Oliver Declan, stop right now," I yell, and he does. Somehow the deep timbre of my voice makes an effective tool when it comes to getting kids to obey.

"Must be the new kid," Pedro says unnecessarily since neither of us have seen him before.

Walking toward the teen, I do a quick assessment. It always helps to make a few pre-judgements on the kinds of issues we could be dealing with. Because of all the privacy laws, I'm not allowed to get a lot of initial information on the disabilities and needs the kids have. I have enough to make sure they're safe, but a lot of times I'm forced to wing it for a while. Once the parents come to visit and take a tour, they usually give me more insight and ideas.

Until then, I must go with what Mrs. Johnson is allowed to tell me and my gut instincts. For instance, this particular boy doesn't have any outward physical deformities. He also doesn't have any distinct facial features like my brother had, so I can safely rule out Down's Syndrome. He doesn't seem to be avoiding eye contact either. If he's on the autism spectrum, he must be pretty high functioning. However, he's a little on the heavy side and lumbers rather than walks. Maybe muscle tone issues?

No matter what his official diagnoses are, he has a huge smile on his face. That's a good sign.

"Morning. I take it you're Oliver?"

"Don't call me Oliver." His voice is monotone but not angry. Just factual. "My name is Oli."

"Hi, Oli. I'm Ace." I reach out my hand and sure enough, he takes it and shakes it tightly. "Welcome to All Hands Farm. It's your first day, isn't it?"

"Yeah. I like horses."

So far, so good.

"Me too. Have you ever ridden a horse before?"

He shakes his head, still admiring the mare and not paying much attention to me. "No. But I'm gonna be a cowboy someday."

"That sounds great, Oli." I take care not to stand too close and get in his personal space, still not able to pinpoint what kind of reactions he might have. I assume there are some behavioral concerns with him, but that's not unusual for the special ed program. Frustrations can run high when you struggle to communicate or get terribly uncomfortable. "The most important part of being a good cowboy is you have to learn the rules and you have to follow them."

"What kind of rules?" Oli finally regards me, and while his eyes are clear, there is a slight vacancy to them.

"The number one rule is you don't approach any of the animals without permission from either myself, Mrs. Johnson, or my friend Pedro."

Pedro immediately jumps in. "Hey, Oli. Nice to meet you." He puts his hand out to be shaken and Oli complies easily, which has me feeling confident that Mrs. Johnson made a good choice bringing him here.

"Can I pet that horse?" Oli stares right at the mare when he asks.

Shooting Pedro a glare for coordinating a terrible delivery time, I respond, "That horse just got here. You see how she's jumping around and stomping?"

He nods.

"She's still kind of scared, it being her first day and all. So, we're not letting anyone pet her today. We're gonna let her get used to being in a brand-new place."

"Okay." Oli looks over at me again. "Can I pet another horse?"

"You can pet a horse after we get some work done."

His shoulders slump. "Aw man. You're gonna make me work?"

This is more along the lines of what I was expecting. It doesn't matter how many times the kids are told work comes first and hanging out with the animals comes second, it doesn't completely translate until they've been in a routine for a couple weeks. It's a struggle in the beginning, but one that's well worth it after they've learned the ropes. Even better, once they get used to the reward system, the kids almost always start to enjoy the productivity of a job well done.

"Hey Oli, why don't you come with me?" Pedro offers. "I'll give you a tour. Show you where everything is and get you set up at your first job. The sooner you finish your work, the sooner we can pet the animals."

"Okay." Oli doesn't even hesitate, just walks away with Pedro as he points to the normal things he shows on the tour, like where the bathroom and the water fountain are located. We've learned over the years those are the two most important things.

Mrs. Johnson comes to stand next to me as I watch them walk away. "Sorry about that," she apologizes, hands on her hips. "We went over the rules several times, but he was so darn excited to be here. It's been a struggle all day."

"He doesn't seem disabled." I know that sounds awfully ignorant to Mrs. Johnson, especially coming from me. I know just as well as anyone there are some disabilities you can't see. Mental ones most often. But Oli just seems extremely highly functional.

"Oh, you'll see." She smiles sardonically. "He's been doing really well, but his mother told me to warn you once the honeymoon is over, it's on."

"Can you give me any more information than that?"

"Yeah. They recently moved here from Kansas. He's lived in the suburbs all his life. This is his first time out in the country. I can't give you specifics, but he has defiance issues and impulse control problems. We're hoping the animals will help calm him. Mom's considering getting him some sort of an emotional support animal when he's old enough. Figured this program would be a good stepping off point to see if that's an option before spending all that time on paperwork to apply."

I nod. "Smart. Are you going to head back to school or hang out in the main office today?"

"I'm gonna work in the main office, if that's okay with you. I have a lot of paperwork to catch up on. I could go for a quiet place free from distractions."

"I think Jill is having one of her Metallica days. I hope you brought ear plugs." She crinkles her nose in disgust. Mrs. Johnson hates heavy metal, but when the office manager gets here first, she gets to control the music. "Oh, it's not all bad. Brittany found some of that nasty vanilla Coke you like so much. She put a twelve pack in the fridge just for you."

Her eyes light up with delight. "Oh! I may have to work

at the kitchen table with her instead. She spoils me rotten."

"She spoils all of us rotten." And she does. Running all the meals and the main house has been Brittany's job since she and Pedro got married. She's damn good at it.

Mrs. Johnson tells me she'll find me when she's finished, and I head off into the farm, catching up to Pedro and Oli, since the others have already disappeared to their stations. The workday is already half over, but my new project with a smiling, lumbering teenage boy, just began.

Chapter Three

Greer

Stretching my arms over my head, I give my eyes a break from the manuscript I've been working on all day. Maybe that's a bit of an exaggeration. Closer to three hours.

I love being an editor. I set my own hours. I choose my own projects. I get to be part of the creative process behind the scenes. It's literally my dream job.

But so help me, if this client does not learn how to use an Oxford comma, I am liable to tattoo it on her forehead.

The front door clicks shut as I'm rolling my head around to stretch my neck.

"Hey Julie!" I call out.

Her head pops in the doorway. "Are you still working?" she asks, her straight black hair swinging like a curtain over her shoulder. It's ridiculous how much she resembles her father. Tall and lanky. Dark hair. Dark eyes. Dark complexion. People used to always question if I was her biological mother because I'm so fair compared to her. Once they see us sitting side by side reading, the questions go away. Then we're like mirror images of each other.

"Just getting ready to finish up for the day." I relax my stretches and lean back in my chair. "How was school?"

She doesn't respond. I know that look, though. It hasn't been an easy transition for her.

"It's fine." She plops herself down in the extra chair.

"Make any new friends today?" She shakes her head, avoiding eye contact with me as she picks her nails. "Are the kids really that bad?"

She finally glimpses up at me, revealing the crinkle in her brow. "No, it's not that."

When we moved here, I wasn't expecting her to have such a hard time. She's never had a hard time making friends before. It's obvious by her expression I was mistaken.

"It's just… these kids have all grown up together, ya know? They started school together in kindergarten. It's different than where we lived, when new people came in and out all the time. I'm the first new kid they've had in how many years?"

"I don't know. How many years?" I ask, trying to lighten up the mood.

"I haven't actually asked, Mom." I know by her eye roll my playfulness isn't helping the situation, so I give up and stick with validating.

"It'll get better," I tell her.

"I know. It's just… I'm kind of glad to be able to start over where no one knows me. No one knows my story. I'm not the daughter of the most hated man in town anymore. But part of me, wishes I could go back."

"Have you heard from Jamie yet?"

She shrugs half-heartedly, which is discouraging. She and Jamie were inseparable for the last couple of years. They weren't quite boyfriend and girlfriend, but they were more than friends. It's complicated in the world of high school freshmen. But I'm still surprised by her answer.

"I think he's moved on. I guess with me not there every day, he's forgotten about me."

My heart breaks for her and once again, my mom guilt kicks in.

I have never doubted moving here was right for all of us. It got Oli into a great program at All Hands Farm. We were away from the judgmental stares of people who still blame me for my ex-husband's illegal activities. It even gave Julie a fresh start to be someone besides "the daughter of that retched thief." She knows it, and I know it. And while it was the right move for us, it doesn't mean it's an easy transition.

After such a hard conversation, I don't want to switch topics on her, but I don't have much choice.

"We got another letter today."

Julie groans and leans her head back, draping her arm over her eyes. "Why doesn't he just give up already?"

"Because he's your father, and he's never going to give up."

She snaps her head up. "He was a terrible father before he was arrested. Now, what? He has nothing better to do with all his downtime?"

"Julie," I warn.

"I know, I know. He's still the only dad I'll ever have." She rolls her eyes again as she says it, in a move every teenager across America has perfected at some point. This time, I choose to ignore it.

"Right. Don't burn that bridge."

"Mom, I'm not the one who is burning anything. Dad is the one who made it a priority to work instead of coming to any of our activities or being home for dinner. It's been what, six years since Dad moved out of the house so you could get divorced? Do you know I have no memory of him sitting down and having dinner with us? And not just after he was arrested. Ever."

My gut twists at her words. Nobody wants to hear their child has no memories of their father making them a priority. Even if it's painfully obvious what a scumbag he is now.

"The only times I remember him with us was when we went on family trips. And even then, his face was stuck in his phone the whole time."

"I know, honey. I know. But he wants an answer, and I need to give it to him."

She sighs deeply and sits back in her chair again. "And you need me to decide if I'm going to go visit him in prison before presenting any of it to Oli."

I try to smile but my lips don't cooperate. "If you're not going to go, I'm not going to open that can of worms with him. It throws him into too much turmoil," I remind her. "But if you are going to go, I can't keep him from visiting too."

"That's a lot of pressure to put on me, Mom."

"I know. And I don't mean to. I'm not trying to pressure you. It's just what our lives are."

She doesn't begrudge me. I know that. She's just had to grow up faster than most kids.

"You don't have to decide now. And you can reserve the right to change your mind. Always. If you want to say no for now, that's fine. And if you change your mind, let me know. Just don't change your mind if you decide to go, because you know Oli wouldn't handle that well."

She pretends not to be paying attention to me, instead staring at her fingernails again when she weakly says, "I know."

I hate this. I hate that her life continues to be in upheaval all the time. It doesn't matter where we move or how settled we get, there will always be a sense of chaos. Always be a sense of being unsettled. I know it's part of having a special needs child, one who will never not be in your care, but how do I provide enough attention to my "normal" child while taking care of the one who will always need me more? It's a mom guilt battle I fight every day.

Still, I do what I can and while we have this moment, I try to take advantage of it.

"What else happened at school today? Anything exciting?"

"Well, there is one thing." A small smile graces her lips as I nod my head in encouragement. "Since we just moved here, the swim coach is going to let me try out for the team."

I clap my hands together and hold them against my chest. "Oh honey, that's wonderful!"

"I might not make it, though. You know I'm not that fast, and this is a college town. Everyone's chasing a scholarship around here." Despite her reservations, her face is beaming with the new possibilities that have opened up for her.

"You know I don't care about that. I'm proud of you for going out for the team. Do you want me to see if there's a pool around here you can use to practice for a few days?"

Opening my computer, I begin searching gyms in the area

that have pool facilities.

"I probably should," she starts. "I need a little practice with my flip turn, and I need to make sure I don't disqualify myself on my breast stroke entry."

As my fingers click over the keyboard, I narrow down a few gyms within a couple miles of our house. "Do you have a lot of homework tonight? Oli won't be home for another hour or so. Maybe we can head over to one of them and check it out real fast—"

I barely finish my sentence when my phone starts ringing. It's a number I don't recognize, but it's local. That can only mean one thing.

Oli's having a meltdown.

Looking up at Julie, she shakes her head, visibly deflated because she knows too. "It's okay. We can go later."

As she stands up and walks away, I call out, "I'm sorry, Julie. I'll find you a practice gym tomorrow while you're at school."

She doesn't respond, but I know she hears me. She's hurt that she has to be accommodating to her brother again. The problem isn't that we've had to delay setting up practice times. It's that we *always* delay setting things up for her, and there's no way to fix it. When the choice is between one child who is possibly in a dangerous situation and one that needs to go swimming, there's only one option.

Mom guilt in full force again, I pick up the phone before it goes to voicemail. "Hello?"

Bracing myself for what's coming, I pinch the bridge of my nose with my fingers.

"Mrs. Declan?" a female voice says on the other end.

"Speaking."

"This is Mrs. Johnson, one of Oli's teachers. We need you to come to the farm."

Chapter Four

Ace

We've had some stubborn kids come through our program. It's kind of the nature of what we do. We're used to all kinds of behaviors. But even I have to admit, this new kid, Oli, he's as stubborn as they come.

Mrs. Johnson warned me. She said he would honeymoon for a while, but eventually his behaviors would surface. And boy have they. With a vengeance.

He's been here a couple of weeks, and he's done really well. But he's never gotten over his fixation on that new mare. The one I warned Pedro no one could touch except him. But of course, that's the one Oli wants to pet, which we can't allow.

So today, after helping muck a stall and pitching some hay, it was time for the reward part of the day. Petting a horse.

Oli immediately went for the mare and when he was told no, that's when things went south.

"You said when I was done with my work, I could pet that horse." He'd obviously forgotten the details of our conversation.

"No, Oli. We said you could touch *a* horse. Not that one. The black one is off limits. You know this. We've talked about it before."

"You lied to me! You're a liar, liar, pants on fire!"

"Oli, I need you to calm down. You're scaring the animals," I warned. "You don't want them to be afraid of you if you're going to pet them."

That stopped him for a few seconds as he processed my words, but not for long. "I wanna pet the black horse! You promised!" he continued.

"Again, Oli, we told you you could pet a horse, but not that one. She is off limits," I said patiently. As much as he was trying to push my buttons, it wasn't working. "Your choices are to calm down and go pet a different animal, or you don't get to pet any of them."

That was it. As soon as I laid it on the line, Oli went into a rage.

Now, rage is a relative term. I've seen way worse. But it sure wasn't fun watching one my stools and my brand-new sawhorse go toppling over. And I was damn sure surprised he didn't break his hand when he punched the wall, since that drywall didn't give one bit.

When none of that fazed me, he threatened to throw a cow pie at me, but gave up when I told him the only thing he'd do is get poop on his hand because fresh dung isn't solid. Thankfully, that eliminated me getting covered with cow shit. Pedro would love nothing more than to see that, but it's a hard pass for me.

Instead, Oli sat down on the ground and refused to get up. If I've learned anything over the years, when a one-hundred-fifty-pound kid sits on the floor throwing a tantrum, you wait them out.

Mrs. Johnson stayed as long as she could, waiting for him to become compliant. Finally, she had to go. Oli isn't her only student. She's responsible for several kids that need to get back to the school for pick-up time. So we did the thing we hate the most. We called his parents.

Now here we are, an hour later, with Oli still sitting on the floor.

Leaning up against the door jamb with my arms and legs crossed, I ask him for the umpteenth time, "Are you done yet?"

"Mmm," he grunts as an answer, which I interpret as a no.

"Hey man." Pedro claps me on the shoulder. "I figured you'd still be here." He's trying not to chuckle, but I can hear it under his breath. He finds the fact that I've been standing here pretending I'm not bored out of my mind for the last hour hilarious. Especially since he got to do the fun stuff like working right along with the kids. But since I'm the one who's trained in restraints and de-escalation techniques, I'm the one who gets to deal with meltdowns.

Making a mental note to sign Pedro up for his own certifications so he can have his turn waiting out a pouting kid, I turn to concentrate on our conversation. Lord knows it's the most exciting thing I've done in the last sixty minutes.

"The crew started the evening milking, and the vet is gonna stop by and make sure our Bessie is done with her antibiotics and can be moved back with the herd."

I nod my appreciation. "Make sure she's marked, and we

dump her supply. I don't want to accidentally mix her milk in with the rest of it and get dinged for antibiotic residue."

"Already taken care of."

"What does that mean?"

Pedro and I look first at each other than over at Oli, who has spoken his first real sentence since his tantrum began.

"What does what mean?" I ask.

He stares up at me, clearly interested in our conversation. "About the cow's milk having antibiotics or something."

"Oh." I peer over at Pedro, and he shrugs. I don't think either of us were expecting Oli to talk to us for a while. But this is good, and I'm not going to waste the moment to educate him. "When a cow gets sick, we have to put her on antibiotics. Kind of like when you get sick. You know how you get put on medicine?"

"I'm on a lot of medicine. You mean like that?"

I can't help but smile at his innocence. "It's kind of the same. Except it's the kind of medicine you only stay on for as long as you're sick."

"It's not for forever, like mine?"

"Exactly. But when a cow stops taking it, it's still in her body for a few weeks, which means we can't drink her milk until we know good and well that the medicine is all gone."

"Then what do you do with the milk?"

"We have to dump it out."

He thinks for a second before saying, "That seems like a big waste of milk."

I nod in agreement. "It is. But it's better than having someone get sick from drinking milk that had cow medicine in it."

He scans the barn, and I squint my eyes, watching to see

what he's going to do next. Finally, he seems to come to a decision. "Are the cows nice?"

"They are. Very nice."

"Do you think I could pet one?"

I gape at Pedro who shrugs. "I don't have anywhere I have to be right now. They've got it under control in the milking parlor."

Focusing back on Oli, who seems completely calm and compliant now that he's been distracted from that damn mare, I say, "As soon as you pick up that stool you tossed and help me put the sawhorse upright, Pedro will introduce you to our Bessie. Can you do that?"

He nods and scrambles to his feet, immediately following my instructions. Within seconds, he and Pedro are out the door and headed toward the parlor. I shake my head and make yet another mental note that the fastest way to get Oli to stop fixating on a horse is to talk about the cows. Go figure.

They no more than duck into the other building when I hear gravel crunching underneath tires, and I turn to see a little black Mazda inching toward the open barn door. Having never seen the car before, I assume it's one of Oli's parents. I make sure to pick up the odds and ends from the ground and take them inside the barn. Usually when the parents first get here, they take a second to inspect where their child is spending so much time.

Sure enough, when I make my way back outside, a tall blonde is standing with her back to me, taking in the scenery. It's no wonder. The wildflowers are blooming; it's a sea of purple out in the fields. I really should make a point to stop and enjoy the view more often. It's easy to get used to seeing the terrain so you don't notice the beauty.

"You must be Oli's mom," I call out, hoping I don't startle her.

Instead, she surprises me when instead of introducing herself, she immediately begins the interrogation. "Has he calmed down yet?"

I chuckle, liking that she gets right to the point. She's not rude or dismissive. Just clearly a mom who knows her son well.

"It took him a while," I admit, "but I finally found what distracts him."

Her eyebrows shoot up. "Oh yeah? It wasn't something electronic, was it?"

"Nope. Cows."

"Cows?" Her eyebrows furrow in confusion.

"We were just as surprised as you are. My farm manager and I were talking about one of our sick Bessies while Oli sat on the floor. Apparently, meeting her was more important than waiting us out."

"Oh yeah." She walks toward me, a smile on her face. "There's nothing Oli hates more than a sick or injured animal. Keep that in your back pocket for next time."

"Trust me. I've already made a note." I tap my temple with my finger and smile at her. She's not dressed for a farm— yoga pants and a white T-shirt. Neither of which would stay clean or be without holes if she worked here. But her no-nonsense attitude is refreshing. We never know what kind of parent we're going to get when a child is raising holy hell. I can already tell I'm going to like working with this one. "He's over in the milking parlor right now, getting to meet her. If he's lucky, he'll get to see the vet do an assessment of her before we put her back with the herd."

"Oh no. Is she really sick?"

"Nah." We begin walking the same path Pedro and her son took a few minutes ago, albeit at a slower pace. "Just standard safeguard procedures. I'm Grayson Whitman. My friends call me Ace."

I reach out my hand and she takes it, her grip not too tight, but not that girly shit where you only shake with your fingers. I like it. I also like the way her palm feels against mine, which is a very strange thing to notice in the moment, but there it is.

"Greer Declan. Nice to meet you, Ace. And I'm sorry about Oli. He's been having a rough go of it lately, and I have a bad feeling he's testing you."

"Funny you say that. I got the exact same vibe from him. I think he'll be good here, though. Especially now that we know his weakness."

She laughs, and the warm sound goes straight to my core. She's clearly a woman who knows her son well, but refuses to be brought down by his struggles. "You've figured it out faster than most. I can't tell you how appreciative I am of that."

"It's what we do here," I say with a shrug. "Working with the animals really helps kiddos with special needs. And Oli has a lot of potential. If we can get that stubborn streak under control, he could make a decent farmhand. He's strong, and he's not afraid of any of the animals. Those are two huge hurdles he doesn't have to tackle."

Her face seems to relax, and I know I've hit a nerve. "Thank you for saying that," she says quietly as we meander the final yards to meet up with the others. "Not everyone recognizes his potential. I see it. But I know it's going to be hard to get there. Knowing someone else sees it too, means a lot."

Contemplating her, I take in how this must feel from her perspective. Oli is the new kid in town. New house. New school. New program. I'm sure it has to be hard on her as a mother, knowing there is going to be fallout and hoping the new people around her are equipped to handle it. Suddenly, I'm intrigued in a way I wasn't before, so I go out on a limb and ask what is possibly the most inappropriate question ever.

"How does his dad see it?"

She stops and studies me, assessing me for what, I don't know. Maybe a clue as to why I'm asking. Maybe to see if she can trust me with the truth. Either way, it takes her a few seconds before she answers.

"His dad doesn't see it at all. He's not around to know one way or the other what kind of potential Oli has."

I press my lips together, not sure if I've been put in my place or given a warning. But clearly, I've been given a big piece of Oli's puzzle. One that isn't shared freely, although I do sense there is more to the story.

Still, I feel the need to reassure her that Oli's mental, emotional, and physical well-being are safe with me.

"Well then, I guess Pedro and I will have to work extra hard to make sure Oli knows we believe in him."

A huge smile crosses her face and my breath catches. She's remarkable. I don't know how I know that, but I do. Even in her not-at-all-farm-appropriate attire and hair tied up on top of her head, I can tell she's going to be fun to get to know.

"Well, this is our milking parlor," I say, breaking the moment. "Let's head inside and find your boy, shall we?"

I pause as she turns to the entrance, so I can get my bearings straight and try to shake off my secret hopes that Oli has another meltdown soon, to give her a reason to come out here again. Having a crush on one of my kids' moms is not what was supposed to happen today. But it appears I'm out of luck. And those yoga pants hugging that very fine ass are not helping.

It also looks like I might have a date with Rosie Palm and her five sisters tonight. Dammit.

Chapter Five

Greer

"I wasn't supposed to see him, Greer!" Adeline sounds panicked in my ear. "I was never supposed to see him. Why is the universe conspiring against me?"

I can't help but laugh at her ridiculousness. Not that I don't understand it.

In a weird twist of fate, Adeline's muse, Spencer Garrison, showed up at her book signing event last night. Apparently, his sister is a huge fan of Adeline Snow books. None of us knew that until Spencer showed up with her. Hence, Adeline's panic.

"It'll be fine," I say in the calmest voice I can muster. "He was nice, right?"

"Yes, he was nice. He was awesome. He was beautiful. He was… good lord, that man is attractive." She's rambling at a rapid pace, and I'm trying not to giggle in her ear. Not because I'm laughing at her. But because she's so damn cute.

I get it, though. As much as I'm trying to encourage her and calm her down, I get it. No one wants to meet their idol. What if they're not as wonderful as you've built them up to be in your brain? I, personally, think Diana Galbaldon is a beautiful literary writer. But I never want to meet her because if she's a terrible person, I will never get over it. I've heard she's nice, but that's subjective. Instead, I pretend she and I would be BFFs and never bother finding out where she's touring.

Adeline no longer has that luxury.

"It's fine, Adi. He was everything your muse has always been, and you'll probably never see him again."

"What if he comes to my next signing? What if his sister comes?" Clearly, I'm doing a terrible job of quelling the hysterics.

"Calm down. If his sister comes, you smile politely, you let her smile politely, and you move about your day. But seriously, what are the chances you'll ever see him again?"

"Really not much," she admits with a somewhat relaxed sigh. I guess I'm finally getting through to her. "You're right. I saw him up close. He was everything I imagined he'd be. And god, he smelled good."

"Really. What did he smell like?"

"He smelled like Converse and wood shavings and the tears of Avril Lavigne's haters." I can't help but bark out a laugh as she continues with, "And maybe a little bit of WD-40 from working on the wheels of his board."

"I really hope you wrote that down because that is a fantastic description. Also, I need to find my old Sk8ter Boi CD now," I mutter. "And you need to take your camera, go explore the city and see if you can get your story going."

"I'm trying, Greer. But how am I supposed to get motivated to write a surfing story in Chicago?"

I shrug and swivel my chair back and forth. "Go check out Lake Michigan. I'm sure you'll find some random people who think those are real waves out there."

"I suppose. I feel like it would be a whole lot easier if I had a real-life love interest. You know, like drawing from my experiences."

"I don't know. Drawing from your fantasies seems to be working so far."

"I guess. Speaking of. When are you going to have some real-life stories to tell me? That could be some good inspiration for me. I could move into the over-forty genre."

"You bite your tongue," I quip. "I am not forty yet. Close, but we won't even speak of that."

"Okay, okay. But seriously Greer, you're in a new town. You need to go out an explore. Meet some people."

"No, thank you. I'm going to pass on that."

"Why? You have so much to offer. You're smart and creative and beautiful and loving…"

"And come with a handful of baggage by the name of Oliver and Julie?"

"I wouldn't call them baggage. I'd call them bonus gifts."

I giggle again. Leave it to a romance writer to ignore teenagers are all pretty much the spawn of Satan and twist the situation into something worth loving. "Well, I'm not saying never. I'm saying give me some time to get settled," I lie.

"Okay." She knows I'm blowing smoke, but she's also had a rough day and enjoys when I humor her. "But there is no harm in jumping on an online dating site. I'll even pay for it if it gives you some good stories that inspire me to write again."

"Tell you what, if I decide to go that route, I'll let you know and will give you the exclusive. I'm sure you can twist my life failings into some really great storylines."

"That a girl! And then I'll deduct your membership fee from my taxes and call it research," she says playfully and then takes a deep breath. "Well. Now that I'm calm and not having a mini panic attack, I'm going to head out and see if I can do a brain reset and fix this writer's block. My deadlines are looming, and I'd hate for my editor to yell at me."

"I don't yell," I argue. "I discuss loudly."

She snorts. "Same difference. Anyway, thanks Greer, for calming me down."

"Anytime, babe. You know you're my favorite client. Let me know how the rest of the tour goes."

We say our goodbyes and hang up, but I'm still thinking about what she said. It's been years since I divorced Neil. I haven't gone out on one date yet. I wonder if it's time. I've been hyper focused on getting the kids through Neil's trial and protecting them from the fallout, building my business, and then dealing with Oli through puberty—I guess I didn't feel like I had time to date. But maybe it's time.

Typing "Online dating website" into my search engine, I'm shocked by how many options there are. There's Match and OKCupid and even Christian Mingle. How do you know which ones are the good ones?

As I scroll and search, I realize they all have similar reviews. Each of them has at least one testimony that says, "I met my spouse on blahblahblah.com".

Well that's great, but that means one less eligible bachelor to choose from.

As I keep scrolling, one in particular catches my eye—ranchersonly.com.

My thoughts stray back to Ace, the man in charge of the farm Oli has been working at through the school. At first glance, there was nothing terribly remarkable about him. He was tall, dark hair peeking out from underneath a ball cap, an old ratty T-shirt stretched across his chest and some tight jeans, finished off by a pair of worn out work boots. I didn't stop to really inspect him at the time, too busy worrying about my son and whether or not he was going to get kicked out of the program practically before he began. But the more I talked to Ace, the more I liked him.

He had this manly vibe to him—all callouses and muscles and hard work. Add onto it, his compassion for kids with disabilities and his obvious ability to handle a meltdown or two, and he grew on me quickly. I was honestly surprised he had figured Oli out as quickly as he had. Normally, it takes someone several months, if they ever do at all. For Ace to figure it out this easily, I admit, it made him intriguing.

My finger hovers over the hyperlinked website. Should I click on it? Do I even dare? What would I find if I clicked on a website like ranchersonly.com? Would I find more gentlemen like Ace? Or would I find people who are trying to find someone who will move in and help them run a farm. Because I can live on land. But I'm not helping. My dainty, suburbian self wouldn't know the first thing about helping out.

Before I can make a decision, my email pings. Glancing down, I see it's from the school. I guess my decision is made for now.

Clicking on the preview box, the email opens.

Dear Mrs. Declan,

"Ms," I grumble under my breath, wondering when people are going to finally catch on that I'm not married. For goodness sake. Julie wasn't even in double digits when we moved out.

This is a notice to remind of you the ARD committee meeting for your son, Oliver, tomorrow morning at 9am. We will be discussing his placement in our program. If you cannot attend, please let us know at your earliest possible convenience so we can reschedule and/or schedule you to participate by phone.
Thanks for your cooperation.
Sandra Marshall
Special Education Educator

Sending a quick reply confirming I will be in attendance, I go back and close out my search engine. There is no use in paying money for an account on any of these sites.

This is my life. I need to get used to it.

Chapter Six

Ace

Once a year we like to open the farm to the parents of the kids in the co-op. It's a fun and more relaxing day than we normally have around here. The parents all come wearing jeans and boots and are ready to work right alongside their child. Well, it's not more relaxing for them. But it is for us.

What we find is the more the parents know what the students are doing and seeing them in that environment, the more they appreciate the program and encourage their kids to be part of it.

Simultaneously, when the kids see their parents putting in hard work, it gives them a boost of motivation.

It's my favorite day of the year, and today is that day.

All eight of our current kids are already here, waiting for their parents to arrive. They arrived about an hour ago, so we could prep them for what to expect and they could put up a few decorations, including some great snapshots Mrs. Johnson took of them hard at work. They really get into making it a party.

It gets really hot when you're leading a herd of cattle from one pen to another, so we always have plenty of drinks. At the end of the day, we have a picnic dinner, and I have no doubt Brittany outdid herself. She loves this event almost as much as I do.

Donnie, one of our oldest kids, is the first one to see his parents arrive.

"Mom! Dad!" he yells and takes off across the yard like his britches are on fire. He and Pedro were heading over to fix part of the south fence, but now poor Pedro is left alone to finish loading tools and supplies in the back of his truck. Looks like we may need another day before getting that task done.

Wrapping his mother up in a big hug, Donnie almost knocks her over.

"Oh! Careful, Donnie," she calls out, hugging him back. "I know you're excited, but you forget you're bigger than me."

His dad just chuckles, learning his forearms against the top of the car.

"Come see what I'm doing. I'm helping Pedro." Donnie grabs her by the hand, but never makes eye contact.

"I'd love to see," she says gently, as she tries to slow him down. "But let's not be rude. Let's say hello to Mr. Ace first."

"Oh yeah. Mr. Ace, my mom's here. My dad's here."

I laugh and reach my hand out to shake theirs. "I see that. It's nice to see you again Mr. and Mrs. McMillan."

"Same here. I love what you've done with the place," she says politely. "Did you get the main house repainted?"

"Yes, ma'am. Did it right after Christmas last year. I figured my mama was probably rolling over in her grave with as much as I let the place go, so I brightened things up a bit."

"Well, it looks great. And the herd seems even bigger this year than last year. Is that right?"

"Maybe by a little. We had a dozen or so calves born over the last few months. But also, part of our south fence got knocked over, so we had to combine everybody today. That's probably what you're seeing since we usually keep the herd split for their different milking times

"Oh, maybe that's what it is."

"Mom," Donnie interrupts, unimpressed with idle chit chat. "You don't need to keep talking to Mr. Ace. You need to come see what I'm doing."

"Okay, okay, Donnie. Let's go talk to Pedro. Nice seeing you again, Mr. Ace."

"You too, Mrs. McMillan," I say with a smile.

Mr. McMillan watches them go, his own smile crossing his face as Donnie drags his mother through a mud puddle, not even noticing he got them both filthy. Mr. McMillan is not a man of many words so when he stays behind, I know he's got something important to say.

However, he could probably stand in silence all day, so I decide to start the conversation myself. The McMillans are great people, but there's still tons to do around here. "How's it going?"

"Fine, fine. We're immensely pleased with Donnie's progress since he's been in this program."

"Yeah, he's done amazingly well. Making more eye contact with people, getting some tasks done. And I swear he's built some muscle since he's been here."

Mr. McMillan chuckles again. "He's definitely lost some weight. We were having a hard time keeping him out of the junk food when we first put him in the program. Now he's all about eating meat and potatoes."

"It's amazing how hungry a growing boy can get when he's working out on a farm. Even if it is only a couple days a week."

"Tell me about it. I'm just glad I'm not having to buy a jar of peanut butter every two days anymore."

My eyes shoot up in surprise. "Seriously?"

"Oh yeah," he says with a nod. "I couldn't keep that boy out of the stuff. He would go through a jar every two days. It's no wonder he was so heavy when he first started. Manual labor has done him and his heart a lot of good."

"I like to think so."

"Which is why it worries the Mrs. and me that he's going to be leaving the program in the next couple months."

I knew this conversation was going to happen today. Crossing my arms over my chest, I watch as Donnie is animatedly telling his mother all about the fun of putting two by fours in the back of a truck. It's great that he enjoys it, but unfortunately, it's not the kind of work we can hire him on full-time to do. And therein lies one of the biggest issues for parents with a special needs child.

At twenty-one years old, Donnie has been working out here for about four years. When he turns twenty-two, he'll be rolled out of the public school's special education program. That means the skills he has now are what he has to find a job and become as independent as possible.

"I've thought about that a lot lately. And I put out some feelers."

"You have?" Mr. McMillan sounds genuinely surprised that I would go to that kind of effort. Which is weird because

I've worked with Donnie for a long time. It doesn't seem like going the extra mile to me.

"I have. I would love to keep him on, but we've talked about his functioning level, and I don't think it would be safe for him to work here in an unsupervised capacity."

I can practically feel him deflate next to me. He was hoping I would say something different. "But I have a friend at the no-kill animal shelter in town who has been trying to expand into a co-op of sorts as well. I told her about Donnie."

His head whips around to scrutinize me and my words. "What did you tell her?"

"I told her he's part of this program and he's getting ready to roll out of it, but he's a hard worker, he's made really good strides with following through on basic tasks, he's strong, which they need, and if there is someone he could work side-by-side with to get things done, he could be a good fit."

He pauses briefly before taking a deep breath like it's too good to be true and he needs to be prepared that he's having false hope. "What'd she say?"

"She said she wants a couple more months to get things arranged, and then she'd like to see if Donnie is interested in part-time job over there."

The noise that comes out of Mr. McMillan sounds like he's strangling a sob while trying not to yell "Hallelujah." "Oh, Ace, that would be wonderful. He has such a sense of purpose working here, and we don't want to take that away from him."

"I know," I reassure him. "I get it. My brother was the exact same way. When these kids... hell, when anyone has a purpose and a place to go to everyday, you're just happier."

"I agree. Have you mentioned it to Donnie yet?"

"No, sir. I wanted to talk to y'all first. Not knowing if that was an option or if there would be transportation issues, I didn't want to spring anything on him until y'all were involved."

"Absolutely. If you have the information, you can forward it to me, and I'll get a hold of the woman in charge there to take that off your plate."

"That would be great. I'll shoot her an email and cc you on it to introduce you guys, so we can see what happens."

"That sounds great. I appreciate it, Ace." He turns and shakes my hand again, clasping my one hand between his two. "Thank you so, so much."

The look of relief on his face is so strong, I can't help but smile. As he turns and walks away, going toward his family, the extra stiffness in his posture is gone. It feels good to know one five-minute phone call could have that much impact.

I don't watch him for long. Mostly because I hear a car driving up and that means another parent is coming. Only this time I'm the one stopping in my tracks. The car is a black Mazda.

I know who that belongs to.

It's Greer Declan. Also known as Oli's mom and the woman I haven't been able to get off my mind since she left here last time.

Stepping out of her vehicle, I notice she brought someone with her. It's a teenaged girl who has similar features to Oli but carries herself differently. This girl seems to be all teenager—right down to the phone in her hand and single ear bud dangling out of her ear.

"Ace." Greer approaches me with an outstretched hand, the girl following behind her.

"Ms. Declan," I respond.

She scoffs. "Please, please call me Greer."

I nod and take her hand in mine. "Greer. I can do that. I see you brought a friend with you this time."

"Ace, this is my daughter, Julie, Oli's sister. Julie, this is Mr. Ace, he's the guy who runs the program and manages the farm."

Julie gives me a shy wave and pushes her black rim glasses up her nose. "Nice to meet you."

"You as well," I respond with a nod. "If you guys are thirsty at all, Brittany put some drinks out on the picnic table. It can get awfully hot out here. She'll bring out dinner from the main house later."

Greer gives me a strange expression, but I don't have time to decipher what it means before we hear Oli yell, "Mom! Mom! You're here!"

I chuckle. As independent as these kids want to be, it never fails. They get overly excited for their mothers to show up, so they can show off exactly how independent they really are.

"Hi, Oli. I take it you're having a good day?" Greer hugs him tightly, then shoves her hands into the back pockets of her jeans. This, of course, drives my attention to where her hands are. And down the back of her legs. All the way down to the cowboy boots she's wearing. They're scuffed enough that she's had them for a while, but not like it's from regular use. I'm only distracted for a moment, though. Oli's excitement brings me right back to the conversation at hand.

"Yeah. I'm learning how to milk the cows."

She takes a step back. "You are?"

"Uh huh." His eyes are as wide as his smile while he talks about his new job. "The Bessies are so sweet and they lick my finger with their big long tongue and it feels really weird. But we put them in the big stall and put the machine on them. It's like, I don't know what it's called but it's like their boob—"

I burst out laughing. "It's their udders, Oli."

"Yeah, that thing. Their udders. And we make the milk come out and then we put them in the pasture, and they can eat and they're so happy, Mom. I really like the cows."

Greer looks over at me, stunned. "How come I haven't heard about these cows before? When did this happen?"

"Just this week," I say. "You remember how interested he was in the cows? We figured, why not? We needed the help over there so we decided to try it out."

"Come on, Mom! Let's go see the cows!"

Oli turns and runs off, while Greer turns the opposite direction. "Hey Julie, you wanna come with us? Oli wants to show us the cows."

Julie glowers at us like only an incredulous teenager can pull off. "No thanks, Mom. I'm good." She walks to the picnic table and sits down, never taking her eyes off her phone.

"I take it she prefers the wonders of Snapchat to the farm?"

"Maybe." Greer smiles at me, and I swear it short circuits my brain. "But it's more likely she's reading a book."

"Big reader, is she?"

"She's read the Percy Jackson series at least four times. She's read Harry Potter so many times in paperback, the cover fell off. She is definitely the reader in the family. Makes my book nerd heart happy."

We begin walking slowly toward the barn. Something about being with Greer makes me feel like I'm not in a hurry.

We don't need to get there any time soon. "You're a big reader too?"

"I'm actually a literary editor. So yes, reader by hobby. Editor by trade."

"Nice. I love that you made your hobby into your job. I didn't realize there were any publishing houses in the area. And that means you get to work from home, right?"

"There aren't, and yes, I work from home."

"Oh, that's nice.

"Yep. It works perfectly around Oli's schedule."

"Speaking of Oli's schedule," I switch topics on her. "He's doing really good around here."

Her face lights up and I know instinctively she needed to hear that. "Really? I was afraid after that first meltdown, he wouldn't be allowed to come back."

I shrug. "Meltdowns aren't that uncommon around here. Especially when a kiddo first starts. But we changed his job and that seemed to help a lot since he's interested in what he's doing. He helps with the clean-up and the guys are really good with him. They're actually teaching him how to use the equipment so he can do the milking himself."

"Really? But what if he hurts a cow?"

I chuckle. "Our Bessies are stronger than Oli will ever be. And the milking machines are calibrated so he can't really do much damage attaching it to the udders wrong."

She puts her hand on my forearm, and I feel a zing all the way to my chest. It's like her touch is electric.

"Thank you, Ace. You don't know how much I appreciate that. As a mom of a special needs child, having someone take the time to help him… well, it really means a lot to us, and it's important to his future."

I return her smile. Not because of what she said, but because of how it makes me feel. In a weird way, it makes me feel manly, and worthy, and all those feelings that go along with your ego being puffed up. Which is odd, since I've been doing this for so many years. I should be used to the compliments. But it's not the words. It's the woman. I can't explain it, and I don't even want to try. I'd rather just enjoy the feeling. It's been a long time since I've felt this way around a woman. Hell, maybe it's the first time ever.

"He's a good kid," I finally say quietly and continue with our steps.

"Hey Ace!" I hear over my shoulder and turn to see a very pregnant Brittany walking toward us. "Everything's ready to go. You want me to set out all the food now, or do you want me to wait?"

"Um…" I think for a second, trying to remember how many parents are already here. "I think we could wait about an hour. Just to make sure everyone is here."

"Yeah sure. Whatever you want, hon. I know this is your favorite day of the year." She pats my arm and I cover her hand with mine. She refuses to admit it, but I know walking all the way out here winds her these days. "I made sure to make your favorite pimento cheese sandwiches." She winks my direction and turns to waddle back to the house.

"Go sit down and put your feet up," I call after her. "Your ankles are swollen, which means you're pushing it too hard. You know the doctor warned you about that."

"Don't you worry about me, Grayson Whitman," she shoots right back. "I'll sit down when this kid is born, and then what will you do? Starve. That's what you'll do."

I chuckle and turn back to see Greer sporting a strange

expression I can't quite interpret. I open my mouth to ask her what's wrong, but Oli comes barreling through the parlor doors.

"Mom!" He accidentally yells in her face and practically runs her over. The look on his face is priceless when he realizes how close she actually is. "Mom, come on," he says in a much quieter voice. "Let me show you."

Walking inside the milking parlor, it's nothing special. Just a barn. But it's set up to make it the most efficient for milking. There's a couple dozen stalls, each decked out with the latest and greatest equipment to keep things running smoothly. Each stall is occupied by a cow in different stages of the process.

Taking it all in, Greer seems overwhelmed by what she's seeing, so of course I launch into my normal explanations. "It takes about seven minutes to milk a cow. Once we're done, we unhook them and send them back to the field to go on about their day, just like Phillip is doing over there." I point his direction as he smacks one of the Bessies on the hind quarters, sending her on her way. "She'll head over with the rest to eat, graze, and lounge in the sun."

She turns and squints at me. "They lounge in the sun?"

"Oh yeah. Our Bessies seem to be a lazy bunch."

"Why do you call them Bessies?" she asks, as I pat one on the hind quarters.

"I don't really know. It's something that started years ago, and it kind of stuck. Maybe it makes us feel more bonded to the animals, a term of endearment."

"Hey Mom, look." Oli leads us over to where one of the cows is getting hooked up. "Look what I can do."

Freddy, one of my long-time farmhands, patiently works with him, helping Oli get everything set up and the machine started. It's not necessarily a complicated system, but there are quite a few steps involved. Low and behold, Oli's got it. I can tell Greer is impressed.

"That's fantastic, Oli. I'm proud of you."

Oli puffs up, same as I did a few minutes ago. "Yeah, Mom. I'm really good at this. I'm gonna get a job here someday."

"Well, keep working hard and we'll see," she says non-committedly.

"Oli, you wanna keep helping for a while? Or you wanna come show your mom around some more?" I ask him.

"I wanna keep helping with the cows."

"Okay, do you mind if I show your mom around the rest of the farm?"

"No." He doesn't pay attention when he answers, too engrossed in what he's doing.

We meander our way out the door and continue around the farm. Before I lose my nerve, I turn to her. I don't know if she'll feel like I'm crossing a line, but I can't help myself.

"Hey listen. I know you're new in town, and I know how rough that can be. If you're interested, I'd love to show you around."

She pauses and glares at me. "Are you asking this as a friendly gesture, or are you asking me on a date?"

I can't help but laugh at her candor. "It could be a friendly gesture, but honestly, I was hoping for the date part."

Her jaw drops, and I can see fierce anger in her eyes. "Are you kidding me?"

Taking a step back, I wonder if I completely misinterpreted the chemistry between us. "I'm sorry, I don't understand. It's not against any school policy since I don't actually work for the district."

"Your pregnant wife just came out here and offered us dinner, and you're asking me on a date? How disrespectful is that?"

I bark a laugh. "Um… Brittany is not my wife."

Greer takes a step back. "She's not?"

"No, she's Pedro's wife," I say, still chuckling. "She runs the main house and feeds all the farmhands. She's my employee. But she is also very much Pedro's wife."

"Oh." A blush creeps up her cheeks. "I'm sorry. I guess I assumed since she came out of the house, and you knew about what her doctor said…"

"I know, I get it. It's a different dynamic when you work on a farm. We're very much like a family. But as close as we are, we are not *that* close."

Greer presses her lips together, and I can't tell if she's trying not to laugh or buying herself time. "Can we try that again?"

"You want me to ask you out again?"

"Yes. If we could have a do-over, please."

I decide to humor her. "Greer, now that you know I'm not married"—she quirks an eyebrow at me playfully—"I'd love to take you out and introduce you to our town. Would you grace me with your presence on a date?"

She snickers. "Yes, actually, I think I would enjoy that."

"Ace! Hey man, we need some help in here." One of my guys calls me back to the parlor. Lord knows what could possibly be urgent enough that they need my help. I'm almost afraid to know.

"If you'll excuse me, duty calls."

"No problem. I'm going to walk around if that's okay."

"No problem at all. Just don't go in any pens without a staff member with you. No matter how inviting the animals might look."

She laughs. "Don't worry. I love animals as much as the next guy, but not nearly as much as my son."

I turn to walk away, a huge grin on my face.

Chapter Seven

Greer

Scanning the neighborhood while we wait on the front stoop, I'm impressed by what a cute area Joie and Jack live in. The entire street is older, one-story homes. Craftsman style, so they're all really cute, but very much cookie-cutter.

I like the neighborhood. There are kids riding bikes and parents sitting out on lawn chairs. Just from the little I know about Joie, I can see her living here. My brother, on the other hand, that's a different story. He's never been the quaint, cookie-cutter type.

Then again, he spent a handful of years in his tiny shoebox apartment, probably not even picking up after himself. This is a huge upgrade.

A small pang of guilt runs through me as I think about how my brother has moved on. How we all have moved on. I still miss my sister-in-law, Sheila. She was wonderful. She died shortly after my ex-husband went to prison. I don't know if I ever properly grieved her passing. Or maybe I did, and I was grieving everything all at once. Or maybe I had already grieved so much when her third cancer diagnosis happened, it was a different feeling. I don't know the answer. The only thing I do know is I still miss her sometimes. She was one of my bridesmaids. She was the first one at the hospital after both my kids were born. She took over and planned both my parents' funerals. She was family.

That's not to say Joie hasn't been good for Jack. She really has. From the times we've all interacted, they're fun together, very low-key and loving. It's like she got him out of his work-induced bubble and brought him back to life. Plus, they laugh almost constantly. It's one of the reasons I'm excited to be here having dinner with them. I hear they have their hands full right now and could use an extra set of eyes.

The door finally swings open, and my jaw does the same when I take in my big brother's appearance.

"Do not. Say. A word," he growls at me, eyes narrowed.

Julie tries hard to stifle her giggles next to me, but Oli blurts out what everyone else is thinking. "Why do you have bows in your hair, Uncle Jack?"

He hrmphs and opens the door wider to let us in. "Because somehow I got suckered into babysitting a bunch of little girls who have nothing better to do than play fucking hair dresser."

Joie comes around the corner already chastising him. "Watch your mouth with kids in the house. And quit complaining. You sound like a grumpy old man. Don't even try to convince me you aren't loving it as much as they are."

In the distance, I hear giggling. A lot of giggling.

"How many little girls did you end up with anyway?" I

ask Joie as we embrace in a quick hug.

"All of them. And what is this? You didn't have to bring anything," she gently chides as she takes the supplies for my famous fruit salad out of my hand and turns toward the kitchen. Or at least, I assume that's where we're heading. The floor plan is a little more closed off than I expected, but it's still nice in here. The living room itself is huge.

"It's no big deal. It's a super easy fruit salad."

"Well thank you. We're only ordering pizza so at least I can feel like I'm giving the girls something healthy. Anyway," she continues with our original conversation, "you knew we had Elena's three girls for a few days, right?"

I nod because Jack had mentioned it the other day. Elena's ex-husband was none-too-pleased she was getting married to Joie's brother, Greg, and refused to help out by taking his own kids for the week so they could go on a honeymoon. Not a shock. I know too many women who have those kinds of ex-husbands.

"Elena's mother will take over on Monday, but she found out about her fortieth high school reunion after all the wedding plans were made, and we didn't want her to miss it. It's too important. We offered to take my three new nieces while she's out of town. It seemed to work out for everyone."

"Everyone except Jack, who has turned into the World's Ugliest Barbie Doll," I jest, making Joie laugh.

"You know he's a big softy. He likes to complain."

"Don't I know it. So you have three little girls here. Wow."

"Four."

"Four?"

She nods. "All four. Libby is only a parent when she feels

like it, that's Greg's ex-wife, so I'm not surprised, and her mom basically raises Peyton. But her mom got really sick yesterday and called to ask if we could take her. Speaking of… we probably need to peek in and check on them. They're awfully quiet all of a sudden."

I follow her out of the kitchen and down the hall, picking up a bright colored children's book that was clearly discarded on its way down the hall. "Travis's Troubles" I read to myself. Flipping it over, the synopsis on the back catches my eye.

Travis has lots of good in his life, but sometimes he has trouble making the right choice.

"Looks like someone has been writing books about my son," I snigger to myself.

Catching up to Joie, I say, "I feel bad Peyton's grandma is sick."

She shrugs. "I'm sure she'll be fine. I think Libby was a late-in-life baby, which makes sense as to why she grew up to be an entitled brat. I think being the main caretaker for a toddler, even her own grandbaby, wears her out."

Walking through the doorway, I see what used to be Jack's man cave. But from the amount of crafts, baby dolls, and nasty cheap nail polish, I would say there's too much estrogen in here to call it that again. I also don't feel bad for tossing the book on the shelf. There's going to be a lot of "Clean Up, Clean Up" later on.

"She's a nice lady," Joie continues. "Too bad her daughter is such a witch."

"Let's play witches, Aunt Joie! I need a witch hat!" One of the girls yells, her blonde ringlets bobbing up and down as she bounces. I can see why Joie agreed to watch this many kids at once. They're precious.

Joie smiles fondly at the girl. "That's a great idea, Maura! I bet you can make a witch's hat out of some black paper and the stapler," she says handing over the supplies, much to the girls' delight. Very quickly, they're all sitting on the floor trying to figure out how to imitate Joie rolling up the black paper just enough to make it a cone shape.

"Aunt Joie?" the oldest one of the bunch asks, eyes never leaving her craft. "When is Uncle Jack coming back? We want to paint his finger nails."

Joie's face lights up mischievously, and I can already tell she's keeping my brother on his toes. It's a good thing too. He has such a weird sense of humor. It's nice knowing he found someone who can keep up with him.

Joie puts her hands on her hips and cocks out her knee. "I think that's a great idea. I'm gonna go get Uncle Jack right now."

"I'm right here," he says from the doorway, looking resigned to being back on mannequin duty. I, on the other hand, am very happy by this turn of events. Who doesn't love when the big brother who used to put bugs in her hair finally gets his payback in the form of pink strawberry-scented nails? "But I brought someone with me."

Julie comes in, her smile bright and the girls immediately forget their crafts and gravitate toward her. She sits on the floor, criss-cross applesauce much to their delight, and my and Joie's disappointment.

"Hi, I'm Julie. What are you playing?" The girls immediately clamor around her, one trying to sit on her lap, another one picking up brightly-colored beauty items to show her. Before I know it, one of them is brushing her hair and another is putting blue eye shadow on her. Badly, at that. It's like watching little monkeys climb all over the mama monkey at the zoo.

"Oh man. I was having too much fun seeing all the latest male fashions," Joie says under her breath and then turns to Jack. "I guess you're off the hook."

"Thank god." He yanks the barrettes out of his hair, grimacing when one of them doesn't let completely go of a strand. "And thank Julie for always keeping her nose stuck in a book instead of a glamour magazine. I can't believe I've never gotten suckered into this before. You're my favorite, Julie!" he yells over my shoulder.

"I know!" she calls back, not even flinching as stubby little fingers twist strands of her hair around some fake curling device.

"Aw," Joie patronizes, patting his arm. "You do realize Isaac is almost old enough to have one of his own. Pretty soon, you'll be Grandpa Jack!"

"You are an evil, evil woman," he says before kissing her on the lips.

"Where'd Oli go?" I ask, as we make our way back to the kitchen. I need to get started on the fruit salad I brought.

"I set him up on the Xbox." Jack tosses more bows on the counter and runs his fingers through his hair. He missed one in the back, but none of us seem too keen on telling him about it. "I'm sure he's playing some random game I'll never be able to figure out."

"Wait, what?" The smile on my face isn't reaching my eyes. "He's playing video games?"

Jack's posture immediately changes. "Was I not supposed to do that? I thought it was only his tablet he couldn't get until nighttime."

I sigh and realize this is one of those times I need to just let it go. "No, no. It's okay. I've been limiting his electronics by a lot lately. I've been reading about electronics addiction in children, and he has every single marker."

"You can be addicted to electronics?" Joie asks when we get to the kitchen. "Like really, truly addicted?"

Unloading the supplies, I get distracted momentarily. "Do you have a big bowl I can use?"

"Yeah sure." She reaches under the counter and grabs one for me as we chat.

"Thanks. As it turns out," I say, getting back to the topic at hand, "just like some people are pre-disposed to having the alcoholism gene, others are pre-disposed to having an electronics addiction gene. I don't really get why or where it comes from, but it's apparently a thing. People, particularly children, get obsessed with various forms of electronics and it begins to affect their ability to function. All those things you think of when it comes to a drug addict, that's basically what happens to Oli. I'm really trying to limit it. It's not realistic to keep it away from him completely. But if I can give him his 'fix' once a day, it helps curb his behaviors. It's like incentive to act right."

"Oh shit," Jack mutters. "I'm sorry. I can get him off the Xbox if I need to."

"No, wait, don't," I interrupt quickly. "There are four little girls in this house who don't need to see one of his epic meltdowns. The electronics will be a good distraction for him now. I'll just deal with the fallout later."

Not that I want to, but in this situation, it's the better of the two choices.

"I'm sorry, Greer," Jack apologizes again. "I didn't even realize. I feel stupid."

"Don't beat yourself up about it. I learn new things about Cli every day. You never know what the next thing we're going to pinpoint is. It just happens to be electronics this time. But honestly, I think his new job is helping him."

Joie watches closely as I dump the frozen fruit into the bowl, pouring the French vanilla coffee creamer over the top of it and mix.

"Wait, I wanna hear about Oli's job in a minute." She holds up her finger to stop us and stares into the bowl, fascinated by what I'm doing. "But what is that? Is that dessert?"

"You can definitely use it as dessert. I usually don't, but you can."

"And that's all it is. Two ingredients?"

"Two ingredients."

She claps her hands excitedly. "Jack! I think we finally found something I can make."

"I don't know, babe." He doesn't appear convinced. "I have this bad feeling you'd still be able to screw it up."

She smacks him on the arm as he snatches a frozen strawberry out of the bowl in and pops it in his mouth. "Oh shit, that's cold," he mumbles around the berry while sucking in a breath.

"Uh yeah. It's frozen," I say, sounding more like "duh".

"Serves ya right," Joie says. "That's what you get for making fun of me."

He smacks her on the ass as he makes his way out the door, presumably to hang out with Oli for a bit. I know he likes spending time with his nephew and really does see himself as a pseudo-father figure. But I'm not fooled. Mostly Jack's hiding from the gaggle of little girls who are armed with hair spray and combs.

"Okay, back to the other topic. How is Oli's job going?" Joie leans a hip on the counter and crosses her arms.

"I think it's going well," I respond honestly. "We had some trouble at first with the new routine, and he doesn't like being told no, especially when it comes to animals."

"Mmm... The dreaded 'n' word no kid ever wants to hear."

"It's really true," I admit, "and with his emotional intellect being around eight years of age, I know he can get really frustrated."

"He's emotionally only eight?"

"Yeah, that seems to be the age he gravitates toward in public. He always wants to play with the kids, which makes him look creepy."

Joie giggles, making me smile. "I'm sure it can."

I shrug. "I guess it goes with the territory. I've had to explain the situation to a few parents, but usually once they know what's going on, they're okay with him playing. Can you only imagine what they first think when this seventeen-year-old kid comes barreling up wanting to play Pokémon with all the third graders?"

"He'll find his place. Sounds like his job is already helping with that."

"Yeah. Ace picked up on Oli's love of cows, so they moved him over to what they call the milking parlor. And he seems to be doing really well there."

"Ace?" she asks.

I clear my throat. "Grayson Whitman. He runs the program. Most everyone calls him Ace."

Joie pauses long enough that I start to feel like I'm missing something. Looking over at her, she's making a face. Like she knows something.

I narrow my eyes. "What? Did I accidentally spit in the fruit salad?"

Please say I spit in the fruit salad.

"I think someone might have a little crush on teacher."

I gasp. "I have no such cru—"

I don't bother finishing my sentence when she gives me a "mom" look. I know that one. I use it on my own kids, quirked eyebrow and all. I'm busted, and there's nothing I can do about it.

"Fine." As much as I don't want to have this uncomfortable conversation, I will admit, it's fun having some girl talk. I didn't have many girlfriends in Kansas after Neil's arrest. People tend to distance themselves from you when you're under federal investigation, so it was no surprise. And realistically, I didn't have the time or energy to be a good friend during that stage of our lives, so it was kind of a blessing. Plus, it appears I've been busted by Joie and there's nothing I can do about it except thank my lucky stars Jack isn't standing here. He used to be the biggest brat when I would go out on dates. I doubt that's changed. I'm hoping Joie won't be as obnoxious. A little womanly advice might be nice. "He's a little bit handsome. And he gets along with the kids really well."

"And do you know if he's single?"

I press my lips together before finally answering quickly. "Maybe."

It's Joie's turn to gasp. "He asked you out, didn't he?"

Whipping around, I stare at her in disbelief. "Ohmygod, are you a mind reader? How did you know that?"

She steps forward, way too excited by my news. "I could tell by the look on your face. You're easy to read. Are you going to go?"

"I told him yes," I begin, her squealing excitedly, "but I think I'm going to cancel."

Her face falls. "Why wouldn't you go out with him?" She sounds sad. Like she's just as invested in my dating life as I am.

"I don't know." I turn back to the fruit salad, even though I don't need to actually stir anymore. At least it keeps my hands busy. "I just… dating me is a lot."

"What do you mean by that?"

"I mean, I'm a package deal, ya know? I have an ex-husband who is in prison. I have a special needs teenager. I have—"

She interrupts before I can finish. "—a successful business. Your own home. Your own money. Your own independence. So what? So you come with a little extra baggage. Everyone does."

"Yeah, but Joie, it's a lot to take on Oli. Remember how nervous you were when you first met him?"

She regards the floor sheepishly. "But then I asked questions and got to know him, and I love him now. He's difficult, but we all have parts of us that are difficult."

"That's a lot of parts, Joie."

She steps forward and takes my hand, clasping it between hers. "And Greer, this guy already takes on Oli several times a week. Voluntarily."

I bite my lip. She makes a really good point. "But what if it goes bad?"

She shrugs. "What if it does?"

"You don't think that would negatively impact Oli?"

"You planning on moving out to the farm any time

soon?"

"No," I say rolling my eyes. "But someday, what if?"

"Greer you can't think about the somedays. You can't. I learned the hard way with your brother. Be honest about your life when you first start dating, but also be honest with your kids. You deserve to go out on a date. And if that's all it ends up being, you went, had a good time, explored the town—no harm, no foul. And if it does go somewhere, you take it one day at a time."

The doorbell rings at this exact moment, giving me a chance to absorb what she's said. High-pitched cheers come from the back room and a low-pitched squeal comes from the front room making me chuckle. Oli does love his pizza.

"Come on." Joie puts her arm around my shoulder and guides me to the front of the house. "You can think about it later. Let's go wrangle up these kids and get them fed."

And by wrangle, she means herding a bunch of feral cats.

Chapter Eight

Ace

The blast of cool air as I walk in makes me shiver. I don't mind working in the heat. I've been doing it all my life, so I'm used it, but it means air conditioning on a warm fall day can feel a little chilly on my skin.

Searching the signs around the bookstore, I try to decide where to begin. I know what I want, but hell if I know where to find it. In the animal section? Business? Who the hell knows? I finally give up and make my way around tables full of sale items to the information desk.

"Can I help you?" the woman behind the counter asks me in a flat tone, never taking her eyes off the monitor she's staring at.

"Yeah. I'm looking for the new Temple Grandin book. I can't seem to find it anywhere."

She continues observing the screen, clearly not interested in this conversation. "What's the author's name?"

I crinkle my brow. You'd think someone working at a

bookstore would have heard the name before. "Uh, Temple Grandin?"

"What's the last name?"

"Grandin?" I'm starting to question whether or not I'm actually saying words out loud. Am I speaking too quietly?

A few clicks of the keys later and she finally gets a little animation to her face. "Aha. Here it is. Author's name is Temple Grandin. It just came out a couple months ago. Follow me."

I just shake my head at how odd this entire exchange has been and follow her to the "self-help" section. Of course, it's the one place I didn't look.

It takes her only a few seconds to locate the book and grab it off the shelf. "Here ya go." Then she turns and walks away.

This is why I don't like big chain stores. I can't seem to run into people who actually like their jobs. Mom and Pop shops are more my style, but this is all we have in the way of bookstores around here. Besides, it's always possible I attract the wrong kind of customer service personnel.

Speaking of attracting people, after flipping through the book quickly, I turn around only to see the woman who has been starring in all my latest fantasies across the aisle. Greer is dressed in blue jeans and a plain white shirt, hair pulled up on top of her head and sunglasses holding the rest of her hair off her face. She's got her nose in a book, and her effortless beauty takes my breath away.

Before I can stop myself, I'm walking her direction, my focus squarely on her.

"Scoping out the competition?" I jest as I approach. I know the second she recognizes me because her face lights up.

"Ace. What are you doing here? I'd expect you to be on the farm right now."

Holding up the book to show her I respond with, "Just grabbing some research material."

Her eyebrows rise, making her forehead wrinkle slightly. "Temple Grandin, huh? I'm impressed."

I shrug nonchalantly. "I like to hear what she has to say. She has good insight into how best to work with our Bessies."

"She knows a lot about how to work with the kids too."

I chuckle. "That she does. I always take away a few nuggets of wisdom when I read her books. What about you? I see you're in the"—I glance up at the sign over the shelves—"romance section. I guess I was right about why you're here."

Reshelving the book she was holding, she smiles at me. Little lines around her eyes form. I like the way they look on her. They don't age her, even though most women would probably call them crow's feet. On Greer, though, they show how much she's lived.

"Just market research, I suppose. I like coming here and seeing my clients' books on the shelves and what other things are being picked up by publishers. Keeps in me the know with my clients. Plus, it gives me an excuse to have someone else make me a cup of coffee," she says, referring to the small coffee shop on the other side of the DIY books.

I don't know if she dropped a hint about wanting to share a table with me, but I jump on that idea quicker than a bull jumps on a heifer in heat.

"Well, I was just about to pick up a cup. Would you like to join me?"

This time, a grin crosses her face slowly. It almost feels seductive, even though I don't think that is her intention.

Down boy, I chastise myself internally. *It's coffee. Not a roll in the hay. Although that would be fun, too…*

"I'd love to."

Snapping out of my wayward thoughts, I reach my hand out and gesture. "Lead the way."

The line is short, so we get our drinks quickly and snag a table overlooking the rest of the store. I like that the little café is up a few steps. It makes it feel like you have a view, even though we're inside. But I guess that's the effect they're going for.

"How long have you been running the farm?" she asks, her lips pursing as she blows away the steam curling up from the hot liquid.

I don't know what's wrong with me, but I have to practically force myself to stop thinking of what those lips must feel like. Either it has been way too long since I've been with a woman, or she and I have a very strong connection. Considering we haven't set a day for our date yet, I don't know which it is.

Concentrating on the conversation at hand, I rub the scruff on my chin. "Gosh, I guess it's pushing twenty years now."

The muscles in her smooth neck move when she swallows, another physical attribute I shouldn't be noticing. "That's a long time. It's a family-owned business, right?"

I bob my head back and forth as I think about how to respond. "It used to be, but since it's just me now, I'm not sure we can call it family-owned anymore."

"Oh? Where's everyone else?"

Oh boy. She opened a very depressing can of worms. None of it's a secret; it's just a lot at once. Still, even if I didn't like her in a romantic sort of way, her child spends a whole lot of time on my land, and the story is going to come out eventually anyway.

"About six months before I was supposed to graduate from college, my dad dropped dead in one of the fields."

She throws her hands over her mouth. "Ohmygod, that's terrible!"

"Yeah. Massive heart attack. Doctor said he never knew it happened. One second he was working in the field and the next second he was singing with the angels."

"At least it was quick."

"Yep. And honestly, it wasn't that surprising. Don't get me wrong, we were all crushed. But the doctor had been telling him for years he had high cholesterol. Stubborn as he was, he refused to change his diet. And my mother would never force him to. She always said life was about quality, not quantity, and she'd rather we live full, happy lives than live longer in misery."

"Hmm." Greer responds. "I never thought about it that way. There's some wisdom in that."

"I suppose. I feel like she missed out on a middle ground, though. Especially since her own enjoyment of life ended up killing her about five years after my daddy."

She leans in, eyes wide in disbelief. "Are you kidding me?"

"Nope. The woman loved her cigarettes. Refused to quit, until lung cancer took her. I'm glad I came back after my daddy passed to run things again. It meant I could take care of her and my brother, John."

"I didn't know you have a brother." Her smile is so genuine, I feel bad about continuing on with the unfortunate truth.

"Had."

Her face immediately drops. "Oh my gosh. I don't know if I can take any more past tense in your life."

I chuckle at her reaction. When you tell the story, it all seems to happen back to back. Reality is, there were years between their deaths. It was a struggle, sure. But I had time between. For that, I'm grateful.

"John had Down Syndrome and, while he was really smart, he was also really babyfied in some ways. He was so close to my mother. When she died, and I became his guardian, we did well together, but it wasn't the same for him. He cried, wanting his mommy every night, saying I didn't sing the same way she did. Finally, his heart gave out. He had a congenital heart defect, but really, I think he died of a broken heart."

"Literally and figuratively," Greer interjects, mirroring what I've always thought. She pats my arm. "I'm sorry Ace, that's... wow."

"It's really okay, Greer. It's been over a decade. I've gotten used to being on my own. The nice thing is at first, we put together the co-op to give my brother and kids like him a place to learn skills. Now I keep it going in his honor. I like to think all three of them are looking down watching, and are really proud of us and what we've accomplished."

"Well if they aren't, I certainly am," she says.

Peering up at her again, I smile. She's beautiful, inside and out. But now I feel like I'm being a Debbie Downer.

"Anyway, enough of the depressing talk," I announce, slapping my hand on the table. "How is Oli adjusting to the new school. And Julie, that's your daughter, right?" She nods. "How is she settling in? I know transition can be rough."

Her face practically glows as she tells me all about how Oli is handling all the changes much better than originally anticipated. It makes me feel good, knowing I'm a part of that. Julie, on the other hand, is still struggling with fitting in. I suppose that's not unusual. The teenage years seem to be the worst for everyone.

Before I know it, we've run out of coffee and out of time.

"I'm sorry," she says kindly, "but I have to run if I'm going to make it home for Oli's bus."

Looking at my watch, I realize we've been sitting here for over an hour. "Oh wow. I didn't realize how late it was. Yes, definitely."

As she begins to stand, she stops and turns to me. "Thank you for the coffee, Ace. I really enjoyed visiting with you."

And just like that, my focus is back on those lips.

"Good. Are we still on for a real date?" I raise one eyebrow in question and get a flirty smirk in response. I take that as a good sign.

"Absolutely. You have my number. Text me and we'll coordinate our schedules." I stand when she does, because I'm a gentleman like that, and watch as she walks away after patting my arm.

My hand immediately covers where she touched, like somehow, it'll make the electric feeling I had when she touched me stick around longer.

When I finally pull myself together, I toss my coffee cup in the trash on the way out, leaving the book I spent so much time tracking down sitting on the table.

Chapter Nine

Greer

Turns out, coordinating schedules with a farmer isn't that easy. Especially if he's the head honcho of the whole operation. Apparently, not only does he run the business side of things, with help from his office manager, he also does a good chunk of the physical labor as well. I'm not sure why that surprises me. You can tell by his physique and tan he works hard. But it's not as easy as deciding to go on a date. He has to make sure all his duties are covered.

The animals won't feed themselves. Actually, they will. But not if no one gives them the food.

The nice part about constantly trading our schedules back and forth is it leads to other conversations. Ace and I now text or talk on a near daily basis. I've learned all about how close he and Pedro are. He's learned all about my parents' unfortunate car accident that took them together. I've learned more about how a farm runs than I ever realized there was to know. He's learned that the only thing I hate worse than a scary movie is an X-Men movie. That lady in blue freaks me out.

I feel like we've gotten to know each other a lot the last couple of weeks, which makes me more excited when the stars finally align the right way.

And my babysitter is available. There's only one person I trust with Oli. My brother, Jack.

"You're late," I complain as I open the door and let him in the house, still in my fluffy white robe with my hair wrapped in a towel.

"Got stuck in a meeting with Hank," Jack grumbles. "Got any leftovers?"

I follow him into my new kitchen where he starts raiding my fridge. "There should be some pot roast in here." He grunts his approval and grabs the right Tupperware, placing it on the counter while he gathers everything he needs. "Why'd your meeting run late? Did you get in trouble with teacher again?"

He snorts. "Hardly. Hank was being… Hank."

"Meaning…?"

"We went over our normal stuff—line up, plays, all the stuff. And then he got sidetracked. Went on a rant for twenty minutes about why curling shouldn't be an Olympic sport."

I blink a couple of times at the randomness. "Um, it's October. And not an Olympic year."

"Yep." He licks a drop of gravy off his thumb. "That's Hank for you."

"How did he get on that subject?"

"Who the hell knows? Probably because Renee wanted him to take her ice skating or something at the new rink that just opened on Park Place. I guess he tricked her into going curling instead."

"That is very odd." I cock my head as I'm suddenly trying

to figure out why curling was added as an Olympic sport when wrestling was removed. Same thing with archery. Would the original participants consider these sports? Or are they considered skills? And why am I spending precious time thinking about sports instead of getting ready for my date?

Shaking my head like I'm clearing my brain, I glance up at the clock. I'm running out of time. I better get a move on.

"Okay, enjoy your pot roast." The microwave door slams shut right on cue and beeps as he sets the time. "I need to finish getting ready."

Jack turns and leans against the counter, crossing his arms and legs. "Where are the kids, anyway?"

"Julie is in her room reading"—he gestures like he's not surprised—"and Oli is in his room playing on his tablet."

Jack crinkles his brow. "What happened to limiting his electronics?"

I shrug. "You were late, and I had to shower."

Groaning, he runs a hand down his face. "I'm gonna have to find a way to get him off it, aren't I?"

"No. It's set for the Internet to go off at eight anyway, so you don't have to do anything except listen to him complain when he's knocked off his game."

Jack sighs but forgets what he was worried about when the timer dings. *That man and his love of food.* I shake my head in amusement on my way to my room. Before I get very far, I turn around and glare at him. "I should be ready before Ace gets here but if I'm not, I need you to let him in."

Jack freezes and my hackles raise. I know that look.

"Jack," I warn.

"Greer," he counters.

"Don't you dare give him the third degree." We're a little

more than five years apart so Jack wasn't around a lot when I started dating. But when he was home, well, let's just say I didn't get many second dates after Jack was through with the inquisition.

Jack raises his hands defensively. "I'll be on my best behavior."

"Nope, not good enough." I cross my arms. "You better be on *my* best behavior."

He scoffs. "What's the difference?"

"The difference is I can show Joie the pictures of your 80s rock star hair."

He narrows his eyes at me. "Those pictures were destroyed."

I narrow my eyes back. "You think I didn't make copies first? I don't care what your prom date said. You looked nothing like Jon Bon Jovi."

He purses his lips while he thinks, but finally nods once. Good enough for me. I don't believe for a second he'll be good, but at least it won't be as bad as normal.

Before I can get to my closet to decide on an outfit, I notice the flashing light on my phone.

Picking it up, the text is from Adeline Snow.

Adeline: *Quit freaking out. You're going to have fun. You deserve this.*

I chuckle lightly. I wasn't going to tell her I had a date tonight, but when she called to give me an update on her writing progress, it sort of came up.

I really should be getting ready, but I stop to shoot off a quick response.

Me: *Shouldn't you be writing?*

Adeline: *Pffftt. I'm waiting for you to come home with a fantastic story I can swipe for my book.*

Me: *So you're saying you don't ever plan on publishing?*

Adeline: *Don't ruin this for me! Go! Have fun! Have drinks! Have sex! You only live once. Do it for the both of us!*

Me: *Lol. I'll talk to you tomorrow. You better have some words written!*

Adeline: ***runs to hide***

Dropping my phone on my bed, I realize I spent more time conversing than I should have. Now it's a mad scramble to get ready on time.

I go through all the motions as quickly as I can, still taking care to present my best self.

Makeup.

Hair.

Lotion from head to toe.

The only thing that takes more time than normal is clothes. Normally, I'm in yoga pants and a T-shirt. Going out is a treat I don't usually have, so I want to spruce myself up a bit.

I groan when the doorbell rings. I thought I had more time. Oh well. I guess I have to trust Jack believes me about those pictures. I know I have one somewhere, but I really don't want to have to dig it up to make good on my threat.

Grabbing my blue jeans, I finally decide on a flowy white

top with a matching camisole. It makes me feel sexy and alluring. Or at least, not frumpy.

A few minutes and I can't primp any longer. If nothing else, I may need to save my date from my brother's harassment.

Chapter Ten

Ace

The door swings open and before I can react with the excitement I feel, I realize this is not who I was expecting.

"Uh, hi," I say to the scowling man standing in front of me. "I'm here to pick up Greer. Am I in the right place?" Leaning back to inspect the number on the outside of the house, I could have sworn this is where she said she lived.

The man widens his stance and crosses his arms over his chest, clearly trying to show who's in charge. But I'm too busy trying to figure out where my GPS went wrong to feel intimidated.

"Yeah," the man finally says.

"Yeah, I'm in the right place?" I try to clarify.

"Yeah."

I tilt my head waiting for more information when a female voice comes up behind him. "Ohmygod, Jack, quit it." Greer shoves him out of the way and then turns to me, apology written all over her face. "I'm sorry, Ace. Please come in. This is my brother, Jack, and he seems to think it's funny to try and play the role of bad cop when I go on dates."

Jack shrugs and sticks his hand out, his demeanor doing a complete one-eighty. "It's my job as big brother. Jack Pride."

"Ace Whitman, nice to meet you." Turning to Greer, I half joke, "You go on dates often?"

"No, I haven't since high school, which is why I wasn't expecting him to play this little game again, or I would have warned you. Clearly, I underestimated how much time he has on his hands and how much he really needs to get a hobby."

Greer is glaring at him, but Jack flashes a grin at me. He's having too much fun with this.

"Now can you make nice for a few minutes, Jack, while I go finish getting ready?"

He gapes at Greer's words, but I can already tell it's sarcastic. "I'm always nice."

"Mm-hmm," she responds and turns to me. "I'll be right back."

She crosses the room and turns the corner, I assume to her room to finish getting ready. I follow Jack into the living room where there's a random football game on.

"You a big football fan, Ace?" he asks as he plops himself down on a giant chair with a matching ottoman. I sit next to him on the couch and make a mental note that it is way more comfortable than it looks. I need to go furniture shopping. I bet it'd be great for a Sunday afternoon nap.

"I've been to my fair share of college football games."

"Really?" Jack's interest is piqued. "You ever been to a Vikings game?"

I nod. "A couple. It's been years, though. My best friend

used to go to school there, so he would get an extra ticket sometimes."

Jack makes a slow non-committal nod, like he approves of my answer. "You ever play?"

"Nah. I grew up on a farm. I was more of a rodeo rat. My sport of choice was always bronc riding, not tossing the pig-skin."

A low whistle sounds from between Jack's lips. "You're a real life bucking bronco rider. Like that movie *Eight Seconds*."

I grimace. "That was a shitty movie about bull riding, but I suppose you could compare it."

"That's kind of hard core, man," Jack says enthusiastical-ly. "Trying to stay on a horse like that and getting tossed in the air like you're a ragdoll, without any pads. I'm impressed."

"I guess it's kind of impressive. I used to love feeling the sheer power of the animal underneath me, squeezing my thighs with all my might so I didn't get thrown. And trying to keep good posture to not lose points."

"You ever get stepped on?"

"Nope." I sit back, relaxing into the conversation. "Hell no. That's the first thing you learn when you try to tame a bronco. The minute you hit the ground, you damn sure better get up and run for your life."

"Hi, Mr. Ace."

Oli is standing against the wall giving me a shy wave. He's wearing pajama pants and his hair is dripping onto his shirtless chest. I assume he's just gotten out of the shower. He seems awfully subdued, but I guess that's because we're not in our normal element, so he isn't quite sure how to respond to my sitting here.

"Hi, Oli." I don't get up. I don't want to accidentally get

into his personal space. He needs to get comfortable with me here first, since social cues aren't his specialty. I don't want to accidentally agitate him.

"Oli, you know you're not supposed to come out here without a shirt on," Jack reprimands.

Oli looks away, clearly not happy he's been called out. "But I don't have one."

"Now Oli, I know that's not true. You have a lot of shirts in your room, probably in your drawers. You just need to go find one."

"They're all dirty."

Jack doesn't even pause. "Well then I guess you better get all your dirty clothes and put them in the washing machine."

Oli smirks, knowing he's been caught in a lie. The inappropriate effect is something I see all the time. Smiling when you get caught. Laughing when you're in trouble. In some ways, it always makes it easier to figure out when you're not getting the whole truth.

"That's what I thought," Jack says. "Now that we've established you have a clean shirt in your room, tell me, did you wash with soap?"

Oli's eyes widen, this time getting agitated. "Don't talk about my business in front of people."

Jack doesn't back down. "Don't worry about Ace. He takes showers just like you and I do. And he uses soap too. Please answer me. Did you?"

Oli looks up at me sheepishly, and I nod. "It's true. I took a shower before I came over. Even washed my butt crack."

That makes Oli laugh, which means he's relaxing around me. "Yes, I washed with soap, Uncle Jack."

"Did you wash your pits?"

He laughs some more like it's the funniest thing he's ever heard. Lifting his arms up, he says, "Wanna smell?"

Jack throws his hands up in front of him. "No, that's okay. I'm good. Did you wash your butt crack?"

Oli blushes but keeps laughing. "Yes."

"And your squirrel food?"

I furrow my brows, thinking. It takes me a second to figure out it must be an inside joke about washing his private bits. But now Oli is full on belly laughing.

"Yes, Uncle Jack! I washed everything!"

"Okay then. Go put a shirt on, and you can come back out here."

Oli complies and turns around, heading back down the same hall he came from. I know it's not my place to be happy about the exchange that just happened, but I can't help appreciating Jack handles him gently. Extended family can have a hard time knowing how to treat disabled family members. I know my parents use to complain about that, and I like knowing Greer isn't having a similar experience.

I don't say any of that out load, though. Instead I say, "Squirrel food?"

Jack's eyes flash with amusement. "His mother hates it when I call it that. Says it gives him all kinds of ideas for inappropriate slap stick jokes."

"That's why you keep doing it?" I say with a chuckle.

Jack shrugs. "She's my baby sister. It'll never not be my job to torture her in some way."

"Torture who in what way?" Greer asks as she saunters back into the room.

My breathing hitches for a second when it finally registers how good she looks tonight. Long, blonde waves falling over her shoulders, with just enough skin peeking out to let me know her flowing white top is off the shoulder with some sort of frilly thing underneath so she doesn't show too much. Dark blue skinny jeans and, of course, those gently scuffed boots.

Good lord, she's like a fucking wet dream.

"Oh nothing." Jack keeps his eyes glued to the TV. "Just chatting about how much fun Oli and I are going to have."

She puts her hands on her hips and glares at him. "Do. Not. Watch that stupid *Tommy Boy* movie again."

"Why not?" Jack complains. "It was a bonding moment for uncle and child!"

"Your bonding moment turned into me spending weeks trying to get him out of the habit of yelling 'Holy Schnike' over everything!"

Jack laughs while I stifle my own. "That was awesome."

"Jack!" she yells.

"Okay, okay. We won't watch that. We'll find something else to do."

I'm not sure I believe him, and I don't think Greer does either, judging by her narrowed eyes and arms crossed over her chest. "I'm gonna have Julie keep an eye on you."

He gapes at her for a second and finally relents, shifting on the couch. "Such a buzzkill."

"Mom, are you leaving?" Oli asks coming back out of his room, this time with a shirt on. It doesn't do much to cover up his pot belly, though, being that it's about two sizes too small.

"I am." She puts her arms around him and pulls him in for a hug. "Mr. Ace and I are going to go out for a little bit. But I'll be back soon."

"Where are you going?" He snuggles in more, a smile on his face. Such a mama's boy.

"Actually, I don't know. I'm just along for the ride."

Standing, I throw my two cents in. "I was going to take her to go dancing, Oli. Think she'd like that?"

"Oh yeah," he says. "She dances around here all the time. It's very embarrassing."

I chuckle. "Well then, I guess I better get her in the middle of a dance floor with a bunch of people, so no one can see her through the crowd. How about that?"

"Good idea."

Greer kisses him on the top of the head and we say our goodbyes.

"Julie, I'm leaving," she calls down the hall on the way to the front door. "Keep an eye on your uncle."

"Okay!" is the only response we hear coming from the other room, except for Jack yelling, "Hey!"

As soon as the door closes behind us she turns to me. "I am so sorry about my brother. He is like a forty-something-year-old teenager."

"He was fine," I reassure her, as we walk to my truck. "Kind of enjoyed talking to him. He seems like a fun guy."

She snorts a laugh. "*Fun* is not how I'd describe him. Annoying would be a better description. I'm glad we're finally in Texas. It's good being around family, and my kids really need him. But when he gets in one of his ornery moods, there is no telling what is going to come out of his mouth."

Opening the door of my truck, I help her climb in, and she settles in while I make my way around the front, taking a few seconds to tamper down my excitement. It's been a while since I've been on a real date. Not for any other reason than I never met anyone I was interested in enough to leave my normal routine for a few hours away. I hope she enjoys what I have planned.

Once I'm situated beside her and we drive away, the conversation continues to flow.

"Did I hear you tell Jack that you were a bronco rider?"

"Sure was." I turn to smile at her while simultaneously trying to keep my eyes on the road. "I wasn't the best, but I held my own."

"Do you do rodeos or something?"

"No. When I was in high school I kind of wanted to, but I wanted to go to college and get away from the farm more. There's not a lot of training time available when you're studying for a degree too. Not to mention there're no facilities when you're inside city limits. I did get close once, though. I missed making the circuit by half a second and two points. But it turned out all right. The farther I got into my degree, the more frat parties and tailgating became important."

"Why did you want to get away from the farm?"

"I don't know." I shrug. "I think I wanted to find my own way, ya know? Like it was always expected I would come home and take over the business, but I had too much I wanted to do first. Funny how life has other plans."

"Yeah. Nothing ever turns out the way you think it will."

I pause for a second, taking in her words. She really does understand what it means to not end up with the life you expected. But she also seems to make the best of it regardless. I like that.

We sit quietly for a few minutes, but the silence drives me crazy. It makes me feel like I'm being a terrible date.

"Are you okay with going dancing? Do we need to get something to eat first?" I blurt out, more to fill the silence than anything.

"No, I'm good. I had to feed Oli, so I ate with him. Dancing sounds great. I haven't been in so many years I forgot how much I enjoyed it until you mentioned where we're going."

"You don't get out much, do you?"

She shrugs. "It's hard finding a babysitter for a seventeen-year-old boy. But now that Jack is close by, I'm hoping to venture out more and enjoy myself."

"I think it's great he's so good with the kids. And their father is okay with you guys living here now?"

She snorts humorlessly. "He doesn't have a choice. He's in Leavenworth for the next fifteen years, seven if he has good behavior. So no, I'm not at all concerned about what he thinks."

I pause, trying to gauge her mood when she shares this part of her life. I knew her ex was in prison, but I've never asked and she's never shared. Somehow, it seems personal even if she wasn't the one at fault. And considering this is our first date, I don't want to make her feel uncomfortable. She doesn't say anything else about it, so I don't push.

Instead, we continue to chat about tamer things like the farm and her job and her daughter, Julie, who she seems to worry about a lot. Not because there's anything wrong with her, but because she's the child without disabilities. I get that. I was the Julie in my own house.

Before I know it, we're pulling into the parking lot of Ranch Road Dance Hall.

"Is this it?" she asks, leaning forward to see more clearly.

It's a small building from the outside. Almost looks like a shack. But the parking lot is packed and every time the door opens, we can see how crowded it is on the inside.

"I promise it's bigger than it seems once you get inside."

She smiles at me. "It looks like fun."

"Well then, let's go."

We jump out of the truck and I lace her fingers through mine as we walk toward the door, country music blaring every time it opens, the beat pulsing through me. Or maybe that's just the hammering of my own excited heart.

Chapter Eleven

Greer

I'm excited to explore the dance hall. This kind of dive is right up my alley. I love hole-in-the-wall places like this, where you can't tell from the outside that it's the best local haunt in town.

The door opens, confirming everything I was expecting—loud, country music played by a band of locals, a bar with nothing but beer and high-end whiskey, and a dance floor half the size of my whole house. It's perfect.

Ace leans into me so I can hear him over the music. "Do you wanna get a drink?" he yells.

I smile and shake my head. "I wanna dance."

A wide grin crosses his face and he takes my hand, leading me through the crowd to the dance floor.

He finds us a place and pulls me into his arms, which I don't mind at all. It feels good being up next to him and his broad shoulders and solid chest. It's been a long time since I've been this close to a man. But it's not just being this close to the opposite sex. It's being close to Ace.

I can't describe it, but it's like we fit together like a puzzle. Not just physically. We seem to align with our ideals and priorities. Never mind the fact that we understand each other for things like losing our parents too early or how important family is.

Taking my hand in his, we begin our two-step in time to the music. Or at least attempt to. Only a few steps in, I crash into the couple behind us.

Ace heeds the man I've run into and mouths "Sorry."

The man gives us a friendly nod and dances away. I laugh when Ace gives me a sheepish look and says, "Oops." But pretty soon, we find our rhythm.

Quick, quick, slow… slow…

Quick, quick, slow… slow…

It's not the kind of two-stepping I've done before. There are a few more steps involved, but it sure is fun. I'm not sure how many songs go by before he's adding a spin.

It feels good to let him take charge, follow his lead and not have to think about where we're going or what obstacles are in the way. It's just… freeing. Like I don't have a care in the world. Like no matter where he leads me, I'll follow because he'll make sure I won't run into anyone.

Well, not again.

We dance for I don't know how long before I have to lift my hair up and fan my neck, because I'm sticky with sweat. Ace wipes the droplets off his brow with his sleeve, so I know he's feeling the same way.

"You ready for that drink yet?" he asks, still beaming from how much fun we're having.

I nod and he laces our fingers together as we walk off the

dance floor. I gesture that I'm going to grab the small empty table that just opened up. He nods and heads to the bar.

The music is infectious, and I find myself tapping my toe in time with the beat while I wait. Apparently, I'm not the only one who thinks so. That couple we first ran into is still going. They're something else.

They have to be in their fifties, but boy can they command a dance floor. They're dressed in matching plaid shirts, blue jeans, and boots, topped off with cowboy hats that seem to stay on no matter how fast they spin. And the way they move together, it's like they can read each other's minds. You can tell they're not just partners on the dance floor, but in life too.

Ace places a tray in front of me, capturing my attention. Two beer bottles, a basket of chips and two small bowls, one salsa and the other guacamole, sit on top.

"I know you said you already ate, but I figured after all the calories we burned off, you might be hungry again."

I love that he's thoughtful. Especially since I love a good guacamole. "Thank you. You're right. I worked up a bit of an appetite." Grabbing a chip, I dip it and take a bite. I like thinking guacamole counts towards my vegetable intake. Even if avocados are technically fruit.

"I hope beer is okay," he says as he unloads all our goodies and pushes the tray to the side.

"Yeah, I think it is. What kind is this one?" I inspect the label. "Is this a local brew?"

He chuckles. "That's Shiner Bock. It's a staple of Texas."

I take a swig, making my assessment. "Not bad."

"It's even better like this. May I?" He holds up a lime wedge, and I nod giving him permission. First, he squeezes the juice inside the beer, then he pushes the wedge down inside the bottle as well. "Now try it."

I do, and he's right. The addition of the citrus gives the beer a whole different flavor. I nod my appreciation. "I like it."

"Now you're truly a Texas woman."

I laugh and keep munching while we watch the dance floor. The band finally decides to take a break, making it much easier to talk over the lower volume of recorded music.

"How long have you been divorced?"

"Um," I clasp my hands in front of me and lean on the table, staring up as I do the math in my head. "I left, gosh, what was it, six years ago? Our divorce didn't take that long. I guess I've been divorced about five years."

"Wait, five years?" He smirks at me. "You haven't been on a date in the last five years?"

I shrug because dating is hard. And it sucks. People don't tell you that part when you're getting divorced.

"I've tried, but I'm not a dating kind of girl. I'm a relationship girl. It's different. There's no online website for that. All the dating sites seem to be for booty calls."

"That's weird because Pedro met Brittany on an online dating site."

"How long ago?"

"Gosh, they've been together for close to ten years."

"Yeah, that's what I've found. The people who met their spouse online, it was like ten years ago. All the decent people are gone. Now it's a meat market for those wanting random hook ups. Or the crazy ones who were the reason they're divorced in the first place."

"Oh, come on. Surely it's not that bad."

I raise my eyebrows. "I'm on a date here with you instead

of in a relationship with someone else, aren't I?"

He laughs, a deep chuckle rumbling from his chest. I can't help but wonder why the sound seems different somehow—sexier than when other men laugh. Is it because of his job? Like working outdoors gives him an abundance of testosterone or something? I've always seemed to date white-collar men. This is the first time I've gone on a date with someone who's a hard-working guy for the sake of working to live.

No, that's not right. I've dated some blue-collar men before. Long ago. Like before I got married. But somehow, this feels different. *Very* different. And not just because we're older and wiser.

"Forgive me for laughing," he says as a small blush creeps up his cheeks. "It's hard for me to wrap my brain around how you've been divorced for five years and someone hasn't snatched you up yet."

"Thank you." I warm at his compliment, but recognize he doesn't see the reality either. Resting my hands on the table, I level with him. "There are not a lot of men out there who want a woman with a special needs child."

He almost looks like I slapped him, he's so shocked by my words.

"That can't be true. It's not like special needs are uncommon."

"No, they're not. And women who have children with special needs date all the time. And sometimes it works out. But in my experience, the older our kids get, the more that reality kicks in. Eventually, other people understand this is my life permanently, not until he's eighteen and goes to college, or until he's twenty-two and graduates and gets a job. This is my life forever. He won't magically get better once he's an adult, so I'm free to travel. He won't be bringing grandkids over for me to dote on and then leave with his wife to live their lives. There won't be any of that."

I can see my words sinking in as I continue.

"Unless I magically come up with millions of dollars, there will be no private residential facility where he is taken care of and monitored by a loving staff at a facility for adults with special needs. There are state-run schools, but we don't qualify for any of them. This is my life. Oli will always live with me. I will always be fighting over keeping him off the Internet. I will never not have locks on my closet to lock up anything of value or electronic. This is it for me. I will always have to monitor if he's getting too violent. I will always have to monitor if his meds need to be tweaked. Even when I'm ninety, I will still be monitoring my son. That's a lot for any man to jump into. I'm sure there are exceptions to the rule, but that's been my experience so far."

He swallows hard, and I watch his Adam's apple bob. I can tell he's thinking about how to respond, because he knows I'm right. Dating post-divorce is hard enough as it is. When you add a child with a permanent disability, especially one that is behavioral, that's a whole different ballgame.

I could fall into the pity party, but millions of single moms do it all the time. Marriages that include a child with a disability fall apart at an astronomical rate. If the birth dad can't hack it, how in the hell is a stepdad supposed to?

"Well, I'm here, aren't I?"

It feels good hearing those words coming from a man as wonderful as Ace. I want to take them to heart. I want them to give me hope, but I've seen this before. Just because I haven't been on dates, doesn't mean I haven't been flirted with. I've met quite a few nice men over the years who expressed interest. It never came to fruition once they saw what my life entails. Ace's words are nice. He's a nice man. But he doesn't get it.

"And I keep waiting for you come to the realization that my life comes with more than you really want."

He smiles sadly at me, knowing I'm right.

"Come on." Standing up, he reaches his hand out for me. "Let's dance."

I slide my small hand into his larger one and he leads me to the dance floor, pulling me close to his chest with our fingers clasped between us.

Resting his forehead against mine, we sway to the music, enjoying the feel of each other. I breathe him in, trying to memorize everything about this moment because I'm not sure if this is him trying to comfort me, or if he's saying goodbye.

Chapter Twelve

Ace

Brushing down my favorite horse, I find myself whistling a little while I work. The morning milking and clean-up is complete. The kids have all been assigned chores. Mrs. Johnson is working in the office. And I'm pretty sure Brittany has a nice little spread for lunch ready to go. It's a good day.

"Why are you still smiling?" Pedro asks, finishing up his own chores in the barn.

I glower at him. "Am I not allowed to smile?"

"You are. But you've been smiling nonstop for the last couple of days. Is this about your date?"

I refuse to answer him, instead continuing with my task. Even though he's right. My smile has everything to do with Greer.

I had a great time with her. We danced. We talked and laughed. We drank. It felt really low-key and easy. But something about it was just… right. I haven't had that much fun in years. Didn't even realize I was missing it in my life. And honestly, I can't wait to see her again.

We've texted a bit back and forth over the last couple days, but we're both busy. Still, there doesn't seem to be any pressure on her part to move faster and I like that. I like that she has her own life and her own goals. I like that she's not out searching to find some magical true love. She's making her own way. It's admirable.

"Maybe it is," I finally answer. "What of it?"

"Whew!" he shouts. "You got it bad. Was she a good kisser?"

I turn and glare at him. "Why would you ask me a question like that when you're a happily married man?"

He holds his hands up defensively. "Don't act like I'm stepping out of line. I don't need many details. I'm trying to figure out why you're happy these days, and nothing makes me happier than kissing my woman, ergo, I'm trying to figure you out."

I roll my eyes because he can defend himself all he wants. "You are the biggest gossip on this farm. I know it, and you know it. And I'm not ready for all my employees to know my business. *Ergo*," he chortles at my dig, "I'm happy because I had a good time. And no, I didn't kiss her."

"Well, why not? If you like her that much, you should have gone for it."

I snort a laugh. "Because unlike some of us in this room"—I look around even though we both know we're the only ones here—"I'm a gentleman. I like to take things slow and wait for the right moment. That's not on a first date."

"I did more than kiss Brittany on our first date," he grumbles.

"I know. You told me. Way too many times and in way too much detail." It still makes me cringe that he made her call him Daddy. There are some things a man doesn't need to know about his best friend. "I get it. You ended up marrying the girl because you fell hard for her. But that doesn't mean I'm you. I like to take things slower. Her life is busy. My life is busy. This isn't going to be love at first sight where we end up walking down the aisle in a Vegas quickie wedding."

"You loved that I had a quickie Vegas wedding," he retorts.

"Only because we got to play real poker for your bachelor party, and I didn't get dragged to the Felicia Does Flinton strip club down the way," I retort, making him laugh.

"I'm saving that for the next bachelor party I'm in charge of coordinating. I'm hoping it's yours. I know how much you loved getting a lap dance from Marsha Harris last time."

I groan. "I still don't know how the most popular girl in high school ended up there. I'm truly wounded that all my high school fantasies were obliterated that night, and I blame you for it."

He belly-laughs at the memory of my grimace when she stumbled over to me, after clearly one too many shots, and trying very hard to give me a sexy dance, probably hoping for a big tip. But the fantasy wasn't working, what with lipstick smudged on her teeth, hair that may not have been brushed in a few days, and her husband standing off to the side making sure I didn't touch. It was possibly the weirdest moment of my life.

"Enough of those traumatic memories." He tosses his supplies to the side and leans against the stall. "Are you going to take her out again or what?"

Slapping my horse on the hind quarters, I walk back to

the supply table, putting everything away. I can hear all the farmhands hooting and hollering as they make their way from the milking parlor to the main house. That must mean Brittany is making an appearance with the promise of food.

"I hope so," I say honestly. "I know it's hard for her to find a babysitter for Oli so we're just taking it one day at a time."

"Well, don't take it too slow. It's long past time for you to get back in that proverbial saddle again, if you know what I mean." He makes a lewd gesture with his hips, and I have half a mind to punch him in the junk.

"I really hope you are eluding to things that are none of your business."

"Of course, I am. It's been a while. You need to get laid."

I turn to gape at him, crossing my arms. "How do you know when I got laid last?"

"Easy. It's the last time you whistled while you worked. That was what, five years ago?"

Rubbing my hand down my face, I question, not for the first time, how this obnoxious man became my best friend. "You can leave well enough alone there. Do you know how creepy it is that you're keeping tabs on my sex life?"

"It's not creepy. It's me looking out for you—"

Before he can finish his sentence, we hear a weird sound coming from one of the pens and both stop what we're doing. It sounds like one of our animals is either freaking out or in pain.

"What the…?" Pedro quickly heads for the door. When he makes it outside before me, he starts running. That's when I know something is terribly wrong, so I pick up my pace.

"What the hell?" As soon as I hit the door and see all the

commotion, I take off running. Oli, despite repeated warnings and thinking I finally got through to him, broke into one of the pens. And not one with any of our mild-mannered animals. Oh no. He broke into the pen holding that damn wild mare Pedro's been trying to break.

Clearly, he's too close because she's freaking out and Oli obviously doesn't know what to do nor does he recognize how much danger he's in.

"Oliver! Get away from that horse!" Pedro screams and jumps the fence faster than I've ever seen before. He immediately goes after the horse to try and calm her, and I'm right behind him, grabbing Oli and shoving him out of the way.

"Get out of the way, Oliver! Go!"

"I just wanted to pet her," Oli says defiantly.

"I don't care! Get out of here!"

Several of the guys recognize the predicament we're in and run up, climbing through to help Pedro which only spooks the mare more.

"Everybody get back!" he yells, trying to approach her slowly to calm her so we can get everyone to safety. But she's not having any of it. She's bucking and stomping, shaking her head back and forth in agitation. He's taking it slowly.

But in an instant, the entire scene changes. Something blows by her feet and, as if in slow motion, I watch in horror as she rears up and kicks him right in the chest. It happens so fast, he doesn't have time to react. He goes flying and lands on his back with a thud.

"Pedro!"

I vaguely register Brittany screaming in the background, too busy scrambling to get to my friend and help him. I can't lose him. He's been part of my life for too long. Brittany can't lose him. His unborn baby can't lose him.

Trying not to panic, I shout, "Call 911!" Then, I turn back to him, looking for any trace of blood. "It's okay, buddy. You're gonna be fine. We called an ambulance. Someone get this horse outta here!" I yell, hoping we're not still in harm's way.

As I continue to talk quietly to Pedro, one of the other guys holds Brittany back from her husband before it's safe. Someone else grabs Oli and manhandles him out the gate.

Finally… finally after kicking down part of the fence, the mare takes off running to the grazing field, but I don't care. We can get her back later. Right now, my only priority is making sure Pedro is okay.

Chapter Thirteen

Greer

The drive to All Hands Farm usually takes twenty minutes.

I make it in ten.

As I drive up the long driveway toward the barn, an ambulance passes me and the fear running through me intensifies, makes my blood run cold.

When I got the call that I needed to get out there ASAP because Oli was involved in a major incident, I didn't stop to ask questions. Granted, they didn't offer me any; they only said to hurry and hung up, so my mind has been reeling on the entire drive about what he could possibly have done.

Did an animal get hurt? Was there a fight? A fire?

Now that I've seen the ambulance, I'm more frightened than ever.

Pulling up to the side of the barn, I throw my car in park and jump out the car door.

"Oli! Ace!" I yell, feeling like I'm halfway to hysterics

from the anticipation of what's coming.

Ace appears somehow, but I don't know from where. I know I'm wide-eyed and disheveled in front of the man I have a huge crush on, but I can't make myself stop to care.

"Where's Oli? Is he in that ambulance? Is he okay?"

Recognizing my emotional state, Ace immediately comes to me and pulls me to him. "Oli is fine, okay? He's fine."

I breathe a sigh of relief, but quickly realize if he's not in that ambulance, then who is?

Pulling away, I regard Ace. For the first time, I realize he's as ruffled as I am. He's not wearing his normal baseball cap, and his hair is sticking up in all directions, like he's been running his fingers through it. "Oli's fine," he reiterates. "He's in big trouble. But he's fine."

"But the ambulance… What happened?"

He doesn't back away from me, but starts running his hands up and down my arms in comfort. "Take a deep breath."

I follow his instructions and realize how badly I need it. I guess I was shallow breathing the whole way here.

"Oli is fine. We had a little problem though, and we're gonna need to figure out how to fix it."

The words *Oli is fine* register, so my heart rate starts to return to normal. But that doesn't eliminate my fear.

We've had a little problem, and we're gonna need to figure out how to fix it.

I know what those words mean. They mean Oli did something to cause a really bad chain of events. I know it without him explaining, and my heart plummets.

"Do I want to know?" I ask Ace, hoping he'll say it's not a big deal, but I know he won't.

He gives me a sad smile. "You need to know." He grabs

my hand and pulls me into the barn. Oli is sitting on the floor, a scowl on his face and arms crossed over his chest. "He won't get up."

"Why not?"

"I just wanted to pet the horse," Oli grumbles.

Turning to Ace, I know there is question in my eyes. What could possibly have happened?

"Oli broke into the pen with our wild mare."

"What?" My head swivels around to stare at my son again.

"We have talked to him multiple times," Ace continues. "He's been warned about the danger and told he is not to go near her." He lowers his voice and leans in to speak quietly enough that Oli can't hear him. "Greer, I'm sorry. I thought his fixation with her was over, and we wouldn't have any more problems. I feel so guilty that I didn't see it."

"Don't talk about me!" Oli yells, startling a chicken that wandered in with us.

I close my eyes and swallow, trying to get myself under control. I can't look at Ace when I ask, "Who got hurt and how bad is it?"

He sighs. "Pedro tried to calm the mare down, so we could get Oli out of the pen. She reared up and kicked in the chest, knocking him out cold."

I gasp and throw my hands over my mouth. "She kicked—that could have killed him."

Ace nods. "Could have, but didn't. His vitals were good once the ambulance got here. He's heading to the county hospital where they can run some tests on him. Maybe keep him overnight. But he was awake when he left. Chances are he'll make a full recovery. Brittany on the other hand—"

I groan. "Oh, please tell me she didn't see her husband almost die."

"She saw. But she's okay. She's going with Pedro, and I asked the EMTs to check her blood pressure every once in a while, just in case. They'll probably want to monitor the baby for a bit."

A myriad of emotions runs through me. Part of me wants to yell at my son for being selfish and stupid. Part of me wants to cry.

This is why he's hard to live with. He doesn't get cause and effect. It doesn't matter how many times I tell him touching an outlet is dangerous or not wearing your seatbelt can hurt you. Until he experiences the consequence for himself, there's a disconnect. He doesn't know how to take anyone's word for it. Not even mine. And because of that disconnect, this kind of thing happens. Only this time, it wasn't him who got hurt, it was someone else.

Ace seems to recognize my struggle and grabs my hand. I want to lace my fingers through his, but I can't. There's too much unknown now. My son almost got Ace's best friend killed because of his disobedience and his defiance and his fixations. Yet, I'm the one who's feeling guilty. Not Oli. Me.

I take a breath to steel myself, drop Ace's hand, and turn to look at my son.

"I just wanted to pet the horse," he repeats angrily.

Standing in front of him, I cross my arms and make the only threat that seems to work these days. "Oliver Declan, I have a spoon with me and you have three seconds to get off that ground and in my car. Three... two..."

As soon as I start counting, he starts scrambling to his feet. "I'm going! I'm going!"

"You're not going fast enough. One…"

Before I can get to zero, he runs out the barn door. I listen until I hear the slam of the car door behind him. Somehow, in the middle of all this, Ace starts laughing.

"Did you just threaten him with a wooden spoon?"

My lips quirk to the side. "Yeah, one time when he was eight, I spanked him with a wooden spoon, and he hated it. I have threatened hundreds of times, but I've never once had to follow through since then. It's the one thing that seemed to make an impression, so I try to use it only in extreme circumstances."

Ace belly laughs, and I don't understand how he can find humor in all this. Normally I can see the funny side of things, but this is too much.

"If I had known it was as easy as that, I would've been threatening with a spoon too. Especially if I don't have to follow through."

I smile at him, my arms crossed, knowing there is more seriousness to be addressed.

"What happens now?" I'm not sure what I'm asking. Or maybe I'm asking about it all—Oli's enrollment in the program or Pedro and Brittany.

Or us.

My brain is trying really hard to wrap around all of this, but it's a lot to process at once.

Ace loses his smile and looks at me. I know I'm not going to like his answer. "I don't know. Mrs. Johnson shuffled the kids out of here before the ambulance came, so I haven't had a chance to talk to her. I think we're going to need to sit down and discuss things before we know where to go from here."

I nod and clear my throat from the lump that's formed. I

guess it stands to reason that the number one question on his mind is whether or not my son is too much of a danger to be here. I don't know what I'll do if Oli is kicked out of this program. It's the first time he's seemed to have found purpose. It's the first time he's been excited about going to school and doing manual labor and learning a skill.

But I don't tell Ace all that. It wouldn't be fair to him to try and cloud his decision-making process. Instead I blink back the tears trying to form and say, "I understand. Let me know what you guys decide. I'm assuming he's suspended for the next couple days at least."

"I don't know that either. That would be Mrs. Johnson's call. But I assume she'll reach out to you within the next couple hours to discuss the immediate plan."

"Mom!" Oli yells from the car. "Mom, I'm ready to go!'

I close my eyes and shake my head, frustrated that my son created all this chaos and yet he still can't see past his own boredom.

I'm so angry. I'm so tired from being his mom. I'm so tired of feeling guilty for feeling this way. He's not like this on purpose, but that doesn't change how exhausted I am and how defeated I feel. What am I going to do?

"I better go." As I start to pass Ace, he grabs my arm, stopping me.

A single tear slides down my cheek. I wipe it away, embarrassed that it's there at all.

"Greer, none of this is a reflection of you as a mom."

I nod, even though it's hard to believe him in this moment. "That doesn't change that I still have to deal with the situation this time. And next time. And every other time he defies the people in charge. This is every day of my life."

Ace looks back and forth between my eyes, trying to find the answers to something, but I don't know what. Finally, he nods once and lets me go.

Climbing into my car, I back out and drive away.

"I just wanted to pet the horse," Oli says again. "I didn't mean for anybody to get hurt."

Those simple words from my simple child are my undoing. That's when the dam breaks and the tears come flooding out.

I cry the entire twenty-minute drive home while Oli pats my arm trying to comfort me, still not understanding he's the reason I'm crying in the first place.

Chapter Fourteen

Ace

I didn't sleep worth a shit last night, too busy reliving the day's events in my mind. Not just Pedro's injury. As horrible as it was, it comes with the territory of breaking a wild horse. Granted, it wouldn't have happened if Oli hadn't been where he shouldn't have been. But it could have easily been a dog that spooked her or, hell, someone's hat blowing by.

No, the vision that keeps haunting me is the look on Greer's face before she left. The defeat that was plain as day. Just looking in her eyes, I suddenly understood all those fears she talked about the other night. Whereas before, I could play her concerns off as an exaggeration because she hasn't found the right man yet, but now I get it. Now I know why she has never bothered trying to bring anyone else into her fold. Because she's right.

Single moms have to put up with shit all the time, but to

have a child with a disability and a conduct disorder at that, makes it that much harder. She can't trust that anyone would want to be a part of her life because it will always be hard. There is no light at the end of the tunnel. What her life with Oli is now, will be her life forever.

What Greer doesn't understand, though, is I think she's worth a shot.

Pulling up to her house, I see her car in the driveway. Good. I didn't tell her I was coming, so I'm glad she's home. I don't want to wait to talk to her. I have too much to say.

Grabbing the flowers from the passenger seat, I hop out of my truck and set my plan in motion.

Her expression when she swings open the door isn't surprising. I know she wasn't expecting me. She's dressed in sweats, hair up on top of her head, and not a stitch of makeup on that I can see. I like seeing her like this.

"Ace." It's not a question about why I'm here. More like a statement making sure she's not seeing things.

"Hi, Greer. Can I come in?"

She hesitates momentarily before snapping out of her thoughts. "Oh! Yeah. Sure. Come in. Um, can I get you something to drink?" she offers, closing the door behind us.

"I'm good, thanks. These are for you." Handing her the flowers, she brings them to her nose and inhales.

"How did you know I'd like purple daisies?"

"I saw you admiring the field when the wild purple flowers were blooming. They reminded me of that day. You were beautiful, staring off into the horizon, your hair blowing in the breeze."

"Ace," she whispers, and I know she wants me to stop. I know she doesn't trust I'm man enough to handle anything Oli can give, which is exactly why she needs to let me show her.

So I stop divvying out compliments and decide to give her what she really needs—truth.

"Can we sit?" I gesture to the couch, and she nods.

It doesn't go unnoticed by me that she puts distance between us in the form of an entire couch cushion's worth of space. Placing the flowers on the table in front of her, she turns her body toward me. "Oli's out of the program, isn't he?"

I can't stop myself from moving forward and taking her hand in mine. "No, Greer, he's not."

Her eyes snap up to mine, and I can see disbelief written all over her face. "What?"

"Oli isn't the first kid to disobey, and he sure won't be the last. Yes, he broke some trust, and for that, he's going to lose some privileges, but he is exactly the kind of kid we started this program for. He has a shot at learning life skills that will help him become independent and productive. We're not gonna throw in the towel at the first major incident."

The tears are flowing freely down her face now. "But Pedro could've been killed."

She's right. But I wave her off anyway. "Pedro's got nothing but a concussion and some wounded pride."

A laugh bursts out of her through the tears, and I like that some of her anxieties are being relieved.

"There's more." She takes a deep breath before nodding for me to go on. "I've been thinking a lot about the conversation we had the other night at the dance hall, and in light of recent events, I think I understand."

She looks at me quizzically but doesn't interrupt.

"I understand why you don't trust that anyone would want to be part of your life, because it's hard and it always will be."

"Ace." She quietly turns away, but I reach over, cupping her chin and turning her back to me. I want her to hear what I have to say. To really focus on what I mean.

"Greer, just let me say my piece, okay?"

She nods again, and I know I only have one chance to get this right. "My baby brother was a late-in-life baby. Almost immediately, my mama knew something wasn't right. Even when she was first pregnant. But she didn't care. She wasn't planning on another baby, but there he was, and she was going to embrace the challenge. She and my daddy both.

"When he was born, he was diagnosed with Down's Syndrome. And that made not one bit of difference to her. It made not one bit of difference to my father and made not one bit of difference to me. My mama and my daddy agreed they were going to take it one day at a time. Do the best they could and trust it would all work out.

"When my daddy passed suddenly, I came back home because somebody had to run the farm. That fell to me. I couldn't let it fall apart. I didn't necessarily want to come back, but I knew I needed to. But it was more than that. I knew, we all knew, at some point John's care would fall to me. And that's when Mama and I came up with the idea to do the co-op side of All Hands Farm.

"Since that time, we've built up the facility to teach skills to kids like John, like Oli, so they would have a place to go. A place to belong."

I turn to face her, our knees touching, and grab her hands.

"I know I'm not biting off more than I can chew by dating you. The lifetime care of my brother fell to me when my mama died. I know what that felt like. It put everything else on hold. I knew my life would never be my own, but what choice did I have? I could either grow to resent the situation, or I could find the joy in the hand I'd been dealt. That's when I decided to continue building the farm. To branch out into other areas like a little bit of breeding and letting Pedro break in some horses."

"He really does do that anyway?"

I chuckle, because of all the things I've just said, she's still most concerned with Pedro's safety over her own happiness. "Yes, baby. He does it all the time. Breaking horses is part of his job. This particular mare is proving to be a little more difficult."

"Oh." She sniffles and rubs her sleeve-covered hand over her eye, grimacing when some mascara ends up on her shirt. There's some under her eyes too, but I don't care. She's beautiful to me.

"Greer, there is no better person in the world to date than me, because I *get* it. I get that raising Oli is a lifelong thing. It doesn't scare me away. If anything, it makes me feel like fate intervened with us. Who else is going to understand his issues more than I do? Who else is going to be able to help you better than I will? I don't know what the future holds for us. This thing between us is still new. But I would like to see you more. And I don't want you to hold back because you're afraid Oli is going to do something to scare me away. He's not going to make me change my mind. I've already been where you are, so I know exactly what I'm getting into."

A stray tear falls down her cheek, and I wipe it away.

"We could last forever. But if we don't, it's going to be because we aren't meant to be. No other reason. But I'd really like to see if we're meant to be. If that's okay with you."

She nods, and I hold myself back from hooting and hollering like my best friend would be doing right about now.

"I've never met anyone who doesn't treat Oli like he's different, ya know?" I nod because I do know. We used to get the stares and whispers. "But you treat him like he's just a person. Like he's important and special."

"He *is* important and special. Just like Julie is. And just like you."

When she looks up at me with her big brown eyes, I realize how close we've gotten since the conversation started. I glance down as she licks her lips, and I realize what perfect timing really is.

Leaning in a few more inches, I capture her sweet lips with mine. Our kiss is slow and deliberate. Nothing rushed or hormone fueled. Just two people getting to know the feel of each other, the taste of each other, the scent of each other. Breathing each other in so deep, there's no way we'll be able to untangle from each other again.

We pull apart, foreheads still touching and smile at each other.

"I hate that Pedro was right." She crinkles her brow in confusion. "He said I needed to stop being gentlemanly and kiss you already."

She laughs out loud. "Pedro was right." Her giggles are cut short when I take her lips back in mine.

We kiss for what feels like hours, never doing anything more than that. There's no need. There's no rush.

I already know this is the beginning of something amazing.

Amazing Grayson

THE CONTINUATION

Chapter One

Greer

One by one, I gently place my feet on the basement stairs, cringing every time one creaks. Despite my pounding heart and the fear that I'm feeling, whatever, or whoever is down here, will be facing the aluminum end of the bat clutched tightly in my fist when I find him.

As soon as I make it to the bottom of the stairs the door flings open and…

"Ah!" I jump out of my office chair and scream when my phone rings. Grabbing it, I don't recognize the number which just freaks me out more. "WHO ARE YOU AND WHAT DO YOU WANT FROM ME?" I yell into the receiver.

The female voice on the other end remains calm. "Uh, it's Joie and what I want is my ear drum back now that you blew it out of my head screaming."

Clutching my chest to try and calm my racing heart, I collapse back into my hair. "Ohmygod. I'm so sorry, Joie. You scared me."

"Really. I hadn't noticed." Unsurprisingly, I sense sarcasm in her tone. "What are you doing that caused you to react like that to a phone call?"

Dropping my head on the desk, I continue trying to get my breathing under control. I recognize the ridiculousness of the situation. I'm never going to hear the end of it once she tells Jack about it. "I'm working."

"Uh huh. I'm guessing there's more to it than that."

Scrunching my nose, I fess up to my less than stellar idea. "I picked up a new client who writes thrillers. And, well, I don't do scary."

"What do you mean you don't do scary? How scary is scary?"

I begin ticking it all off on my fingers. "All the lights are on, all the blinds are open, it's the middle of the day, I'm currently listening to Jingle Bell Rock and I still screamed when my phone rang."

"Oh my. That is bad," she says, not even trying to hide how hard she's laughing. "Why did you agree to do this if you knew you were going to be scared?"

Because I'm an idiot, I think to myself. "Because I had to turn down a few jobs when we moved so I wanted to get back on track."

"Greer." Joie's tone turns motherly. "If you're struggling to make ends meet, you need to let us know. Jack and I can help out while you get settled."

I smile, even though she can't see me. "I appreciate the offer, but I promise we're doing okay financially. I just meant I need to keep my name out there and making sure the community knows I'm active with my business. The second these Indie authors think you're no longer working, they find someone else to do the job instead."

"That's good to know. But the offer still stands any time."

"And I appreciate it." Swiveling in my chair, I relax into the seat and lean back to look at the ceiling, resting my shoulders. "Anyway, what's going on with you guys? I assume this is a pleasure call?"

She giggles and I can only imagine where her brain has gone—the same place mine did the second she started laughing. It's an industry hazard when you edit romance books. You end up with the humor of a twelve-year-old boy. Oli was one just a few years ago and his giggles used to come at the same types of conversations.

Joie finally clears her throat and suppresses her laughter. "That depends on what you choose to do with my offer."

I crinkly my brow. "Your offer? You have my full attention."

"The Vikings have a home game this weekend. I would love to take Oli and Julie to the game on Saturday and then they could spend the night with Jack and me. Maybe go to a movie Sunday afternoon before bringing them home that evening."

Sitting up in my chair, the idea of having a little bit of freedom for a whole twenty-four hours makes me really excited. It's been, gosh, I don't even know how long since I've had that much time away from the kids. Not that I don't love them and love being around them, but I could use some time to not be in supervisor mode. I could take a nap. Or see a movie. Or work.

Scratch that. I'm not working during a momcation. The possibilities feel endless.

Still, years of feeling like I'm being judged for my parenting abilities make it hard to let go. "Are you sure you want to? You know how Oli can get and I…well, I can never guarantee he'll be on his best behavior."

"I know. We both know. But I've been reading up on de-escalation techniques and Jack will be there."

"But during the game—"

"—Jack will be just a couple rows away if it comes down to it. But I don't think it will."

I bite my lip and try to tamp down my own personal insecurities. I'm here in Flinton for a reason… to be closer to my brother and have a small support system. I need to take advantage of the opportunity for Oli's sake, but also for my own.

"They would love that," I quickly respond before I change my mind. "But make sure you lock up all your electronics that night. Oli's, uh… well, he's struggling with sticky fingers again."

"Again?" she asks and I know she's not being judgmental, just a concerned almost-aunt.

"Yeah. He's struggled with it before. Dumb things like picking up a cell phone if he sees it and hiding away to download games. We usually have it pretty under control but I think maybe he has some anxiety from me dating, or left over from moving or something. I never really know what triggers his setbacks, just try to push through them."

I hold my breath, waiting for her to change her mind about having the kids visit, but I shouldn't underestimate her. "Well, that'll be easy. I have a small fire proof safe in my closet for important papers. I'll just store everything in there for the night."

Letting go of that breath, I feel nothing but relief. "Thank you, Joie. It'll be nice to have a night off."

"And," she singsongs, "this way you can go on a date with that hunky cowboy you've been seeing. Maybe you should pack an overnight bag. Just in case."

My jaw drops open at her insinuation because, holy cow. I could get some sex.

I start making a mental list of what I need to do before this weekend. Pedicure. Bikini wax. Rewind the clock and spend two years in the gym prepping for this opportunity.

Okay, so hindsight is 20/20, but at least I can get the nails and waxing done.

"Greer?" Joie's voice cuts through the line. "So that's a definite yes?"

"Yes!" I practically yell making Joie laugh again. "I mean, that would be great, thank you."

"That's what we're here for, Greer. It's why Jack was hoping for so long that you would move close. We know how hard it is… well, Jack does. I haven't been around very long, so I'm just now learning what it all entails. But I'm guessing the last date you had was last month when Jack babysat? When you went dancing?"

I bob my head from side to side because she's right, but she's wrong, too. We talk on the phone every night and we've seen each other at least twice a week for over a month. Sometimes it's lunch. Sometimes it's a matinee. Sometimes it's a coffee. But lately it's always ended with a make out session. Depending on where we are, maybe even some heavy petting. Of course I don't tell Joie any of that.

"The last time we went out *at night* was then. But Ace has been really sweet, trying to meet up during the day sometimes, too. He has to come to town for supplies and stuff about once a week, so we try to do lunch. He took me to get snow cones at this really great little shack on the side of the road."

"Oh I've seen that place! I wonder if they're still open."

"Nope. Closed for the season. I wanted to take the kids the very next day but they were already shut down."

"That's a bummer. Now I'm craving a snow cone." I can't help the giggle that bursts out of me. Partially because Joie is funny, but mostly because of the nerves that are suddenly over taking me.

Am I ready for this? Am I ready to spend the night with Ace? I think I am. I like him that much. But it's been so long. Surely it's like riding a bike, right? Well not a bike, but like riding…

I giggle again because, twelve-year-old boy humor.

"Um, that wasn't funny?"

"What? Oh. Sorry, Joie. I got lost in my thoughts. What did you say?"

"I asked if noon was too early to pick them up. I'll take the kids to lunch and maybe we can walk around the tailgating party in the parking lot before the gates open for the game?"

"Yeah. Yeah, noon would be fine."

"Okay," she announces. "I'll pick them up then. And Greer," she adds. "Enjoy taking some time for yourself. Even if you don't go on a date, you're not allowed to work."

How is it possible for her to know me that well, already? My automatic instinct is to always work when I don't have to keep a close eye on anyone else.

"I promise," I reply. "I won't work. I'll take a nice, refreshing nap instead."

We work out more of the details, like how the kids need to dress for the game and the medications Oli is taking. When we hang up, I stare at my phone for a while, thinking.

Am I really going to do this? Am I going to make the first move?

No. I don't want to be presumptuous. What if Ace already has weekend plans?

But what if he doesn't?

Decision made, I grab my phone and open my text messages.

Me: *My brother and his girlfriend are going to keep the kids Saturday night. You wouldn't happen to already have plans would you?*

Placing my phone back on my desk, I nod once and mentally pat myself on my back for being cool about all this. While I wait, this is a good time to get back to editing. I'm not sure I can be engaged enough in the story for it to feel as scary, so I continue reading.

As soon as I make it to the bottom of the stairs the door flings open and Pumpkin, our cat saunters through.

Lowering my bat, I lean down to pet him. "What are you doing you silly cat. Are you the one making the noise down here?"

Out of nowhere, I hand grabs the back of my neck and...

"Ah!" I jump out of my chair and scream when my phone pings. "Dammit! Is that going to happen every time?"

Picking up my phone, I'm still breathing heavily as I open the text. It's from Ace.

Now I'm breathing heavily with anticipation about what he's going to say, not just because White Christmas isn't buffering my fear factor at all.

Stupid, useless Christmas carols.

Ace: *I have no plans at all, unless you consider taking you out as plans.*

Me: *If that's your way of asking me on a date, I accept.*

Watching the three little dots start and stop, my anxiety ratchets up a notch. Is he thinking the same thing I am? Is he just busy and I'm distracting him? I want to distract myself from waiting for whatever it is he's about to say, but I'm not sure continuing with this edit while the kids are gone is a good idea.

I snort a laugh at my own ridiculousness. Because waiting for my teenaged children to come home and protect me from the hand that just grabbed her at the bottom of the stair case makes so much sense. Besides, I should be able to finish this in the next few hours before they come home right? I'm on page…

"Fifty-seven of one hundred and eighty?!"

Groaning, I lean back and look at the ceiling again. Why did I think this was a good idea? It's going to take me three more days to finish at this rate, and I'll have nightmares for twice that long.

My phone finally alerts me of another text.

Snatching it up as fast as humanly possible, I have to read it three times to make sure I'm not seeing things.

Ace: *Would it be presumptuous of me to ask you to pack an overnight bag?*

Biting my bottom lip, I try really hard not to squeal with excitement. Ace wants me to spend the night.

I'm going to have sex.

I think.

Well, crap. Now I'm being presumptuous.

Me: *Not presumptuous at all.*

Ace: *Good. I'm in the middle of cleaning stalls right now, but I'll get with you later tonight to work out some details, if that's okay with you.*

Me: *Perfectly okay. Talk to you then.*

Placing my phone back down, I'm practically giddy with excitement. I don't know what will happen Saturday night but it never hurts to plan ahead.

Pulling up Yelp, I scroll until I find what I'm looking for, pick up my phone again and dial the number.

"Um, yes, I'd like to schedule an appointment for a bikini wax," I say when the receptionist picks up.

Nope. Doesn't hurt to plan ahead at all.

Chapter Two

Ace

Sliding my phone back in my pocket, I'm grinning from ear to ear. I'm excited to be taking Greer on a date this weekend, and honestly, I'm excited about the possibilities that go along with her spending the night, too. The idea that she likes me enough to want to sleep with me makes my heart swell and my jeans tight.

As I keep mucking, I go through ideas of where we can go. I keep coming back to the same thing, though—the rodeo.

I want to introduce her to anything and everything that I enjoy. I want to know if they might be things she enjoys, too. I want to show her that the life of a cowboy can be fun and exciting and it's not just… well, slinging shit like I'm doing now. Besides, she looks amazing in jeans and cowboy boots.

Oh lord. I'm turning into a pansy.

The sounds of squealing and scraping across the floor of the back room catches my attention. "What the hell?" I prop my pitchfork up against the stall wall so I can go investigate.

Rounding the corner into the large room we use mostly as storage, Pedro is grimacing as he pulls on the machinery.

"What are you doing with the mechanical bull?" I call out.

Just seeing it in all its rusted glory brings back memories. The two of us used to practice on that thing every day, when we were in our bronc riding days. Dreamed of hitting the rodeo circuit, winning every competition, and impressing all the ladies, so practice is all we did when we weren't working the farm.

That was twenty or so years ago, before our dreams changed and other priorities took over. And the spiderwebs overtook the mechanical bull.

He relaxes and wipes his sleeve across his brow. "Good. You're here. Grab the other end and let's get this sucker set up."

Sauntering to the back of the machine, he glares at me when I end up in the "push" position, meaning he has to "pull" again. His own damn fault. He should have moved faster.

"On three. One, two, three." We both groan as we put all our strength into moving it across the floor to the center of the room. "You didn't answer my question," I say with a grunt. "Why are we doing this?"

Panting after getting it in place, he wipes he brow again before answering. "If I'm gonna climb on Rockette any time soon, I need to be prepared for her to buck."

"Rockette?" I question.

"My mare. Named her for her mean high kick," he says with a grin, like this is funny.

Normally, I might find humor in the name he's come up with for that holy terror, but not this time. This time I narrow my eyes, hoping to convey how I really feel. "That mare just about killed you."

He makes a noise like I'm being ridiculous. "She didn't about kill me. Bruised a couple ribs, that's all."

"And gave you a concussion."

"Which wasn't severe and I've already been given the green light to get back to normal activity."

I continue glare at him, hoping he feels the weight of my displeasure over this turn of events. I don't mind her still being here. She's had a hard life. Her scars are proof of that. There are worse things than an old horse living out the last of her years being properly fed and housed. Trying to turn her into a work horse, though, is entirely different.

"Don't look at me like that," Pedro says softly, not looking up from underneath the rig as he messes with it. "I know you think it's a dumb idea and I'm off my rocker. But I'm telling you Ace, she has so much potential to be amazing. I won't get on her before she's ready. I just want to get some of my muscle memory back for worst case scenario."

I sigh and move my head around, stretching my neck muscles. I trust Pedro to know what he's doing. But it also scared the hell out of me when he was kicked. For a few seconds, I honestly thought he was dead. He's my best friend. My right-hand man. Basically my brother. If I had lost him, I don't know what I would have done.

There are two different emotions battling inside me—the one that trusts he knows what he's doing and I need to let him make his own choices, and the one that is terrified something bad will happen.

Before one of them can win out, he's back to his normal, fun-loving self.

"Got it!" he shouts victoriously as the machine hums to life. "Let's get all these mats set up so we can try her out.

As much as I don't agree with this, the thought of getting back in this saddle after so many years does sound fun. Sure, it's been a long time since I've ridden anything harder than a fast gallop across the field, but it can't be hard to get back into the groove.

It takes a few minutes to find all the mats that have been hidden behind various supplies and tools over the years. Its takes even more time to drag them out, set them up and make sure everything is secure. It's definitely not a two-man job, but I don't think either one of us is ready to let anyone else know what we're up to. Just in case it doesn't go as well as planned.

Coughing from all the dust that's been disturbed for the first time in twenty years, Pedro seems to have a change of heart.

"You're up, Ace. Climb in that saddle and let's see what you can do."

My eyes bug out in disbelief at how easily I got suckered. "What the hell are you talking about? This was your brilliant idea."

"Yeah, but I practically broke my ribs a few weeks ago," he spouts off.

Crossing my arms over my chest, I refuse to fall for his shit. "Funny how you've been coughing for the last ten minutes with no pain at all."

He looks at me, then forces a cough for the sole purpose of fake grimacing. "Ow."

Still not falling for it. "Weren't you just spouting off how you've been given the all clear by your doctor?"

"It's not the doctor I'm worried about." Making it clear he

has no plans to saddle up, he positions himself behind the controls instead. "My very pregnant wife would kill me if she found out I was out here doing this."

I pause, considering my options. I don't agree with us practicing so Pedro can climb back on the horse that damn near killed him.

Then again, this machine isn't a crazy-ass mare. It's a mechanical bull that we can control. And it looks like it'd be fun.

Pedro seems to tap into my conflicting thoughts, so he digs the rhetorical knife in just a bit. "Maybe you're right. Maybe you're too old and frail for this."

Shooting daggers, I argue, "I just turned forty this year."

He shrugs. "Over the hill, man."

Grumbling about what an asshole he is, I stomp over to the bull and climb on, careful to make sure the stirrups aren't worn through. After slapping the dust off the thick reign, I nod at him once. "Don't get too crazy. This thing hasn't been turned on in over a decade."

"Understood."

Raising my arm in the air, giving the signal that I'm ready to ride, Pedro starts me off nice and slow. I use my muscles every day when I ride across the pasture or round up cattle. But it's been a while since I've had to adjust my body according to the jerky twists and turns of a bucking anything.

Turns out, Pedro is right. Muscle memory seems to come back relatively quickly.

Spinning my finger in a small circle, I signal for him to give it a little more juice.

Squeezing my thighs together, I push and pull in the stirrups, keeping may balance as we buck and spin, faster and faster, until I feel myself starting to lose control.

I wave my hands in a cutting motion, trying to get him to slow me down. He doesn't. Instead, he speeds me up.

"Cut it off, Pedro!" I yell.

"I can't!" he yells back. "It's stuck!"

That's not good. I have two choices. Either ride it out or let myself be thrown. The mats are soft, but I have too much pride for that. Riding it out it is, with an extra helping of hope that Pedro will fix the problem quickly.

Hanging on for dear life, I strain to keep myself upright. Lean back, push up, hold my form. I'm doing better than I thought I would, mostly out of necessity and not fun, but finally it's just too much. I feel myself lose control and slide to the side.

One quick jerk to the right and the hind of the bull pop me upright, through the air, landing so far back I almost miss the mat and hit the floor.

As I pull myself to a sitting position and shake the dust out of my hair, all I hear is Pedro busting a gut.

"I never knew you could fly that far," he ribs, still fighting with the control panel.

"Shut up, asshole. I told you that was a bad idea."

"But it was fun, right?"

He's got me there, whether I'll admit it to him or not.

"Think you can fix it?" I finally ask once the machine sputters and dies.

Climbing on his hands and knees to look at the electrical wires under the device, he shrugs. "Probably just needs a little tweaking."

"Good. Work on that when you can."

"On it boss," he says with a smile.

He thinks that my caving means he pulled a fast one on me. What he doesn't realize is I just can't wait to take over the controls and return the favor.

Chapter Three

Greer

"Bye! I love you! Have fun!" I yell out the door, waving like a maniac as the kids drive away. They're not even paying attention. They're teenagers. But I'm barely keeping my nerves in check as it is. If yelling my affections at my children while they drive away is what works, so be it.

Eventually, they're out of sight and I have to close my front door. Leaning back against it, I close my eyes and take a series of deep breathes.

Tonight is the night. Tonight, I'm going to take the bull by the horns and enjoy the physical affections of dating.

Even in my head, that pun sounds really cheesy and over the top, but it's been a long time. If I've learned anything about Ace over the last few weeks it's that he's extremely old fashioned and respectful. He won't push me. He won't pressure. And if I change my mind, he'll back off. I know this with every fiber of my being.

No, what I'm the most nervous about is the prep for tonight.

Glancing up at my wall clock, I cuss under my breath. If I don't book it I'm going to be late for my very first bikini wax. I've always wanted to get one, but never got around to it. It seems easy to just do a quick shave in the shower as needed. But with a new house, a new dating life, and some new-found freedom courtesy of my big brother, I might as well try something new. Especially since I got a discount. Aren't Groupon's great?

Grabbing my stuff, I race out the door and into my car, setting the GPS to guide me to the salon.

It only takes a few short minutes to reach the parking lot, not nearly enough time to get my nerves under control. But then I think of my plans for the evening and know I'm doing the right thing. Showing my hoo-ha to a total stranger for the purpose of ripping out my pubic hair is absolutely the right decision.

I giggle at my own ridiculousness and clamor out of the car before I go completely off the deep end and talk myself out of this.

My nerves immediately calm as I walk into the front room. It's decorated in soft blues and greys, relaxing music piping through some hidden speakers, and one of those glass waterfalls off to the side. I love the sound of water. It's so soothing.

"Hello. How can I help you?" The woman behind the desk is older than me. Probably in her 50's. She's dressed impeccably, hair pulled back in a soft chignon. Her eyes radiating warmth and calm.

Man, I really lucked out with this Groupon. This is a fancy place.

Feeling more confident in what's about to happen, I approach with a genuine smile. "Yes, I have an appointment for a waxing."

She looks down at the giant appointment calendar on her desk. Even her handwriting is impeccable. "Oh yes. Greer Declan?" I nod. "You'll be seeing Rachel today. I see you're a new customer, so I'm going to have you fill out a few papers for me."

She hands me a clipboard and gives me instructions on what I'm signing. Within a few minutes, I've signed over my rights to sue for any accidental burns, which admittedly caused me to pause for a few seconds, and have been called to the back by a tiny woman.

Maybe tiny is a bit of an exaggeration. She's definitely short and fit, like an ex-gymnast or cheerleader. She smiles brightly at me, her blond ponytail bobbing back and forth as she leads me into a small room. The walls sport the same color palette as the front and the same music. The biggest difference is the table in the middle of the room.

"I see you're a new client," Rachel remarks as she looks over the questionnaire I answered regarding allergies and treatment preferences. "We're doing a Brazilian wax. Barely there or smooth as a baby's bum?"

Her question throws me for a loop. I'm too busy processing what she just said. I accidentally scheduled a Brazilian wax, not a bikini wax. I may not be current on the latest grooming trends, but even I know there's a big difference between the two. "Smooth as... wait, what?"

She smiles kindly. Obviously I'm not the first newbie she's had. "I try to talk in code a bit. Makes it sounds less clinical. You have your choice of what style of wax you want. We can leave a patch, a strip straight down the middle, or get rid of it altogether. Your preference."

It occurs to me that this is one of the weirdest conversations I've ever had with a stranger. And I'm a romance editor who has social media, so I'm used to weird.

"Since this is my first time, let's leave a patch. But can it be kind of small? I know completely bare is the trend and all," again, romance editor so I know things, "but that's just weird."

Rachel laughs and reaches into a cabinet, pulling out some clean towels. "It's not as much of a trend as you think. I have so many more clients that just want to clean up a bit. Now, go ahead and strip off all your clothes from the waist down and put these on." Handing me a paper thong that I'm praying doesn't give me a paper cut and a small towel that gives me flashbacks to my last gynecology appointment, she adds, "Then have a seat on the table and cover yourself with the towel. I'll be back in a few."

Worried I'll be caught with my pants around my ankles, my clothes are off faster than a stripper trying to pay her rent on time. Which leaves me more time to look around the room.

From this vantage point, it reminds me even more of being at the gynecologist. Tiny towel that barely covers me and certainly doesn't cover my ass. A real sheet on the table, so that's an upgrade. Giggling, I think about looking down to see if there are stirrups attached. If so, I might have to question which office I actually came to.

Wait… are there stirrups??

A quick peek underneath the table reassures me that I am in the salon after all. That was a close one. Although I'm pretty sure the paper thong just ripped in half with my stretching.

"Knock, knock." I hear a rap on the door and Rachel sticks her head in the room, still smiling. I suppose she would be happy that it's not her pubes getting ready to be yanked out.

Okay, breathe, Greer. It will be fine. Millions of women do this every day.

"Are you ready?"

Taking a deep breath, I nod Rachel's direction. "A little nervous, but I'll be okay."

She closes the door behind her and crosses the room where a bowl of warm wax in a crock pot looking thing is waiting. Why didn't I notice that before? Oh yeah. I was too busy inspecting the table of doom.

"That's to be expected, but I promise, it'll be over before you know it. Go ahead and lie back."

I follow her instructions, praying the towel doesn't fall off. It's been a long time since anyone has been down there.

She moves my leg so it's bent at the knee, foot resting against my other leg. The good news, I'm more bendy than I thought I was. The bad news... she moves the towel around exposing parts of me that have never seen the light of day.

"Are you comfortable?" she asks, gloved hand resting on my leg.

"Yep," I squeak out, eyes shut tight as I wait for the rip of skin.

Instead, I feel a cool cloth run across my innermost thigh. That actually feels good, in an uncomfortably intimate way.

"I'm just cleaning the area of any body oils so the wax works better." More rubbing. "And now for a nice corn starch powder."

My body starts to relax. So far, this isn't bad at all.

"And now for the wax."

Again, not so bad. It's warm and comforting. Like a mini heating pad on my inner thigh. She pats and presses and I close my eyes to rest. Why haven't I done this before?

Riiiiiip.

"Ah!" I squeal, barely aware of her pressing down on the area of my skin that was just been violated in the most violent of ways. "Ohmygod, tell me you're done!"

I can tell she's trying not to laugh when she says, "That was about a two-inch section. We have three or four more of those before moving inward."

"What?!" I screech, falling into the Lamaze breathing techniques I haven't employed since Julie's birth.

"Give it a second." Rachel pushes down lightly for a few more seconds until the pain is all but gone.

Looking down to make sure there isn't blood all over the table from a gaping wound, I realize, except for that initial sting, it actually wasn't as bad as I thought it would be.

"Huh," I remark mostly to myself at this realization.

Rachel looks down at me with another smile. "It passes quickly, doesn't it?"

I nod, still surprised that I didn't really have anything to be worried about in the first place.

"The first pull of your first time is always the worst," she says, applying more wax to another part of my thigh. "Once the anticipation is gone, usually it's not so bad."

As if she's trying to prove a point, she takes that moment to rip the next strip of wax off.

"Oof." That's the only reaction I give this time. "Wow. You're right. I think my nerves made it so much worse. It doesn't tickle. But it's not horrible."

She finishes up my inner thigh, moving to the next one

where we go through the same process before cleaning up more intimate parts. While she works, she tells me all about how she got into the business of waxing other people's business. I concentrate hard on her story while I try not to notice exactly where her fingers are pressing. Turns out, she is, in fact, a former gymnast and waxing was a regular thing when she wore tiny leotards on a daily basis. Makes sense that now some of her regular clients come from the same gym she used to train at.

Before I know it, I'm done and she's having me sit up.

"Wow, that wasn't bad at all, Rachel," I remark. "You do a great job."

"Well thanks. Now get on your hands and knees."

I'm almost positive my brain shorts out because I'm not understanding the last thing she just said. "I'm sorry, what?"

She waves her hand around. "Hands and knees. We have one last area to wax."

Blinking rapidly, I'm trying to figure out if she's meaning what I think she's meaning.

"Greer? You paid for a complete Brazilian. You know that right?"

"Yes," I squeak out because no. No, I did not know that.

She turns away and grabs more cloths and popsicle sticks and other supplies that are now going to go in my bum. *What is happening?*

"This is actually the easiest part. We'll get you nice and cleaned up back there. You won't need to have it done again for at least a month."

"That's good."

That's good? No it's not good. I'm about to have the hair on my butthole waxed off and I can't even think because I didn't even know I had hair on my butthole.

Following her instructions, I struggle to keep the tiny little towel draped over my backside. Of course, the effort is futile, and pointless as she just pulls it up, exposing my practically naked rear to the world.

Okay, not the world. But it is facing the door. That's going to be awkward if someone accidentally mistakes this room for the restroom.

Placing her hand on my lower back, Rachel moves my last of the paper panties to the side and spreads the wax where the sun don't shine.

Ohmygod, there is hot wax in my ass and lord help me, but it actually feels good.

I'm going to hell. I just know it.

Riiiiiip.

The wax comes off and a cool cloth comes on so fast, I barely register that it's over and done with until she tells me to turn back over and relax.

"Wait, that's it?" I question, just in case she's tricking me again.

"That's it."

"For real this time? I don't have like, hang over the side of the bed or anything to reach some obscure hairs I don't know about?"

She laughs and removes her gloves, making a snapping sound. "Nope. All obscure parts are officially hairless now." She pats my leg again. I'm sure she's used to having to comfort people while they get over the shock of their first time. "Take your time getting dressed. I'll meet you outside."

The door closes behind her and I'm left still feeling a little stunned by the turn of events. One thing is for sure though.

If Ace is having any thought of backdoor action, he can forget about it. I've had more than enough fingers there for one day.

Chapter Four

Ace

"Hi," Greer says with a huge smile, her face full of excitement and anticipation of tonight. I suspect it has less to do with me and more to do with having a night off of being a parent. Either way, I don't care. She's officially a sight for sore eyes.

Before stepping foot inside her house, I have to get one thing straight, though. "Are the kids here?"

She shakes her head. "Nope. Joie picked them up at noon—"

Before she can get the next words out of her mouth, I attack her like a starving man. My lips on hers, my hips pressed against hers, my fingers in her hair. Nipping at her bottom lip, her mouth parts just slightly and I take that as my invitation to enter. I should take my time. Should be a gentleman. But alone time is so infrequent, the only thing I can think is to take advantage of it.

She doesn't seem to mind. Pressing her into the wall so

our bodies are aligned, I press my tongue into her mouth, tasting her, caressing her, enjoying her.

We stay that way for several minutes, her hands tugging me tight to her, small moans falling from her lips when I press my pelvis into hers so she knows exactly how much I'm looking forward to tonight. I take it by her response, she's excited about all our prospects, too.

We see each other a couple times a week and it's never anything special. Just quality time spent together. But tonight is different and we both know it. Tonight, there's no time limit. Tonight we can stay out late or go home early. Tonight, we answer to no one, so I take advantage and enjoy the feel of her, the taste of her, the smell of her.

When I think I'm about to combust, I force myself to pull away, but not too much. I don't want to completely lose this connection. Instead, I press my forehead to hers and lick my lips.

"Hi," I whisper, still feeling the surge of hormones racing through me, but holding tightly to my control. I have plans for tonight that don't' include ripping her clothes off and having my way with her in her front hallway. With her door wide open.

"Oh shit. Your door is still wide open."

I turn to grab the handle and slam it, her giggling behind me. Honest to goodness giggling, which I've never heard her do before. She laughs. She chuckles. But she's never giggled like a school girl with a crush before.

I spin back around slowly, quirking an eyebrow at her. "Are you… nervous?"

Her face turns pink with her blush as she stammers "What? Why would I be nervous?"

"Because I asked you to pack an overnight bag." I stalk towards her, enjoying that she's as on edge as I am. I don't like playing games, but flirting like this is making the anticipation that much more fun.

She presses herself back against the wall keeping her eyes glued to mine. "I'm not nervous about spending the night."

"Oh you're not." I box her in, leaning in as much as I can without actually touching her. We're so close, I can feel her breath on my lips. I know I'm pushing my own limits, but I can't help myself. The prospect of this evening combined with an empty house and her taste now on my tongue has me questioning my own resolve.

"No." She toys with my collar, straightening it absent-mindedly. "I'm ready."

"Are you sure?"

She nods and then says the words I wasn't expecting. "I went and got waxed just in case."

Aaaaaaand my brain shorts out.

I can practically feel sparks coming from my ears. I'm sure my face goes completely blank as I blink. And blink again. And blink one more time.

"We need to leave," I grit out and pull my body away from hers quickly.

This time she just laughs. No giggling. She knows how she just affected me. It was part of her evil little plan. A plan I can totally get on board with.

"Wait." She grabs my arm and spins me around, her thumb coming to my lips. "I don't think this shade of lipstick is your color."

I smile as I watch her concentrate on wiping her lipstick off my mouth. I love being this close to her. I love making her smile and laugh. I love how effortless it is to be with her. We can spend an hour at night talking about an interesting topic. Or we can spend an hour having a silent lunch in the park enjoying the sunshine. We've done both.

"There," she finally says. "Good as new."

Never taking my eyes off hers I whisper, "Thank you," and give her another quick peck.

"Hey!" she protests. "Don't dirty yourself up again."

"Sorry." I'm not sorry. Looking around, I see a duffle bag on the floor by the door. "Are we bringing this with us?"

Her blush returns. "Um, yeah. I know we talked about being presumptuous, but since I'm not under any time constraints tonight..."

"Greer," I stop her, putting my hand on her cheek making her look at me. "Nothing has to happen if we don't want it to. Actually, if *you* don't want it to because I already know I won't turn you down." She giggles again and I admit how much I like hearing it. It's endearing that she's nervous about spending the night with me.

"I know. It's just... it's been a long time."

"For me, too."

She nods and takes a deep breathe. "Well then let's go. You need to wine and dine me and see if this goes anywhere from here."

My heart swells, along with another appendage. I don't give her a chance to change her mind. I grab her duffle, then grab her hand, and out the door we go.

"I can't believe you brought me here," she squeals. "I've always wanted to go to a real Texas rodeo. I didn't even know it was in town."

Her cheeks are flushed and her eyes bright as she takes in the arena. There's a lot to look at. From the professional riders to the rodeo clowns to the people watching, she hasn't looked at me once since we sat down. There's just too much excitement. That's what I was hoping would happen. That she would enjoy herself.

"What? There's at least one ad every commercial break these days."

She shrugs. "I don't really watch TV. I don't even have cable."

I scrunch my eyebrows together. "Then what do you watch?"

"Nothing really. I'd rather read. We have one of those internet stick things so if we want to stream something we can."

I think for a second but I'm still confused. "But our first date, Jack was watching sports."

"Jack set the whole thing up since I'm not that technologically inclined. Who knows what he found. It could have been old games for all I know."

She continues to look around, taking it all in. "So what are we going to see anyway?"

"Whatever we want. We can go see the farm animals or ride the carnival rides."

She scrunches her nose, clearly not thrilled with that idea, making me laugh.

"What? Not a fan of rollercoasters?"

"Oh I love rollercoasters," she says. "Ones that are actually bolted into the ground permanently. I have the weird obsession with not flying through the air and landing in the parking lot."

Squeezing her shoulder because she's so close and yet I can't help wanting her even closer, I laugh. "We'll stay away from the fairgrounds then. You might like the events tonight anyway. They're starting with Mutton Busting in just a few minutes."

She looks at me for the first time since we sat down. "Is that where the little kids ride the sheep?"

I nod, grinning at her because I know she's going to love this event. "Sure is. It's like a miniature version of bull riding, but with little kids. To win, they have to stay on for six seconds."

As soon as the words are out of my mouth, we see a group of kids all dressed in protective gear cross through the arena. Sure enough, the sheep are being set up in the stalls, ready to take off and run.

"Can't they get hurt?" Greer asks, concern on her face.

"I guess they could. But really, they're only like two feet off the ground. I've been watching Mutton Busting for years and I've only seen a hand full of kids cry. And usually it's from getting dirt in their mouths."

Greer laughs lightly, but her eyes are glued down below. I stop talking and just let her take in the preparation. Before long, the event begins and we're smiling and laughing as we watch the mini daredevils as they hang on to a handful of wool for dear life.

Most of them fall off almost as soon as they get out of gate, but a few make it the entire six seconds or longer. You can tell by their reactions which ones participate because they live locally and it's fun, and which ones are hoping to make it to the World Championships. The serious riders immediately look up at their score when the fall. The locals seem more interested in taking a bow for the crowd.

"I'm a little sad I never took my kids to the rodeo when they were little. Oli would have loved riding a sheep," she jokes. "And I would have loved watching it."

"I'm pretty sure Pedro is already counting down the days until his new baby can try. Poor kid isn't even born yet and Pedro's already trying to turn him into a cowboy."

"Can you blame him? It's kind of fun."

Turn my head to focus all my attention on her, I take in her smile and how relaxed she seems in this element. In my element. It fills me with a sense of pride that she appreciates the lifestyle I've always lived.

"This is definitely the glamorous side of cowboy life. I'm glad I get to share it with you."

Her eyes flicker over to mine and she gazes at me under her lashes. "I'm glad you wanted to."

I can feel the sexual tension growing between us, but now is not the time or place, so instead of taking her in a passionate, and all too inappropriate public display of affection, I give her a quick peck and link her fingers through mine. Not only are we joined at the hands, our thighs are touching from knee to hip. If I wasn't feeling somewhat desperate to get her home, I don't think I'd ever want to leave this moment.

Our moment is lost when the announcer begins talking about the next event over the loud speaker.

We watch in mostly silence as the barrel racers guide their horse through a cloverleaf pattern around the fifty-five-gallon metal drums. It's impressive that the horses can make such tight turns. It's hard to comprehend that such huge, solid animals can also be so agile.

But barrel racing is not why we're here. What I really want her to experience is the next event—bronc riding.

"That's what you used to do, right?" She points at the riders who are busy getting themselves focused on the task at hand.

"Not on this big of a stage, but yeah. Saddle bronc riding was my sport of choice."

Her eyes are wide as the anticipation of the first ride builds. It's almost palpable throughout the stadium.

"What happens if more than one rider stays on for eight seconds?"

I shake my head, masking my chuckle. That damn movie has everyone confused even all these years later.

"It's not just about how long they can go. It's about technique," I explain as the first competitor climbs up on his ride in the chute. "It's about form. It's about precision. Now when his arm goes up, that's his signal that he's ready and for them to throw the gate open. Watch where his feet are when they go."

Just then, the rider gives the signal and we watch amid the cheers as he hangs on to the thick reign, barely holding on as he's bucked to and fro. It takes six point seven seconds for him to be thrown. Not good, but I've seen worse.

Leaning over to explain more to Greer I say, "Did you see how his feet where both touching the horse's shoulders when he first jumped?" Greer nods. "That's called marking out. He has to do that or he's automatically disqualified."

"So he has to keep a certain form during the ride?" she asks, fully invested in the events now.

"Yep. The goal is to look like he's barely being jostled.

All while be tossed around like a rag doll."

"Wow," Greer breathes and licks her lips, awe in her voice. "It's so much more intense than I realized."

"It takes a lot of power and a lot of control. But if you do it right, you'll have the ride of your life."

She doesn't speak, just watches as the next competitor gives the signal and off he goes.

Chapter Five

Greer

What Ace doesn't know is how sexy I found saddle bronc riding to be. I wasn't expecting that. At all.

But seeing how hard the riders had to squeeze their thighs together and how much they bucked their hips, well, all I could envision was what Ace would look like doing that.

Naked.

While thrusting those hips into me.

Somehow, I have turned into a horny mess around this man. I'm sure it's from the anticipation of what's to come tonight combined with how long it's been. Doesn't hurt that I read romance books for a living either.

But I can't discount the man himself and how attracted I am to him anyway. He just makes me feel beautiful.

No that's not right.

He makes me feel worthy. Like I'm worth the time and effort and difficulty of putting up with the chaos I'm surrounded with. And *that* is the sexiest thing about him—how he makes me feel about myself.

I spent so many years in a bad marriage feeling unworthy of anything. Like I couldn't do anything right. The house was never clean enough. My stomach was never flat enough. My time was never important enough.

Being with Ace is the exact opposite. In general, he puts others first. But when he decides he cares about you, well. It's just a whole other level of sacrifice. It's so much deeper.

Add onto it the tight jeans, calloused hands, now the visual image of him bronc riding and that's it for me. My self-imposed, although accidental, celibacy is definitely ending tonight.

Driving up to the front of the house, I realize I've seen it from a distance many times when I've visited the farm, but I've never seen it up close.

"How old is this house?" I ask when he parks. Even by today's standards, it's a large home. Two stories with a wraparound porch on bottom and a large balcony jutting out from the second floor.

Ace grabs my duffle out of the back of the truck and walks around to help me down, even though I'm already admiring house.

"My great grandfather built it back in the '20s. They had something like eight kids so they needed a lot of room."

"It's beautiful."

He smiles, never letting go of my hand as he leads me to the front door. One of the stairs squeaks when we step on it and Ace shrugs sheepishly.

"It's creaky. There are a lot of boards that need replacing. But I like living here."

Making our way through the front door, I look around. It smells like an older home. Like cedar and musk and… life. I look up and see all the way to the ceiling, which has a huge old chandelier. A railing on the second floor wraps around the entirety of that level so you can overlook the foyer from anywhere. It gives the illusion that the rooms are set up in one big square and we're in the center of it all. Old pictures that span back generations pepper the wall next to the stairs leading to that balcony. To my left, through a very large door, at least ten feet tall, appears to be a formal living room. To my right, an office.

"This is where the magic happens," Ace says walking into the room and flipping on the light. The switch is so old, it's two buttons that click when you push them. The top one to turn the lights on. The bottom to turn them off. Besides that, nothing really stands out. It looks like a normal office. Except as we walk through, there's a second door. "No one knows why there are two doors in here, but this one leads to the kitchen."

Sure enough, we end up next to a screen door that leads outside, a full bathroom across from us, and the massive kitchen just to our left.

"This is the busiest part of the house and where Brittany spends most of her time."

"Everyone eats here?" I run my fingers down a solid wood table that probably seats more than a dozen people. Long benches made of the same wood are pushed underneath.

He nods. "Breakfast, lunch and dinner."

That explains the bathroom by the back door.

"Must be weird having people come in and out of your house without knocking all day long."

He shrugs like it's no big deal. "They aren't wandering the house or anything. But it would probably seem odd if I hadn't grown up with it happening. The farm hands all have to eat and it's my responsibility to feed them."

"How did Brittany end up working for you?"

He chuckles and the sound reverberates through me. I wonder what it'd feel like for him to make a deep sound like that while he's on top of me.

I blink away my wayward thoughts. *We have all night, Greer. Slow your roll.*

"Pedro actually met her on a dating site. When they got engaged she happened to be in between jobs, but didn't want to get stuck behind a desk anymore. I guess she was tired of corporate America or something. But she liked cooking so we gave it a shot. She's been taking care of us ever since."

We continue walking around the building, making our way through another door into a formal dining room that boasts the largest fireplace I've ever seen in my life. I could stand straight up inside it and still see out. The formal living room I noticed when we first walked in is attached. Ace tells me the history behind some of the pictures on the walls and stories that have been passed down, like the time his great uncles got stuck inside the now non-functional dumb waiter.

Eventually, we come full circle and end up back in the foyer.

Standing at the bottom of the stairs, Ace clears his throat. "Um. The only things upstairs are the bedrooms. I don't know if you're tired, or…"

He stalls his sentence and shoves his hands in his pockets.

"Ace, you don't have to be a gentleman with me anymore."

I watch as his eyes darken and his lids grow heavy. This is the most awkward we've been and I know it's because he wants to make sure I'm ready. "I'm trying to take it at your pace. I don't ever want you to think this is all I want from you."

I bite my bottom lip and take two steps forward, until our chests are touching. "I already know that. And I appreciate how much you respect me. But when we're alone, and especially in the bedroom, I don't want a gentleman. I want all of you."

He blinks once and before it even registers, he has me pinned against the wall, kissing me like our lives depend on it. His tongue is hot and strong, plunging into my mouth with a promise of what's to come. His strong hand wraps around my hair as he pulls my head to the side, giving him access to my neck.

I'm panting and writhing against him as he assaults my neck and collarbone with his lips and tongue and teeth. His erection presses right up against me so I can't mistake this for anything less than what it is… passion. More passion than I've ever felt in my life.

Just as I'm getting my bearings straight, he picks me up by my thighs. "Straddle me."

So I do. Locking my feet together behind him, he pushes up against me one more time making us groan simultaneously with the friction, before pushing us off the wall and stomping up the stairs. I take the opportunity to kiss down his strong jaw, nipping at his Adam's Apple and pulling his shirt to the side to kiss down to his collar bone. I have no idea where we're headed, I just know we need a bed and we need it soon.

Tossing me onto a mattress I didn't realize was so close, I

squeal with both delight and a tiny bit of fear from flying through the air. I already know this is the kind of sex I have desired my whole life. Respectful, loving, and wild with passion.

He rips his shirt over his head before I even stop bouncing from the landing and now I'm looking at the pale, rock hard abs. I'd always wondered if they were under there. I'm no dummy. I know the book boyfriends I help bring to life aren't real, but I always wondered if it was possible for a real man to be that cut.

The answer is yes. Yes he can.

"Don't mind the farmer's tan," he jokes and for the first time I notice that his torso is, in fact, a significantly lighter shade of golden brown than his arms.

"As long as you don't mind a few extra dimples in certain places." I wave down my body and he growls, literally growls his displeasure.

Holy crap, that was hot.

"I think women have a terrible understanding of what really attracts men," he explains as he pulls my boots and socks off. I push the thoughts of how sweaty my feet must be out of my head and try to remind myself that unless he has a toe fetish, it won't be an issue anyway. "Men don't care about a few extra dimples or a few extra pounds. Men care about how women make us feel. And you, Greer, make me feel like I'm on top of the world."

He slowly runs his hands up my legs, making me shiver.

"You make me feel like I'm important. Like I'm powerful. Like I hung the moon. The way you look at me, like I'm the most attractive man in the world is a bigger turn on than a super model figure."

His fingers flip open the button of my jeans and I gasp.

"I want to kiss every dimple, every stretch mark, every scar, and every freckle because there's a story behind each and every one of them. They made you who you are. They represent your journey."

Slowly, oh so slowly, he pulls the zipper of my jeans down. I can't take my eyes off his as he peals me out of the denim and tosses it aside. Reaching my waist, he lifts my shirt up, up, up until I have to lean forward for him to pull it off of me.

Laying back down, I watch as he takes his on jeans off. His eyes peruse my body like I do to him. Biting my lip, I find myself squeezing my thighs together to rid myself of the ache that's formed. Before this moment, the only time I've felt this ache was when I was deep—and I mean deep—into a really hot book. But certainly not during sex. There is definitely something to be said for anticipation.

Licking his own lips, Ace climbs up the bed and over top of me, covering his body with mine. "Still want me to put my manners aside?"

I smile and nod. "Watching those bronc riders gave me very dirty thoughts about what you can do with your hips."

His jaw drops open. "You dirty girl!" he chides, making me laugh. The vibrations create more friction between us, and suddenly we're not laughing anymore, but gasping at the sensations.

As requested, Ace doesn't take things slow. His kiss is hard and demanding. His touch is rough. It's everything I've ever fantasized about.

He is everything I've ever fantasized about. And more.

Chapter Six

Ace

I wake up to a warm body snuggling next to me and a bunch of hollering downstairs. While I'd like to stay in bed because of the former (as would the other head I think with), the latter is what launches me off my comfortable pillow-top mattress that I love so much and has me racing for the door.

"Ace," Greer yells right before I swing it open. "Pants."

Looking down, I realize I'm still naked as the day I was born. "Right. Good call." Grabbing my jeans from the floor I throw them on as fast as I can, stumbling multiple times while Greer watches and giggles. As soon as I'm decently covered, I race down the stairs to see what all the commotion is about.

It's Pedro, also pantsless, but with boots on and a wild-eyed look on his face. Thank goodness he had the sense to at least put his skivvies on.

"What's wrong," I demand, flipping into crisis mode.

"Brittany!" he yells even though I'm right in his face

164

"She's in labor!"

I feel Greer come up behind me, but it doesn't register until she says, "How do you know?"

"There's water! Water everywhere! Water all over the bed! Water all over the floor! Water all down her legs!" He's rambling, still wide-eyed and all I can think is that I can't think.

What are we supposed to do? What do we do?

Why do I know what to do when a cow gives birth but not a person??

Grabbing him by the shoulders, I look him dead in the eye. "Okay. She's in labor," I reassure him followed immediately with, "What do we do?"

He pauses and thinks for a second and then yells, "Call Doc!"

Somehow, that doesn't sound right but it takes a second until I can figure out why. "Doc is a vet."

Pedro crinkles his brow like the words don't make sense and then tries again. "Boil some water!" he yells and runs off into the kitchen.

Brittany takes that moment to walk through the door muttering "Sweet Jesus" and rolling her eyes. Although I don't know why. We're going to need that water for sanitation purposes. She's holding Pedro's pants. If I was thinking clearly, I'd make a mental note to thank her for bringing them in the house. No one needs to see those hairy legs.

But I'm not thinking clearly. "Where's the car?" I ask no one in particular.

Still, Brittany is the one to answer. "Where it always is dumb ass. Right there in front of the house."

"Okay. I'm going to leave a note and text everybody." I

reach into my pocket but nothing is there. "Wait. Where the hell is my phone?"

The words are barely out of my mouth when Greer, who didn't have clothes on when I left her but suddenly does, hands it to me. "Right here, babe. Calm down."

I think quickly and try to be calm when I text anyone who needs to know. Jill, the office manager; Phillip, who fills in as the morning shift supervisor when I can't be there; and Greer, who I don't' know why I'm texting because she's standing right next to me but somehow it seems appropriate and right now I don't have time to second guess my own decisions because WE'RE HAVING A BABY!

In the background, I barely register her saying things like "How far apart are your contractions?" and "How long are they?" and "Why is he texting me when I'm standing right here?"

I snap back to reality when Brittany lets out a moan like I've never heard come from a human being before. All of my thoughts are muffled except one:

It doesn't matter what kind of animal it is—horse, cow, human—a mother in labor still makes the same primal, guttural sounds when they are getting ready to have a baby.

That's my one clear thought in all of this? Well, that and to never ever tell the women in the room I thought it. I like the way my face looks without a handprint on it, thank you very much.

Making my way quickly to the office, I leave a note for Jill in case the text didn't go through. I'm not leaving that hospital until I am an uncle and I know things are fine.

Satisfied that she'll see the sticky note I stuck on the monitor, I make my way back to the kitchen. There's a giant pot full of water on the stove. It hasn't started boiling yet so I'm not sure what we're going to do. The only thing I know is to grab a giant box of oversized muffins from the pantry and toss them in the middle of the kitchen table, leaving one more sticky note on top that simply says "Breakfast". The farm hands are just going to have to feed themselves this morning. I'm assuming Phillip will figure out a contingency plan for lunch. They're not completely useless in the kitchen. Well, not Phillip anyway.

Rushing back to the front room, Pedro is standing there looking around.

"My wife… where's my wife? WHERE'S MY WIFE?" he shouts grabbing onto me and shaking me.

"She's in the car, Pedro, ready to go." Greer says calmly as she walks through the front door. How can she walk at a time like this? Doesn't she know she needs to be rushing? And when the hell did she go outside?

"Okay. She's in the car. She's in the car," he chants like the more he says it, the sooner the words will compute. "Where's the overnight bag?"

"Also in the car."

"Where's the car seat?" he bellows.

"You don't need it yet. The baby isn't here. We'll bring it to you before you're discharged."

"Okay." At that exact moment he looks down and suddenly has some clarity. "Where are my pants?"

"Right here." She tosses them at him, a smirk on her face. "You," she points at me, "go put a shirt and shoes on. And you," she points at Pedro who is now dressing in my front foyer and falling all over the place because he doesn't' stop to take his boots off first. If we weren't so panicked, I'd call him a dumb ass. But considering we're about to have a baby, I'll forgive him. "Get those pants on and get in the backseat with your wife. Stop running around like a crazy loon. Your job is to sit there and hold her hand."

"But, but… but we need towels!"

"They have some at the hospital."

"And hot water."

"They have some of that, too."

"Oh." He shakes his head and runs his fingers through his hair. "So get in the car?"

"Yes. Back seat. Hold her hand."

"Okay." He races out the front door leaving Greer with her hands on her hips and chuckling.

She looks up at me, looks back down at my chest, and back up at me. "Why are you not dressed yet?"

"I…I…" I stutter. I honestly have no idea. "Because my brain isn't really working right now and I'm not sure what to do."

She laughs as she walks toward me, then cups my cheeks with her hands. "Calm down. I've done this twice before. It's going to be just fine. But we need to get going so put on some clothes and meet me back here. I'm going to turn off the stove."

"Right," I say in agreement and give her a quick kiss on the lips before taking the steps two at a time and hustling to my bedroom. I have no idea what shirt I grab—just something out of the drawer that looks like it fits. Thankfully, I remember to grab my shoes as well.

Sure enough, Greer is exactly where I left her, at the bottom on the stairs waiting calmly. I'm glad someone is calm in this situation.

"Okay. Let's go."

"One more thing and then you can meet me in the car," she says.

"Anything. What?"

"Hon. Go put the towels away. We don't need them, remember?"

Looking down, she's right. I grabbed some on my way out of the bedroom and didn't even realize it. "Oh. Shit." I chuckle to myself, suddenly realizing how ridiculous Pedro and I are. Towels? Boiling water? Pantsless?

Thank God Greer was here. Otherwise Brittany may have had to drive herself.

I drop the towels on the stairs. We can put them away later. But for now, it's time.

We're going to have a baby.

Chapter Seven

Greer

Of all the nights to stay at Ace's, I'm glad it was the night Brittany went into labor. Watching those two men run around like chickens with their heads cut off had to be one of the most hilarious things I've ever seen.

I have no idea how they stay so cool and under control with farm issues, because when it comes to humans, they are off their damn rockers.

It only took about three hours from the time we got to the hospital until the baby was born. Brittany had done an amazing job of timing her contractions so she did most of her laboring at home. I was impressed. I was begging for an epidural two months before Oli was even born and Braxton Hicks kicked in. Cause I'm a weenie.

But my favorite part of the night was watching Ace hold that brand new baby. Antonio Pedro Garcia was born just after six in the morning and we were in the room to welcome him to the world not long after that. I've never seen so much love come from a man who was not the father. Actually, I don't' think I saw that much love coming from my own kids' father when they were born. What a depressing thought.

The whole night, though, was just beautiful. And exhausting. I pushed through the work week, despite my lack of sleep, mostly because it was the kids' last week of school before Thanksgiving and I knew it would be exponentially harder to get things done. Plus, Ace convinced me I need to take a day off. A day to relax and enjoy my children and myself. To go out, just the four of us and have some fun.

At first I was reluctant, because a good mom doesn't want to get her kids involved in her dating life until she knows for sure it's going to last forever.

Right?

I'm not positive, but I did have a realization. And that is there is something freeing about dating when your kids are teenagers. I had never thought about it until after our first date, when Ace and I officially started seeing each other. But it's true.

When your kids are little, you worry about them getting attached to someone. Will they see that other person as a father figure and be heartbroken if the relationship doesn't work out? Will it will be traumatic if that person disappears? Will it lead to abandonment issues?

But when they're teenagers, it's so different. Sure, they might really enjoy the person you're dating. They might even come to love that person. But they're also old enough to recognize that relationships ebb and flow; that some relationships don't last forever. They've probably already experienced in their own lives and have come to recognize that sometimes people are just in your life for a short time.

Like I said, when I finally pieced that together, this amazing feeling of freedom took over.

Realistically, I'm still worried about Oli. I'll always worry about him. Since his maturity level is that of an eight-year-old, things that don't bother other teenagers still bother him. But once Ace reminded me that he's going to be the guy in charge of Oli's school program even if we weren't seeing each other, well, it kind of freed me up from worrying about Oli too much. Ace is a father figure to a lot of kids and he hasn't dumped out of any of their lives, even when they've left the program. Sure, some of their relationships have faded away. But if he and Oli lose touch, it won't be because he and I don't work out. They already have their own independent relationship.

Granted, it's only been a couple months, but after our overnight date and being part of Brittany's birth, things have shifted. I don't carry that extra worry. Or maybe it's easy to be with Ace just because he's Ace. He doesn't get his feathers ruffled easily. Even when there's chaos all around him, he's just steady. And if anything makes him afraid, I have yet to see it. Except human childbirth.

Seriously. I happened to be here when a calf was getting ready to be born breach. Ace never once freaked out or panicked, even knowing it could have killed his Bessie. He just calmly stuck his arm up inside the cow to turn the calf around.

I have kids so I can handle seeing a lot of things.

Except that.

We're all lucky I only had a gag reflex when he pulled his arm back out. I almost threw my lunch up all over the barn floor.

Oli, on the other hand, thought it was so cool and hasn't

stopped talking about it since. It's always fun to have to relive the visual images over and over when he brings it up. Aren't fixations the best? Fortunately, his mind is on other things today.

"I can't believe I'm trudging through a field to go fishing," Julie complains.

I'm not shocked she's less than thrilled by today's activities. But I couldn't pass up the opportunity to spend some time outdoors with my kids and my new boyfriend. Especially in a place as beautiful as his land.

Autumn is finally here and it's a perfect day for long sleeves and jeans, which we don't get to wear very often. The lush fields are covered in the last of the blooming wildflowers, a few trees scattered here and there. We can still see the main house and the barn as we walk toward the lake, but it's quiet and feels secluded out here. I welcome the reprieve from our constant chaos through everyday life.

"You're just mad that you can't read your book," Oli shoots back, happy as a clam. He's been looking forward to this fishing trip for a couple days now. He actually woke me up this morning instead of vice versa because he didn't want to be late.

It was a struggle explaining that even the fish aren't awake at four thirty in the morning. I'm not sure he ever believed me, but at least he finally gave up on me dropping him off three hours earlier than expected.

When we finally arrived at a more normal hour, Ace handed us each a fishing pole and off we went. Very quickly, we realized we need to give Oli a wide berth. He seems to forget how long the fishing pole is and that the hook can be dangerous. He actually whapped Ace in the head, the hook snatching his hat right off. It was pretty funny since no one end up in stitches. That doesn't mean any of us are willing to get too close, though.

"No, Oli. That's not it. I finished my book last night," Julie retorts. "I don't like the idea of snakes being in this grass. What happens if we get bit, huh? How far is it to the hospital? Who's to say I'm not going to die before I get there?"

Ace's deep chuckle reverberates through me. "That's why I always carry some anti-venom in my pocket."

Julie's eyes go wide. "Are you serious? There are enough snakes out here that you have to carry anti-venom in your pocket?"

Ace laughs even harder now. "I was kidding Julie. If anyone gets bit, I'll just suck the venom right out and spit it in the grass."

"What?" she practically screeches and stops walking, looking all around her like a snake is listening to the conversation and is going to jump out at her this very second.

"Still kidding," he says, still laughing. "You don't have to worry about snakes. We're all wearing boots and I know the sound of a rattler. Plus, this is close enough to the farm that the barn cats like to come out here and hunt. I can guarantee if there was a nest anywhere around here, they would have already found it and obliterated it."

"Oh well that's comforting." Julie rolls her eyes. "Cats eating snakes for breakfast. This just keeps getting better."

I can't help but smile at their playful banter. It's nice being out here like this. Just being able to enjoy each other's company and learn something new. One of the things I was looking forward to when we moved here was being able to spend more time outdoors. I think my kids got so used to living in suburbia, we forgot what it's like to have fresh air and work our muscles.

"I hope this will make up for it right here." Ace points off in the distance. About a hundred yards away, we can see the edge of the water. Jutting out into the lake is a small pier. "We're not gonna be sitting in the grass or anything. We're gonna be sitting out there," he explains. "Makes it easier to catch fish when you're out that far in the water. Plus, you don't have to worry about any critters sneaking up behind you."

"Comforting," Julie says sarcastically, making me laugh.

"Come on Julie. It'll be fun having the experience." She gives me that look that only a teenager can give. It's a cross between "You're insane" and "I'm trying really hard to trust you, but I don't know if I should".

"I'm serious," I chuckle. "This'll be good for us. See how quiet and peaceful it is out here? It's kind of nice to be disconnected from the rest of the world. Even for a couple of hours. No distractions. No internet. No phone calls."

"No fun," Julie interjects.

I purse my lips at her. "We haven't even gotten to the lake yet. Give it a chance."

She grumbles but doesn't say anymore as we follow behind Ace and Oli, who have now taken the lead on our trek. I enjoy watching him interact with my teenage son. He has such a calm demeanor around him, patiently giving Oli enough time to process through questions he has about things like how to know when a snake is poisonous and if they eat fish, too.

To be honest, I find the whole thing very sexy. I find *Ace* very sexy. And not just because I know what he can do in the bedroom, although that's not far from my mind these days. I'm looking forward to the next time Uncle Jack wants to babysit.

No, there's something about a man who has this much empathy and compassion for the people others usually dismiss that makes me want to jump him right in this field. But since this is a family outing, I put those thoughts in the back of my mind.

"It's so quiet out here," I casually mention. "I love that we're far enough away from the highway, there's no chance we're going to accidentally hear the sound of an 18-wheeler putting on the air brakes."

"Sounds like I'm gonna turn you into a nature buff yet," Ace says over his shoulder, shooting me a flirty wink that doesn't help me put my carnal thoughts aside. Now that Ace has unleashed that side of me, I'm having a hard time going without him anymore.

"I've always been somewhat of a nature buff. I've just never had much opportunity. I've always thought I'd could live on a farm. I mean, I wouldn't help or anything." He guffaws at my clarification. "But it's just so beautiful out here, I can see the appeal."

He smiles softly at me and for just a second I hope he doesn't think I was implying I could live on *his* farm. That would be way too forward. I feel my face getting hot, but he doesn't notice as the grass begins to clear and a small beach front is revealed.

Stepping on the pier, we have to walk two-by-two since it's not wide enough for all of us.

"And here we are," he says when we get to the end. "This is one of my favorite places to be."

"It's so pretty," Oli says and I nod in agreement.

We begin dropping all our gear and organizing where everything will be for easy fishing. There's no schedule. No place we need to be. Just the sun, a cool breeze, and good con-versation.

"I can't tell you how many times my friends and I used to come out here to skinny dip when we were young," Ace re-veals.

Julie starts making gagging sounds and Oli giggles.

"You went skinny dipping?" he asks, thinking it's the funniest thing he's ever heard.

"Sure did! There's nothing like working hard on the ranch all day long and coming out here, stripping down to your skiv-vies and diving in. The lake isn't terribly deep, but it's deep enough the water never actually gets warm. When it's a hun-dred degrees outside and ninety-five percent humidity, that's the best feeling in the world."

Julie scoffs. "You don't, like, still do that now, do you?"

Ace just laughs. "Nah. There's this unwritten rule that once you're passed about twenty-five, you're a little too old to do that in public. Don't wanna make anyone barf by looking at our old wrinkly skin." He winks at me again as I cover up a laugh. Julie keeps making gagging sounds, the little twerp.

I know for a fact there's no wrinkly skin on Ace's body. Mine, maybe. But with all that farm work, he's certainly still fit under those clothes.

It's too bad he never had any kids. He'd make a good dad.

Chapter Eight

Ace

The lake has always been one of my favorite parts of this property. One of my favorite places to be.

When we were young, my friends and I would race out here to go swimming in the summer time because the water was always cool. We'd go fishing and canoeing. It was that ideal childhood everyone always talks about.

By the time we hit high school, we started having bon fires out here. A few times we even convinced some of the girls to skinny dip in the middle of the night. Nothing like some moonlight reflecting off a girl's creamy skin to make the crazy teenaged boy hormones go nuts. It's a wonder none of us drown.

So this place holds a lot of good memories for me. I was excited when Greer agreed to bring the kids out here so we could all go fishing. It's one of my favorite ways to relax and it might be good for Oli to get his hands on a fishing pole. Although I wouldn't know. About forty-five second after the worm went on the hook and it all went in the water, Oli got bored. I don't know what he was expecting. Maybe some sort of giant salmon or a shark. I kept trying to explain to him that no, the guy from River Monsters has never been here. We're just looking for a few good-sized trout. That apparently wasn't good enough for him. And it was taking too long.

So he's off hunting frogs, Greer hanging out on the pier, shoes off, legs stretched out, just enjoying the last of the warm sun on her face and being out of the office, Julie and I sitting on the edge feet dangling toward the water.

There's not much cell reception out here either, which means there's no way she can get sucked back into working. Don't get me wrong, I understand what it's like to be a business owner. You're never really away from the office, even when you're away from the office. But one thing I've learned over the last month or so is that Greer never has any downtime. She has to take advantage of the time Oli is away by working, and when Oli is home, the battles are pretty constant. This may be the first chance she's really had to truly relax in, well, in years.

"How come you don't have any kids?"

Julie's question shouldn't take me by surprise. She's not the first one to ask me. I glance over my shoulder at Greer who just looks at me and shrugs. I guess she wants to know the answer, too.

"Just wasn't in my life plan, I suppose."

"You know that's weird, right?"

That comment actually does take me by surprise. I never thought being single and childless at my age could see strange, but I guess from a fifteen-year-old's perspective it is.

"What makes it weird?"

She gently pulls on the fishing pole like I taught her, trying to entice a fish to bite. "You're just really old to not have any kids and not be married. Or at least divorced. Wait, are you divorced? That would make it less weird."

I bark a laugh. "No, I'm not divorced. I guess the right woman just hasn't come along yet. It's kind of hard to date when you run a farm."

She looks at me like that's the dumbest thing she's ever heard. "Why? You're the boss. You can do what you want."

I chuckle and gently tug on my own fishing pole. So far, we're not having much luck. "There's more to it than just that. My work day usually starts at about four-thirty and doesn't end until about eight at night."

Greer says "Ew" behind us and I know she's thinking about those long hours.

"Why do you have to work so much?"

For being the quiet one, Julie sure is full of questions. I'm going to pretend that's a good sign; that she wants to get to know me better.

"The cows aren't going to milk themselves. And the animals can't feed themselves either. It's a big responsibility taking care of animals. I like it, but it doesn't leave a lot of time for going out and meeting people and since we live in the middle of nowhere, not many people come out to visit."

"Do you want them? Kids, I mean?"

How do I answer that? Do I? Maybe. I guess I gave up that dream a long time ago so it's not something I really think about, but I have to admit, when I held baby Nio at the hospital the other day, I realized how much I missed by staying secluded on the farm. It was never my intention to be this old and still alone, but it still happened.

"I think," I begin, trying to be careful with my words. "If I'm supposed to be a dad, it'll happen. I'm not out looking for that, but if the stars align and it happens, that would be okay with me."

She nods and reels her fishing line all the way in, then casts it out into the water again.

"You're getting really good at that," I remark, impressed with how quickly she's picking it up. Looking over, I see Oli has ditched his shoes and waded ankle deep into the water staring intently at something underneath. I'm curious to know what it is, but not curious enough to scare off any fish that may start being interested in our hooks.

"Do you read?"

Greer sniggers behind us, like she knew this was coming. Honestly, I expected this one long before now.

"A bit."

"So what house are you?"

I crinkle my brows and look at her. She's staring intently at me like my answer is the most important one of this entire conversation. I'm about to fail because I have no idea what she's talking about.

"What... house?"

I glance quickly at Greer for some sort of indication as to what the right answer is. She's too busy snickering to help me out, the traitor.

Julie rolls her eyes. "What house? Harry Potter?"

"Oh. I've never read those."

Another eye roll. "How can you call yourself a reader if you've never read Harry Potter?"

Reeling my hook all the way in, I attach another worm and cast the line again. "Well hold on now. I tried reading the book. Hel…heck… I tried watching the movies but they just didn't catch my interest."

Julie sighs like I've disappointed her. "Fine. What about the Percy Jackson books?"

"Nope."

"Hunger Games?"

"I watched the movies," I say excitedly thinking I got one answer right. She purses her lips and quirks an eyebrow at me, looking at me over the top of her glasses.

"Not the same," she deadpans. Guess I failed that one, too. "Do you read anything interesting at all?"

"Last book I read was Saving Private Ryan. It was fascinating. Did you read that one?" I already know how she's going to answer, but I can't help holding my breath that maybe we'll have found some common ground. Instead, she crinkles her nose like she smells something bad.

"I'm not into historical drama."

"That's not historical drama. It's based on a true story."

"Yeah, no."

Before I can open my mouth to respond, Julie gasps and her eyes get wide. Her pole is bending and her line is moving.

"Ace…" she pleads, not sure what to do.

I secure my own pole on the pier and turn to help her. "Don't panic, Julie. Hold on tight," I instruct. "Now reel it in slowly. Good. Now stop. Let the fish fight for just a little before reeling it in more."

I talk her through her very first catch for the next several minutes, Greer standing over our shoulders watching. Even Oli has noticed something happening and splashed his way over our direction.

It takes a several minutes, but sure enough, Julie reels in a good-sized catfish.

"I did it!" she squeals, holding it up by the line as Greer snaps a pic with her phone. "I caught a fish, Mom!"

"You did," Greer says with a laugh.

Oli, still without shoes or socks and wet from playing in the water, grimaces. "I don't want to eat that."

If it's possible, Julie's eyes widen again. "We can eat that? You mean I just caught our dinner?"

"Of course you did," I exclaim, knowing we need about six more of those to actually have a decent sized meal. I don't say it though. I don't want to ruin Julie's excitement. "What do you think we came fishing for? That is some good eating right there."

Julie dances around for a few seconds, still holding onto her line, until the fish makes one last flop scaring the shit out of Julie and making Greer and I laugh. Oli, still not happy about the idea of eating our catch and sad that it died, wanders away. I wonder if he realizes where all the meat from the grocery store comes from. He might never eat again if he found out what the live version of beef is.

"Greer, grab me the ice chest, will you?" She rolls it over to me and I spend the next several minutes talking Julie through safely getting the fish off the hook. She's a natural so far and I realize she and I are more alike than I first suspected.

We spend the next several hours talking fish and books and the various critters Oli catches. I laugh way too hard when Greer screams when the lizard Oli shows her jumps on her lap, and Julie about busts my ear drum when she catches a second fish.

I've always liked my life. Felt like I landed exactly where I needed to be. But glancing at the people around me in my favorite place in the world, I realize Julie may be more astute than I gave her credit for. This is what I'm missing in my life—family. Complete with kids and a partner and lazy days when the fish aren't biting a lot but we're enjoying it anyway.

Like a ton of bricks has fallen all around me, jarring me from the monotony I've been stuck in for so long I realize this is what I want. It's only been a couple months. It's way too soon. But in this exact moment, I think I've fallen in love with Greer. Not just with her tenacity and her strength. I love how she puts people before herself. I love her humor. And I guess it shouldn't surprise me, but I love her kids as well.

I'm so shell shocked by the revelation, I find myself staring out at the water, deep in thought. I want them. All of them. I want to provide for them. I want to make them smile and laugh. I want to help celebrate milestones, and help pick up broken pieces when they come. I want to find a place in all their lives and them to find a place in mine.

"Ace." I look at Greer who has a strange look on her face. "You okay? You've been staring at that water for a while now."

Smiling up at her, trying to disguise the shellshock I feel, I nod. "Yeah. Sorry. Must have zoned out. You guys ready to head back to the house? Learn how to fry up some fresh fish?"

"Yes!" Julie yells at the same time Oli groans a "Nooooooo."

Greer shakes her head in amusement and then adds, "But we don't have enough for dinner."

"Don't worry." I push myself to my feet and begin packing up our supplies. "I always freeze some when the fish are biting a lot, just for times like these. It's cheaper and fresher than going to the store."

She gives me a mega-watt smile and spends a few minutes arguing with Oli about putting his shoes back on while helping put everything away.

My heart swells with excitement that this could be my future. I just have to take things slow and prove my intentions are genuine since they've all had a lot of hurt. But if I'm honest with myself… I can't wait.

Chapter Nine

Greer

I woke up to the biggest surprise this morning… sweater weather. Finally.

Sure, it's also known as long sleeve weather everywhere else in the country. Maybe even grab-a-sweatshirt-just-in-case-you-need-it weather for everyone north of Kansas.

But whatever it's called, I'm thrilled the cooler temperatures have arrived. It has put me in the holiday spirit, which is perfect since I've been cooking Thanksgiving dinner since six this morning.

Joie arrived around ten to "help". I now understand why Jack warned me she was a disaster in the kitchen. I thought he was exaggerating. When she spread out all her brightly colored and organized recipe binders, I wondered if he was trying to play some weird joke on me.

So I put her on pie duty and had her make the first pumpkin of the season. It's not hard to make—eggs, pumpkin puree, condensed milk and spices mixed together and thrown in a pie crust. Simple.

Apparently not for Joie. I don't know if she mixed up creamer and milk or used the wrong spices, but the second it came out of the oven I knew something was very wrong just by the smell. So I took a discreet bite and promptly spit it out in the sink.

She's since been relegated to washing vegetables and peeling potatoes with Julie, all while rambling on about how she did it last year. "How did it not cook right this year?"

Her organizational skills have come in handy, though. She figured out how we could have a sit-down dinner, despite not having a formal dining area, just by moving the couches forward a bit and bringing in a couple folding tables. With Julie's help, and the magic of tablecloths and placemats, it now resembles a banquet for just the seven of us. It helps that Joie knows how to fold napkins into swans. I honestly never knew her part time job skills of making balloon animals would ever benefit me, but there you have it.

The doorbell rings at the same time the oven timer goes off and I look at the clock. Four on the dot.

"Turn off the TV please, Oli and get the door."

He grumbles about having to turn off his video game but complies. Joie gives me a look like she's impressed and I have to admit, I was also expecting more a reaction. Then again, he knows who is missing—all the men.

There is nothing a teenage boy likes better than having some testosterone around to break up all the girly talk around him. Especially when it's his mother and sister all the time. I wouldn't know if he would feel the same if there were girls his age here but I put that thought right out of my head. There will be no dating prospects for Oli. Ever, if I have my say in it.

The sounds of several deep male voices get louder as our final guests round the corner. Ace, my brother Jack and Joie's son Isaac all meander into the room. Looks like they all showed up at the same time. Can't say I'm surprised considering there is a feast waiting for them. A way to a man's heart and all that crap.

"Smells good in here," Isaac says as he greets his mom with a kiss to her cheek. We've met a couple times in passing. He seems like a nice kid. Glancing at Julie, I notice her blushing and refusing to turn around to look at anyone.

Uh oh. I make a mental note to remind her later that Isaac is a grown man in college, and basically her cousin now. Hopefully that'll deter any crush she might have.

Jack bypasses Joie and heads straight for my whipping bowl. "That's because your mama didn't do any of the cooking."

"Hey!" Joie and I both yell at the same time, her because of the insult and me because he just stuck his finger in the whip cream I've been mixing.

"I'll have you know, I peeled some amazing potatoes," she argues when he licks his finger and finally puts his arms around her.

"I'm sure they'll be great baby," he says, then playfully covers her ears and whispers over her head "Don't eat the mashed potatoes."

As they laugh and banter, Ace takes the opportunity to kiss me on the lips. It's just a quick peck, but enough for Julie to notice.

"Ew," she says under her breath, but of course Jack notices.

"Ew is right," he says. "That's my sister you're kissing."

Cocking an eyebrow, I recognize my brother's ornery mood. It always makes life fun, but being that he's my brother and all, I can't let him have the last word.

Grabbing Ace by the lapel, I warn, "Cover your eyes Julie," and her hand flies up to her face without hesitation. She's been around a while. She knows how her Uncle Jack and I each give as much shit as we take with each other. Apparently no one else does because they start laughing when I pull Ace to me, deepening our kiss.

"Oh come on now," Jack bellows, but that doesn't stop me from finishing what I started.

When I finally pull away, Ace leans into me and whispers "Gentleman in public and dirty lover in the bedroom remember?"

It feels like an electrical charge shoots through my body at the reminder. "Oh I remember. But I figured you wouldn't mind this one time. Just to make my brother squirm. Consider it payback for how he acted on our first date."

Ace chuckles and I smooth his lapel down. When I'm finally steady on my feet after that kiss, I let him go so he can continue leaning against the counter and I can finish cooking.

Turning to Jack so I can gloat in my victory of the battle of the siblings, he's around the counter and stalking my direction. I know that look in his eye. He's headed for the whipping bowl again.

"Stop right there, Pride." I hold my hand up like a traffic cop in an intersection. "You get out of my kitchen before I call Hank and tell him what you thought it meant when there was a sock on the doorknob of your college dorm."

Isaac chokes on the sip of water he was drinking and Ace starts laughing. "What did he think it meant?"

Ignoring Isaac's question while the Mexican standoff music plays in my head, I narrow my eyes at my brother.

He grits his teeth. "You wouldn't dare."

"I would so dare and you would never hear the end of it."

Minutes go by. Okay, fine—seconds go by but he finally throws his hands up in the air with a "Fine! I'll wait for dinner."

"It'll only be about five minutes. You'll be okay." I use his favorite patronizing tone on purpose and turn back to my task, ignoring his glare my direction.

"Wait," Isaac says hesitantly. "You can't leave us hanging like that. What did Jack think that meant?"

"Don't you dare, Greer." I roll my eyes at Jack's attempts at sounding threatening.

"No really," Isaac continues. "We're all family. Who are we going to tell?"

"Your head coach," Jack says through a clenched jaw but Isaac just waves him off.

"I would never hold it over your head to get out of doing burpees. Nope." Isaac pops the "p" over exaggerating his sarcasm. I've made up my mind. I love Isaac. He's my favorite almost nephew ever. "I would *never* do something like that. So spill Greer."

"He thought it meant laundry service was on the way," I spout off, Jack shouting obscenities behind me. "I don't know how his olfactory senses didn't work or if he just had terrible allergies, but his roommate thought it was so funny that any time a girl left, he'd fold all Jack's dirty clothes and put them back in his drawers. He wore dirty clothes for close to a year before someone finally told him the truth."

The room erupts in laughter and all I can do is bat my

eyelashes at my brother who is shooting daggers at me.

"I love you," I mouth to him, causing him to flip me off. Of course that makes everyone laugh harder and even Jack has a hard time fighting the grin threating to overtake his face.

This is what we love. Being surrounded by family who can joke with each other and laugh together. Even if it's about dumb things we did in our youth. It makes us happy. It makes us feel good.

It makes me feel like we're home.

"Julie. Can you go tell your brother it's time to wash up? We're sitting down in about five minutes."

"Sure." She wipes her hands on a towel and goes to find Oli while the adults begin grabbing dishes of hot food, putting them on the table. Several conversations happen naturally around me, as they do when you have multiple adults in one room.

Suddenly, there is a crash and a scream from Julie's bedroom.

"What the hell?" Jack mutters and gives me a knowing look. We've been here before, so I know he's thinking the same thing I am. *I wonder if my fun-filled family holiday just went bad.*

Sure enough, Julie comes barreling out of her room, screaming my direction. "Mom! He is in my room, took my tablet, and when I tried to take it from him, he pushed me."

"I did not!" Oli yells from the other room but doesn't show his face.

I sigh and remove the hot plate gloves from my hands, dropping them on the table. "Are you okay?"

"Yeah," she says quietly, trying to hold back tears as she rubs her shoulder. "I lost my balance and fell into the wall."

Nodding because I'm not sure what else to do, I turn to my guests. "I'm sorry guys. You can go ahead and get started. I need to go handle this and it could be a while."

"No," Jack says with finality. "We'll wait. The turkey needs to be carved anyway. You weren't wanting to make that a new tradition were you?" I shake my head. "Then we'll keep ourselves entertained until you get back. We're fine."

I kiss him on the cheek in appreciation. No one in the world except my family understands our situation like they do. Even Isaac doesn't seem to be fazed by the sudden change in plans.

"I'll go with you," Ace says, moving around the table.

"Ace, you don't have to—"

He holds his hand up before I can finish my sentence. "I know that. But we've been working hard at the farm on taking responsibility for his actions and making things right. I might be able to help remind him of everything he's learned."

I hesitate because there's a difference between disciplining Oli in his school environment and laying down the law at home. It's a different boundary. Not one I know that I'm ready to cross yet. It feels oddly like I'm letting Ace do my job for me.

"He's right." I roll my eyes because of course Jack agrees with him. Jack is always trying to jump in and help me out with Oli, even when I don't need it. "I'm serious," he continues. "Even if Ace just stands in the doorway, you know as well as I do Oli will listen better."

I blow out a breath. "That's kind of insulting."

He just shrugs. "It's a man thing."

"He's right," Isaac interjects. "I listen to my coaches way more than I listen to my mom."

"Hey," Joie exclaims and smacks Isaac playfully on the arm.

Sighing with resignation, I realize they have a point. Oli seems to respond to other men better than he responds to me sometimes. I don't know if it's a quirk of his brain or a character trait, but he just seems to recognize them as more of an authority sometimes. It's frustrating, but what can I do? I have to meet him on his level in times like this.

"Okay, well let's get this over with then," I say to Ace who smiles at me, but I can tell by the look on his face he's not happy about the turn of events either. "The sooner we de-escalate, the sooner we can eat." Turning to Julie, I add, "You stay here."

She plops down on the sofa and mutters how much she wishes she was an only child. The only response I give is to pat her on the shoulder as I walk by. Because really, there's nothing to say. It is what it is.

We find Oli back in his own room, lounging on his bed, tablet in his hand. Ace leans against the doorframe, giving me space to deal with my son.

"Oliver."

"What." It's not a question. More of a statement that he's annoyed.

"Where'd you get that tablet?"

"Julie left it out." He still doesn't look up.

"She left it out in her room, which you are not allowed to be in."

"Okay."

He continues ignoring me and playing on the device he didn't ask to use or get permission to take. Fed up with not being taken seriously, I stomp over to him and snatch the tablet out of his hand. "Hey! I was playing that!" he yells.

I quickly disconnect the game and begin uninstalling the app. It's not a game Julie plays anyway, so she won't mind. "You aren't supposed to be on electronics at all. It is Thanksgiving and we are having dinner."

"I don't wanna eat!" He bellows and stands up to his full height. Out of the corner of my eye, I see Ace move away from the doorway and take a step forward in response. I don't think Oli's trying to intimidate me, but just because of his size I can understand why the movement makes Ace take notice. It also is my last straw.

"I don't care what you want, Oliver. You are in so much trouble right now. Going into your sister's room to stealing her tablet. Pushing her into the wall."

"I didn't push her!"

"Ignoring me. And now not obeying? You had better march yourself into that living room and sit next to your Uncle Jack right now. Do you understand me?"

"No!" he yells in my face, but I don't back down, even when Ace comes to stand behind me.

"You've just lost a minute off of your tablet time. Do you want another minute taken off?"

Oli's eyes get wide. "What? I didn't do anything wrong!"

"That's two minutes," I threaten, knowing the only way to get this under control is to whittle away what little time he's allotted per day.

"NOOO!" he shrieks so loud I know all our guests had to have heard.

"Would you like another minute off or are we finished with this?"

Oliver begins pacing frantically and breathing heavily

through his nose. "I didn't do anything! Why do you hate me?"

Ace puts his hand on my shoulder and gestures that he's ready to take over if I'm done. I'm not as angry as Oli thinks I am, but I am embarrassed. And frankly, I'm hungry. The sooner we can end this, the sooner I get to nosh on some turkey, so I nod my response to Ace.

He steps forward and crosses his arms over his chest, feet apart. "Oli remember how we talk about having to be able to trust each other when we work on the farm or else we can't get the job done?"

"Yeah." Oli doesn't stop pacing, but at least he's listening.

"When you go into Julie's room and take her things, it breaks her trust. It makes her feel like you don't love her and don't respect her."

"I *don't* love her," he spouts off.

"Sure you do. You're just mad right now. But just like at the farm, we need to take responsibility for our actions. So I'm going to ask you a question, and you aren't going to lie about it or else there will be consequences. Did you go into Julie's room?"

"No!" Oli yells.

"That's a lie, Oli. I know you did. That's five minutes off your time."

"What?!" Oli shrieks, mirroring my thoughts, because that's not how we do this.

Ace, on the other hand, stays calm. "Let's try that again because your mother and I already know the answer. Did you go into Julie's room?"

"NO!"

"That's another five minutes off."

"You can't do that!" Oli yells and begins banging his fist on his forehead in frustration.

"I just did," Ace coolly, like he isn't upending everything I've put in place. Like he's going to be here to have to fight it out later when I have to implement this. "The choice is yours Oli. Tell the truth or get more time taken off. Did you go into Julie's room? And before you answer, remember, Julie saw you in there."

"AAAARRRRRRRRGGGGGGGGGGGGGH!" Oli breathes in deeply but finally caves "YES! I went into her room. Are you happy now?"

Ace nods once while I stand there, praying this is almost over. I could jump in and tell him to stop, that he has no right to take so much time off at one time. That I need him to have at least a little bit of a reward or the battle will be even worse later. But to undermine an authority figure in Oli's life means a slew of problems popping up in the future. It's not worth it.

"Thank you for telling me the truth. Next question. Did you take Julie's tablet?"

Oli immediately responds without thinking. "No."

"That's another five minutes."

Oli growls and plops down on his bed, rocking back and forth, gritting his teeth. I make a mental tally that he's down to thirteen minutes of tablet time. If he loses much more, I'm in for a huge fight later.

"Try again. Did you take Julie's tablet?"

"No." Oli begins to cry, knowing he's lying but fighting so hard to get the truth out. The tears used to make me feel terrible, but I learned long ago, in order for him to learn, sometimes it has to break him and it's painful.

Ace sighs. "You know that means I have to take five

more minutes away."

"You can't do that," Oli whispers this time, full on alligator tears rolling down his face.

"Last time, Oli. Did you take Julie's tablet?"

Oli bangs his fist one more time, lets out a sob and says, "Yes."

Ace sits down next to him and puts his arm around Oli's shoulder. "Thank you for telling me the truth. I know that was hard, but that's what a man of honor does."

I stand in the middle of the room watching with both awe at how easy Ace makes discipline look, while also shooting daggers at him because I'm going to have to implement it all later. I didn't want to fight later. I'm so tired of fighting with my son that I choose my battles with him instead. Some people treat themselves with a glass of wine. Some with chocolate. I treat myself to a break by not always enforcing my own rules. It's not necessarily consistent, but honestly, I don't think Oli recognizes the difference between me disciplining because he needs it and for what he perceives to be my own fun and games.

The two of them finally stand, Oli wiping his eyes and smiling up at Ace before Ace pats him on the shoulder and sends him on his way.

As soon as Oli is out of the room, Ace immediately pulls me into his arms. "Oli is a good kid. He's gonna get there."

I nod and flash him a small smile, hoping he doesn't see how conflicted I am. I'm angry at this turn of events, but I'm not quite sure why. And yet, there is still a house full of people waiting on Thanksgiving dinner.

"Well thanks for helping." The words are out of my mouth before I can even think of how much I'm *not* thankful for him helping. Unfortunately for me, Ace notices.

Cocking his head, he looks back and forth between my eyes. "What's wrong?"

I shake my head and press my lips together. "Nothing. Nothing at all. Let's go eat."

Then I turn on my heel and walk back into the living room, leaving Ace behind.

Chapter Ten

Ace

Something is wrong.

Ever since Thanksgiving, whenever I talk to Greer it just feels off. She's quieter, doesn't stay on the phone as long, doesn't laugh. I'm getting a weird vibe from her and I don't like it.

In the few days since the holiday, I have racked my brain a million times to figure out what caused this rift, but I'm lost. I suspect it stems from Oli's meltdown and how embarrassed she is when it happens in front of people, but I thought we were past that. I thought she understood that his behaviors don't change the way I feel about her. That I'm fully equipped to help her. That I want to be a team with her. And that dating or not, Oli's one of "my kids" now simply because he's here a couple days a week with the co-op program.

Since my brain is running ninety to nothing, I've slept like shit. It's only been a few days, but I already miss her. I miss seeing her with an intensity I didn't have before she spent the night. But it's not just the physical. I miss the ease of our conversations. I miss the playful banter. I miss stepping away from the farm for a couple hours just to have lunch.

When I asked if she wanted to go grab a bite today and she declined because she's too busy, I admit that one stung.

So here I am, taking my frustrations out on this mare who has never been brushed so clean in her life.

"I don't think you can get her hide much glossier." I glance up and Pedro's standing in the stall door. He's got deep, dark circles under his eyes; hair is more disheveled than normal; and he looks like he hasn't slept since Nio was born, which probably isn't far from the truth.

"You look like shit, man."

Instead of being insulted he sighs and runs his hands down his face. "Yeah. All the books warned us how exhausting being a first-time parent would be, but whoo-eee. They weren't kidding man. I am wiped."

"Why don't you take off early?" I suggest. "Go take a nap. We got things covered here. Besides, Brittany probably needs you."

"She's fine. She's got a friend coming over in a bit. Besides, I needed to check on Rockette first. I see you're looking as rough as I am. Gonna tell me what's going on or do I have to guess?"

I crinkle my eyebrows in confusion. "What are you talking about? I'm fine."

"Uh huh," he crosses his arms and leans against the wall. "Is that why you've been brushing the same spot for the last five minutes?"

Realizing he's right, I stop my movement and take a step back. Every time I think about Greer these days, I seem to lose focus on what I'm doing.

"Yeah, man. Sorry. I'm fine."

He's not buying it. "That's a bunch of bullshit and I know it."

Blowing out a breath and tossing the brush in the bucket, I turn to look at him and put my hands on my hips. "I don't know man. Something's changed. Something's different."

"With Greer?"

"Yeah. Things were going fantastic, ya know? We went out. She spent the night. Hung out with the kids. Did Thanksgiving. All the sudden, it's like she's pulling away from me."

"A woman backing off has never bothered you before. What's different this time?"

"What's different is I—" I stop before finishing. I know I love her. I know it. But somehow it feels wrong to confess that to Pedro before I do Greer.

He pushes off the wall and walks to the horse, scratching her behind the ears absentmindedly. "I get it. So then have you asked her what's going on?"

"Hell yeah I asked her about it. I can't get more than an 'I'm fine' out of her."

Pedro drops his head and shakes it in amusement. "Ooooh, you are in the dog house."

"What? How do you know?"

"Man. And I thought you were the one who was good with people," he says under his breath, then looks me dead in the eye. "Ace, if a woman says everything is fine, she means she's really mad and you need to figure out why."

I stare at him blankly as I go through my catalog of memories again, trying to decide if he's right.

Nope. Still nothing.

"I have gone over everything in my head a million times and the only thing different is that Oli had a meltdown over Thanksgiving and I helped her out. After that, nothing."

Pedro looks at me incredulously. "You say you helped her out. How did you do that?"

I take a deep breath and relay the story to him as we gather the grooming supplies and lock up the stall. "Well, he stole his sister's tablet. He got caught on it. He lied about it. He was giving Greer a lot of lip so I stepped in, *with her permission*," I emphasize and he nods his approval. "Then I took care of it."

"Took care of it how?"

"He got time off of his tablet every time he lied, which is what she was doing."

"Did you do it the exact same way she was going it?"

"Well, no. She was only taking a minute at a time, so I upped the stakes."

"You what?"

I roll my eyes. "It was exactly like we do here on the farm. I took five minutes away of his play time."

Pedro clears his throat. "Let me get this straight. You stepped in to help her but you didn't do what she was doing. You took over and did it your way."

"Well, yeah. He's used to it. It's no different than taking five minutes off his time here when he plays with the animals."

"But it wasn't here. It was in her home. With her who has to implement it."

I think for a minute and realize exactly where I screwed up. She's not angry. She's frustrated. I gave Oli a punishment that she had to follow through with on her own. My eyes snap up to Pedro's.

"Well shit."

"Yep."

"I can't believe I did that man. I know better."

"I know you do. You used to bitch and moan when I did it with your brother."

"I did," I admit, wondering how I could be so stupid.

"Plus, I'm really wise when it comes to raising kids because I have one of my own," he says with a straight face.

Picking up the brush out of the bucket, I chuck it at his head. He ducks, but not before it ricochets off his palm. "You're an idiot." Sighing I admit, "But you're right. Here I was thinking I was becoming a team with her and instead, I made her life harder."

"Yep. So what are you going to do about it?"

"I think I need to let her know I figured it out, fess up to it, and maybe not do it again. I don't' want to cause her any extra stress."

"That sounds like a plan."

After pausing to let it all sink in, I look back up at Pedro. "You're going to be really obnoxious now that you're a parent, aren't you?"

"Damn straight," he yells without hesitation, a huge grin on his face. "All those people who used to say 'You can't judge someone's parenting style because you don't have kids'. Well I'm a parent now. I can judge anybody I want."

I shake my head. "You've been a parent for ten days."

"Irrelevant. No one gave me a time limit on how long until I had wisdom. It magically showed up that night."

"After you finally put your pants on?"

"Yep."

I make a mental note to get Brittany a t-shirt that says "I'm with stupid" for Christmas. Somehow it seems appropriate these days.

Chapter Eleven

Greer

The smell of the farm permeates through my car window, bringing back memories of the last time I was here. Only then I was driving to the main house. This time I'm looking for a cottage about a mile further up the driveway but still on the same land.

When Brittany gave me their address and explained how to get to their house, it made more sense why they dropped by Ace's when she was about to give birth. They're home is on the property so the main house was on their way. Good thing he did, too. I'm not sure the nurses would have appreciated him showing up in his tighty whities. Not that it would have been the first time, I'm sure. A friend of mine is a Labor and Delivery nurse. She has some stories.

When I make it to the front door and knock, Brittany answers almost immediately.

"I am so glad you're here," she says. "I love my baby, but I forgot what it's like to have arms. Would you please hold him?"

She thrusts the bundle at me and takes the Tupperware out of my hands, getting no argument from me. I could go for some baby snuggles right now.

Waving me over the threshold, she leads me into the house. It's small, but comfortable. Definitely more modern than the farm house Ace lives in with a more open concept and fresh paint. It's also very clear that a newborn lives here, what with more baby supplies than I've ever seen in my life scattered all over the living room, some of them unnecessary at this point. What in the world do they need a giant play kitchen set? The baby doesn't even sit up yet!

"Thank you for the food. What is it?" She peels back part of the lid to peek inside.

"Thanksgiving Mash. It's a recipe I found on line. Basically, it's all our left overs thrown in a pot and turned into stew. It's good."

"It sounds good." She breathes in deeply and sighs. "Smells good, too."

"It is. I tried some to make sure. I hope it helps you out a bit. I remember what it was like to have a newborn and my husband gone to work all day. It's exhausting. This way you don't have to cook."

"And I so appreciate it." She puts the container in the fridge and waves me back to the living room, plopping down on one of the couches. I gently lower myself onto a loveseat, trying not to jostle the baby. "I need to thank you for helping us the night Nio was born. Pedro has taken to being a daddy like a champ, but getting there was quite the shit show."

I snort a laugh. "Really. I don't know how those two get things done around here sometimes."

Pulling her legs up beneath her, she gets more comfortable. "I've seen them dealing with emergencies before and they're usually fine. I guess neither of them have ever dealt with those protective urges over a tiny human before so they didn't quite know what to do."

"I suppose not. Either way, you're going to have a really funny story to tell this little one when he gets older. Isn't that right," I coo at him, bringing him down to my lap so I can get a good look at his sweet face.

He's a beautiful baby, and I don't just say that to be nice. He's got darker skin like his dad, but light features like his mom. Light eyebrows, light eyelashes, light tuft of hair on his head. If he ends up with blue eyes like his mom, he's going to be a heart breaker when he gets older.

Brittany gazes at her baby lovingly as I stroke his cheek with my finger. "Does holding him give you baby fever?"

"Not at all," I say without hesitation. "I am thirty-nine-years-old and have no interest in starting over. This shop is closed. Although I'm sad Ace won't get to experience it." Realizing what I said, I feel my face flush. "Not that there was any talk about that anyway."

Thankfully she ignores my guffaw. "He'll be ok. I think he made peace with that issue a long time ago. I'm sure it helps that he'll end up being a huge part of raising this one."

"Mmm," is the only response I give. I'm not sure I want to talk about Ace. I'd rather talk about breastfeeding, sleep patterns and monitoring bowel movements.

"Are you guys fighting?"

I should have known Brittany would be more observant than that.

Looking up at her, I see only concern on her face. "I

wouldn't say we're fighting, exactly."

"Are you sure? Pedro says Ace looks like shit and has been really irritable since Thanksgiving."

This is news to me. "Really? I thought it was just me having an issue."

She cocks her head and purses her lips. "You know Ace is way more observant than that."

I sigh. She's right. I shouldn't be surprise that Ace is feeling me distance myself a bit. It's not distance from him, per se. I'm just trying to figure out how to feel about him stepping in to help me, and then leaving me hanging for the clean-up.

"I'm just processing through some stuff. You know Oli, my son, has meltdowns sometimes and is really difficult."

She nods because she does know. Oli's defiance put Pedro in the hospital a couple months ago. I'm almost surprised she's letting me in her house after that trauma. If I were her, I might still be holding onto some resentment over it.

"He had one when everyone was over for Thanksgiving. Ace helped me get him calm, but he disciplined him without talking to me about it first."

"Did you not want him to do that?"

"No. It's not that." Nio takes that moment to start fussing. I'm kind of glad. It gives me a chance to try and put my thoughts in order as I pop him up on my shoulder and begin swaying side to side. "He gave Oli a punishment that I had to follow through with even after he was gone. So I got stuck fighting with Oli for a second time after everyone left."

"Was it something you wouldn't have done otherwise?" When I look at her, she holds her hands up defensively. "I'm just playing devil's advocate. I find it helps me when I'm having a hard time sorting out my thoughts."

"Not necessarily. It's just… I didn't have the option to decide if it was worth choosing this battle. But I was kind of forced into following through with it. It just made things harder on me later. He wasn't wrong, but I can't figure out if he crossed a line or not. It's hard to explain."

Brittany presses her lips together and looks at the ceiling momentarily, like she' trying to put her own words together. "I don't know if I'd say he crossed a line. But let me ask you another question…was he wrong in his thought process?"

"What do you mean?"

"I mean, was the punishment over the top or unjust. Or something you would never do because you don't believe in that kind of discipline."

I shake my head and she nods hers in response.

"Ace has been doing this a long time. From what you're telling me, it sounds like it may be less about what he did and more about your disappointment that you didn't do it first."

Her words hit their intended target. Ace didn't do anything wrong. In fact, he did everything right. I'm just so used to doing it myself, and frankly, I'm so exhausted from the last several years, instead of recognizing that Ace's method worked, I've been focusing on the argument Oli and I had later—one we would have had later anyway because we have it every night when he complains about not having enough tablet time.

Finally breaking my own strong will, I sigh. "You're right. I haven't had to share ideas on discipline for well over five years. Longer if you consider that my ex was never home to begin with and would always hide upstairs in our room when he was home. I guess instead of looking at how it worked, I was focusing on the fact that Ace doesn't know our routine."

"Which is why he can see the big picture in a way you can't because you're so close to it. Maybe his suggestion would work."

"It actually did," I admit. "Oli told the truth twice in a row, which is really hard on him. Like it's physically painful for him to take responsibility for his own actions."

Brittany's lips twitch in a half smile. "That's pretty standard with the kids who come here. Emotions aren't their strong suit so one as harsh as conviction is really hard for them to process."

I nod in agreement because I see that all the time in Oli. Emotions make him uncomfortable. Anytime he triggers, there is almost always a big emotion attached to the meltdown. Looks like his mother might be sporting of that same issue.

"Well now I feel bad. I didn't want to make Ace upset. I just wanted to figure out what I was feeling so I could get over it."

She shrugs. "That man is head over heels for you. I'm not surprised he's that intuitive when it comes to you."

A smile crosses my face. "You think he's head over heels for me?"

"Pfft." She waves her hand at me like that's the most insane thing she's ever heard. "I've been working here for over ten years. I've never seen him light up so much when he talks about a woman. And I've never known anyone to spend the night before."

My heart swells with that information. I knew Ace and I enjoyed each other's company, but to know he feels more for me… well, that makes me feel even more desperate to get this misunderstanding behind us.

"The morning milking should be over by now," Brittany continues. "I'm guessing you can find him in the barn if you need to. Probably working on that damn mechanical bull Pedro doesn't think I know about. I swear I need an 'I'm with stupid' t-shirt."

The decision made, I hand Nio back to his mama, kissing him the top of his sweet-smelling head. "Bye baby boy. I'll see you again soon." Standing up, I check my pocket for my phone and my keys. "And thank you Brittany. You should be a therapist."

"I live with Pedro," she says as she kisses her sleeping baby lightly. "Figuring out what the hell people are even talking about has become my specialty over the years."

Laughing, I make my way out the door, closing it quietly behind me. Now that I know what my own issue is, I feel like a weight has been lifted off of me. Hopefully I can find Ace and get the last of those weights off my chest.

Chapter Twelve

Ace

Pleased that I finally have the new remote set up for the mechanical bull, I wonder why the hell I'm putting so much time and effort into fixing it in the first place. Ever since making me help him pull it out, Pedro and I have been tinkering with it way too much.

At first, I thought it was a dumb idea. But it started bringing back memories of when we were young and idealistic. The world was our oyster and all that shit.

Where did the last twenty years of our lives go? I think to myself, even though I know the answer. They went right into this farm.

Normally, it doesn't bother me. I have a full life… a home. A successful business. A program helping to put successful young adults out in the world. Good friends. I love these things. I wouldn't trade them for the world. So why am I starting to question if it's all enough?

I think Nio being born, combined with this weird rift between Greer and I just brought to the surface the insecurities that I don't normally notice. Insecurities that like to convince me I missed my chance. I missed my chance at being a father. Maybe I even missed my chance at finding the love of my life.

I don't know why it wasn't in the cards for me, but every day after my fortieth birthday I get further away from ever having the opportunity for either of those things.

Pushing away my thoughts I focus on the task at hand… trying out the new remote.

I climb up in the saddle, positioning myself as well as possible before securing the remote in its cradle. It's a little awkward trying to get the reign around it, so I make a mental note to adjust the cradle's location when I know it works.

Pressing the power button, the machinery hums to life. That's a good sign. Turning the knob slowly with my left hand, we start moving. Rocking back and forth in a smooth motion. So far so good.

Turning a little more and pressing a button, we go a little faster, slow spins intermixing with the bucking.

I give it a few seconds to make sure it doesn't glitch before turning the knob again, moving at a more respectable bronc riding speed.

Pleased with myself for fixing a thirty-year-old piece of machinery, I relax into the motion and enjoy ride, letting my inner twenty-year-old come out and play.

Spinning toward the door, I glance up to see Greer leaning against the jam, smirking at me.

"I know those hips can go faster than that," she flirts and I know she's referring to that night together.

Pressing the stop button, the machine slows down smoothly, until finally coming to rest with Greer and me facing each other.

"What are you doing here? With the way you seem to be avoiding me, I figured I was going to have to come track you down."

I don't mean to sound rude or angry, but when she grimaces I realize my words have come across snippier than I intended.

Dropping my head, I apologize quickly. "I'm sorry. That came out wrong."

She pushes off the door way and walks my direction. "No, I'm the one who should be sorry. I wasn't avoiding you…"

"You kind of were."

"Okay fine. I kind of was. But not for the reason you think." Teetering around while trying to navigate her way through the eighteen-inch-thick landing mats, she finally comes to a stop next to me. I throw my leg over the bull to stand in front of her and pull her into my arms, hugging her tight. She reciprocates immediately, wrapping her arms around my neck. Breathing in deep, I just enjoy the feel of her.

"I've missed you. I'm sorry I left you to implement a punishment I had no right to give. I wasn't even thinking."

Pulling back, she gazes into my eyes. "You didn't do anything wrong. I would have fought with Oli anyway. It's kind of inevitable."

"Then what happened? Why did you disappear?"

She begins plucking invisible link off my shirt while she speaks. "I think I wasn't so much angry that you punished him as much as I was angry that he has to be punished at all. I'm tired of it, Ace. I'm tired of being embarrassed when people see him melt because I'm afraid of the judgment. I'm tired of having to give these punishments at all. And I think when you did it, and did it better than me, I questioned my own ability."

"Babe—"

"No listen," she interrupts so I comply, knowing she needs to get it all out. "I've spent a lot of years being isolated from everyone except teachers at Oli's school and online friends. Moving here is the best thing we ever did, but I think it's taking me some time to get used to the fact that there's no judgment here. My brother isn't silently condemning me. Neither is Joie. Isaac certainly didn't flinch when Oli started yelling.

I snicker through my nose. "No, I'm pretty sure he was moving onto his second helpings by the time we got back into that room."

"Someone needed to. The fridge is still full and I just dropped half the leftovers off with Brittany."

"Are you who her company was?"

She nods. "Of course. I needed to get my hands on that baby before he stops smelling like a newborn and starts smelling like a stinky toddler."

I want to laugh because I know full well how stinky that baby will be with Pedro as a dad, but I don't. I'm too grateful for her being here, sharing her fears.

"Anyway," she continues. "I'm working on shifting my way of thinking. I'm going to try to remember that we're a team. Taking the dating out of the equation, you are one of his mentors through school and I'm his mom. We work together for his well-being no matter where we are."

I'm not sure if it makes me happy to know she's come to this conclusion. I don't want to support her because of my position in the school. I want to help her because I love her. Not that she knows it yet. But I also don't want to push now that she's finally processing her own issues. "Does thinking about it that way help?"

"It does. It makes me feel less like I'm giving up control and that I'm a bad parent. More like I'm tag teaming with someone who truly understands."

Now that's a statement I feel good about. Cupping her cheek, I stare into her brown eyes. "I do understand. And I promise I will never, ever judge you as a parent. I love you, Greer."

Her eyes widen in shock, but quickly soften as a smile takes over. "I love you, too, Grayson."

She leans up on her tip toes and presses her lips to mine, making my world finally start spinning again. I didn't realize how much it had stopped until now. "God, I missed you," I mumble against her mouth.

"I missed you, too," she whispers in response and pulls away, running her hands down my chest and licking her lips. "Now that we've got that cleared up, what are you doing out here anyway?"

Shifting my body so I can grab the remote, I show her my new device. "Pedro and I have been working on this a little bit and I was testing it out. Making sure it works right."

"And does it?"

"So far so good." Noticing a sultry look in her eye, I cock my head at her. "What? What are you thinking?"

She pushes away from me, walking around the bull, sliding her hand down the back of it and trying to sway her hips. It looks less like a sway and more like she's off balance since she's stepping on eighteen inches of padding. But if she feels like being playful, I'm not going to call her out.

"Can I try?"

My eyes pop wide. "Riding the mechanical bull?"

She flashes me a flirty grin. "I wanna see how hard I can ride it."

How does this woman always make my brain short out? I blink once. Twice. Then scramble to my feet and help her up.

"Are you sure about this?" I ask, double checking that she really thinks this is a good idea. Somehow, I suspect she's never been on one of these before. This is going to be interesting.

"Let me ride, cowboy." She tries to be flirty, but I can see that suddenly she's a bit unsure. Like it was a good idea when it was in her head, but now that she's sitting on top, not so much.

But I admit, I'm a little turned on by this game, slowly I turn the knob, giving it just enough juice to rock back and forth. Her hips coordinate with the motion and I suddenly have flashbacks to the night she was riding me. Remembering how much she liked that, I give the knob a tiny little nudge.

They begin to move faster and Greer throws her arm above her head, trying her best to imitate a bronc rider and failing miserably. In fact, she may be more uncoordinated riding than she is dancing.

"Give me more!" she yells, really getting into it. Her lack of balance is coming out full force, but I can tell she's having fun, so I comply, giving the knob one more nudge.

That nudge is all it takes for her to lose her grip completely and she goes flying off the bull, landing in a heap just a few feet away.

"Greer!" I yell and run to her, dropping to my knees and scan her body for injury. "Are you ok? Where are you hurt?"

She puts her hand on her head and grimaces. "In my pride. My pride is really, really hurting right now."

I can't help the laugh that bursts out of me. "Are you hurt anywhere else besides that?"

"No," she grumbles as she sits up and straightens her clothes. "That was supposed to be an act to turn you on."

"Oh trust me," I say as I grab the back of her neck and kiss her lightly on the lips. "That was sexier than when Deborah Winger tried to impress John Travolta."

She crinkles her nose in disgust. "Urban Cowboy? Seriously? That was a terrible movie."

"I had my first wet dream to that scene."

Her eyebrows raise and her demeanor completely changes with that information. "Really."

"Really." Leaning over her, I press into her body forcing her back onto the mat. She runs her hands down my shoulders and across my back, never breaking eye contact. "I've always fantasized about a sexy woman riding a mechanical bull and then taking her right there on the floor next to it once her hips were nice and warmed up."

Grounding my own hips into hers, she gasps. That's my cue to kiss her again. So I do. Hard and fast, plunging my tongue I her mouth like my life depends on it. She responds, thrust for thrust and before I even realize what's happening, she starts laughing.

Pulling back, I look at her quizzically.

"Urban Cowboy, Ace? Really?"

Smiling wide, I lean down to nuzzle into her. "What's wrong with a teenage cowboy dreaming about a hot chick practicing her bull riding? They were practically forcing me to picture her naked."

She smiles again, making my heart swell. This is the woman I love. The best thing that has happened to me in a long time and if I could keep her right here like this with me forever, I would.

"Trying it out was fun and all, but I don't think you're ever going to get me up on the dusty thing without panties on."

"I wouldn't dream of it." Shifting above her, I rest my hips between her legs and grind for good measure. "Besides, I have other ideas on how we workout those sexy hips of yours."

So we do. Several times.

And it's amazing.

Amazing Grayson

THE CONCLUSION

Chapter One

Ace

"Aaaahhhhh," I groan and collapse on top of Greer, depleted from my release. She runs her fingertips down my back, giving me goose bumps. "I love afternoon sex," I mumble in her ear, making her giggle.

She pushes me off her, which I've learned over the last couple of months is her way of telling me I'm getting too heavy and she can't breathe anymore. "It's 'cause it's the only kind of sex you're getting."

"You think that's what it is? I thought it was just because it's so good." And it is good. Phenomenal, actually. The more we learn about each other's bodies and what each other likes, the more fun it gets. I don't mind exploring new ways to please her. But knowing I've already figured out some of her hot buttons is a turn on too.

I rub my hand on her stomach absentmindedly while I wait for my heart to stop galloping. I love the way her stretch marks feel across my fingertips. The faint ridges are a combination of smooth and rough, and a reminder of why we're careful about our sex life. There are children involved.

When we first started sleeping together, we knew we were going to need to be creative with our time. We don't have the luxury of dropping everything whenever we miss each other or the mood strikes. We've got responsibilities. But what we also have is a running lunch date.

At some point, we finally realized we could have naked lunch if we did it at her place. Naked coffee too. So that's what we do now. It's cheaper than always eating out, and I prefer "eating in" anyway.

Yeeeah. We won't go there.

"How is your stomach feeling anyway?" I ask and pull her hand to my lips, kissing her knuckles.

"I'm not one hundred percent yet, but I'm sure glad that stomach bug is almost finished running through this house."

"No kidding. I'm gonna start stocking the shelves in the barn with vitamin C and pray the farm never gets hit like that again."

Right after Christmas, all my farm hands started getting sick. By the time it was over, half of them had come down with some form of stomach virus. At first, we thought it was food poisoning. But then Oli got sick, essentially eliminating that theory. Then Julie went down. And finally, after resisting it for a couple weeks, Greer came down with it too.

Finally, *finally* everyone is starting to pull out of it. Almost everyone anyway. It seems to be hanging on for some of them. Greer included, which is why I'm hoping she'll fall back to sleep. She has a lot more energy these days. My current relaxation is proof of that. But she still winds easily, so I know she's not quite one hundred percent.

My arms wrap around her, spooning her from behind, as her breathing levels out, and I'm pretty sure she's asleep.

"What time do you have to be back at the farm?"

Or not. Rolling on my back, I resituate us so she's lying on my chest. I like it when she lightly runs her fingertips over my abs.

"I should probably get back since we've been short-handed lately. But I definitely need to be back by the five thirty milking. Phillip is still visiting his religion in the bathroom several times a day."

"Huh?" She raises her head slightly to look at me.

"Praying to the porcelain god?"

"Oh right." She lies back down and snuggles into me. "You really do need to stock up on vitamin C."

"I know. And maybe even some Airborne. Since Phillip can't seem to kick it, I should probably run second shift to-night."

"Do you have some time off this week—?"

Before she can finish her sentence, our ears perk up.

The bus is here.

"What the hell?" she screeches and jumps out of bed. "They're not supposed to be here for at least fifteen minutes. Why is it here early? And where the hell is my bra?"

Grabbing it from underneath the pillow, I throw it at her, and she snags it out of the air one-handed.

"Thanks."

Greer scrambles to find the rest of her clothes; I'm tossing items her direction as I find them. Knowing Oli isn't the one we have to worry about, I take my own sweet time getting dressed. He's come home several times when we're still enjoying our post-coital bliss and has never put two and two together. Julie, on the other hand, seems to know something is up. But I can tell by the look on her face she's in denial, so we don't speak of such things.

Greer buttons her jeans and races out the door to greet Oli. I hear low voices coming from the kitchen as he has likely headed there for a snack. One thing about Oli—the way to his heart is definitely through his stomach.

Slowly, I put on my clothes, making sure to include my shoes and socks, for Julie's denial of course. And then I carefully make the bed. Satisfied I no longer look disheveled and like I just had the best sex of my life, I meander out of the room and into the kitchen where, once again, there is an argument about peanut butter happening.

"Oliver," Greer says gently, "that's too much. You need to spread it on the bread and put the excess back in the jar. We talked about this."

"No, we didn't," he responds and makes no move to follow her instructions.

I walk up in the middle of the conversation and greet him. "Hey Oli. Making a peanut butter sandwich?"

"Yeah."

He grabs the honey, but before he can squirt it on top of the peanut butter, I say, "I'm kind of hungry too. Is there enough peanut butter for me?"

Greer's lips twitch as she fights an amused smirk. Ever since our fight over Thanksgiving, we've come to an unspoken agreement: sometimes "good cop, bad cop" works. Tag teaming seems to be the most effective way to get Oli to comply. Today, I get to be good cop and maybe even get a snack out of it.

Oli looks from his sandwich into the jar and back at his sandwich. "We don't have anymore."

"Sure we do," I say, pointing at his sandwich. "You've got way too much peanut butter there. I bet if you spread it out, you'd have enough to make me a sandwich too."

"I don't know how to do that."

I don't necessarily believe him, but one thing I have learned about Oli: if something is hard for him to do, he'll only try once or twice before he gives up. He doesn't have a lot of patience for accomplishing tasks. At some point, he will forget the technique of how to do something, just because he hasn't practiced.

"Here. Let me show you, and I bet you can do it."

Picking up the knife off the counter and grabbing a piece of bread out of the bag, I scoop some of the peanut butter off his sandwich and put it on mine. Slowly, I show him how to spread it correctly while he watches intently. Finishing it off, I take a bite.

"See? I bet you could do it."

So he does. It takes him twice as long to get it done, but no one is complaining. In fact, Greer looks up at me, shaking her head and trying not to laugh. I can't exactly read her mind, but my guess is she's thinking something along the lines of "If only I had thought to try that years ago."

Once I show Oli how to put the excess peanut butter in the jar and get some honey, he takes his own big bite.

"You did good, Oli." I point at him with half a sandwich in my hand. "That's a real man's sandwich right there."

He smiles shyly around his mouthful of bread, pleased with the praise he's getting.

I offer my sandwich to Greer. "Want a bite?"

She nods hungrily, and I know she must be practically voracious at this point. A week of a liquid diet isn't exactly filling.

Greer no more than chews and swallows than her hand flies over her mouth and she runs out of the room. "I'm not eighty percent like I thought," she calls out over her shoulder. Seconds later, we hear gagging sounds from her bathroom.

Oli makes a face as he swallows. "Ew. That's gross."

I chuckle lightly, not because he's wrong, but because last week he was laughing when one of the farm hands threw up in the back field the bessies were grazing in. Sometimes there's no rhyme or reason to Oli's reactions.

A few minutes later, Greer comes out, rubbing her stomach. "This is not fun. I'm ready for this virus to be over."

Putting my arm around her shoulder, I pull her toward me. "I'm sure it'll only be a few more days. Phillip's been struggling for over two weeks now, and you resisted for a long time. Maybe it hit you harder."

"Maybe."

Kissing her on the top of the head, I tell her, "As much as I want to stay and take care of you, I really need to go check on the farm since we've been short-staffed. But"—I point at her authoritatively—"no more real food for you."

"But I'm hungry," she whines.

"I figured you would be. That's why I put some of Brittany's soup in the freezer a few days ago."

Her eyes widen in delight. "The turkey noodle soup with the really good broth?"

"That's the one. Just take it out and defrost it so you can get a few calories in you tonight. And call me if you need something, okay?"

She nods but has no other reaction as she flings open the freezer door, searching for the food.

Grabbing her, I spin her to me and make sure to look her in the eye. "I love you."

Her face melts into a grin. "I love you too." She lifts up on her toes, and I kiss her gently.

I hear Oli say "ew," amusing both Greer and me. Turning back to him, I just say "bye" to which he doesn't respond, instead finishing off his food.

As I open the front door, I practically run into Julie, startling her. For a split second, I know she's trying really hard not to think about why I'm here in the middle of the day, so I have pity on her.

"Your mom still isn't feeling well. I brought soup."

I don't tell her it's actually from several days ago. I'm happy to let Julie continue believing I've done nothing more than hold her mother's hand. And from the way her shoulders relax, she's happy to let me.

"Thanks, Ace. I can take over from here."

I chuckle as I pass her and head to my truck. If this is the pretense she wants to keep up for a while, I'll just roll with it.

Chapter Two

Greer

Pressing send on my email, I lean back in my chair happy to have that edit off my plate. I love helping with the creative process, but one hundred forty-five thousand words are a lot to go through with a fine-toothed comb. It seems like even more when you've been as sick as I have been.

Glancing at my calendar, I realize I haven't heard from Adeline Snow yet, and part of her book was due to me two days ago.

As much as I'd like to take the rest of the day off, I need to deal with this first. It's not like Adi to be late, and that has me worried.

Grabbing my phone, I search for her contact information and dial.

"I can't do this, Greer," she answers without even a greeting.

I settle into my seat further, already knowing this is going to be an interesting conversation.

"I see the promotional tour is going well."

"We've been here for one day," she begins, "and I'm already practically breaking out in hives thinking about how many times I have to stand next to Spencer in all his athletic glory and try not to barf all over his shoes."

A laugh bursts out at the visual image. Then I think about how close I came to throwing up on Ace, and suddenly, I'm empathetic. And I already felt bad for her. Somehow, word got out Spencer Garrison is her muse, and she ended up on a promotional tour at the insistence of her publisher and his agent.

"Don't you think you're being overly dramatic?" I ask, only half-heartedly trying to calm her down. It's going to take more than a conversation to get her to relax. More like a total body massage and a full bottle of tequila. Even then, it's iffy.

As suspected, my attempts don't work. "Overly dramatic? You've heard the saying 'Never meet your heroes'? Yeah, well, meeting your muse is even worse!"

"Well, has he disappointed you yet?"

"That's not the point." Okay. Obviously, my attempts at rationale aren't going to work. Maybe I should have taken a nap.

"Then what is the point?"

"I don't know!" she huffs and suddenly calms down considerably. "I get this is good cross promotion, ya know? He pulls in some X-Games fans who have never read my books. I pull in some readers who have never watched the games. It seemed like a good idea, but now he smells fantastic, like Red Vines. I just want to lick his neck."

I want to laugh because she's funny and witty when she's anxious. But I'm too tired to have much energy. Instead, I say,

"I would highly advise against licking any part of him without his consent."

"You're not helping."

"What do you want me to say, Adeline? I agree with your publisher. This is a fantastic opportunity."

"It's an embarrassing opportunity, that's what it is."

"Why? Because he knows he's your muse now?" She doesn't say anything, so I continue. "Adi, the only ones who know about the cardboard cutouts you used to stare at are you and me. Someday, if you opt to share that information with him, you can. But until then, we're going to keep it our creepy little secret."

"Fine," she acquiesces. "But tomorrow when the headlines say, 'New York Times Best Selling Romance Author Passes Out as Spencer Garrison Points and Laughs,' that's on you."

I chuckle lightly. "That's definitely a more likely headline than you barfing on his shoes, so I'm more than happy to take the blame for it. I assume this is why I don't have your manuscript in hand."

She groans and I hear a thud like her head just hit the desk. If she keeps banging her forehead on things, she's going to give herself a concussion and definitely pass out in front of Spencer.

"This whole thing threw me for a loop. I was starting to write my story and then it just... well... it sort of changed when he came into the picture," she explains. "Spencer Garrison as a fantasy is amazing. But Spencer Garrison for real is... is..."

"Is your wet dream come to life?"

"No!" she yells through the phone, forcing me to pull it

away from my ear while I laugh. "No, that is not what I was going to say! I was going to say it's even more amazing."

I can't help being amused she's this off-kilter because of one man. I think it's sweet. And while I'd never tell her this, secretly I hope they fall in love. I've seen a couple pictures of the tour, and they are cute together. Her with her '50s poodle skirt dresses and coifed hair. Him with his baggy jeans and skater boy qualities. They're precious together. It's one instance where the real-life love story would be so much better than a book.

"Okay, I'm focusing now," she says. "When was the manuscript due to you?"

"Two days ago."

She pauses. "Wait. It took you this long to track me down? What's wrong? Are you ill?"

I laugh because she's right. Normally, I'm contacting her a couple of days before it's due to make sure she's on track. This time, I wasn't willing to keep a trash can on my lap so I could message her without worry.

"Actually, I have been sick, thank you very much."

"Oh no. Is everything all right?"

"Yeah. Just a stomach virus that seem to be running around town."

"A stomach virus," she deadpans and puts me on alert.

"Yes," I say defensively.

"Uh huh."

"Exactly what are you insinuating, Adeline Snow."

"I'm not insinuating anything. I just think it's awfully coincidental you started riding your rodeo cowboy a couple of months ago and all of the sudden you have a stomach bug."

I can practically hear her fingers being used as italics.

Snorting through my nose, I retort, "If you are suggesting I'm pregnant, then Julie is also pregnant. And Oli. And half of Ace's staff."

"So you weren't kidding. A virus really is running around town."

Smacking my own face this time, I can't help laughing again. "Yes, Adi. There actually is a stomach bug running around town."

"Yeah, okay. When was your last period?"

"It was…" I stop to think because I honestly don't know. "November? December? Something like that. I stopped paying attention about a year ago when Julie started her cycle because we seem to throw each other off all the time."

"Hmm," she says again, and it's starting to irritate me. "You don't know when your last period was…"

"Stop. Adi. I'm not pregnant."

"Okay. I'll take your word for it."

"But Adi…"

"Yes?"

"I'm hoping you will be soon with Spencer's baby," I singsong.

"You shut up right now!" she yells. "Don't you put that kind of pressure on me!"

A belly laugh rips out of me as she yells curses and grumbles about how unfair life is that her muse has been taken away and how she's going to have to start following Jason Mamoa to come up with a storyline, and she doesn't even like the DC movies. Her rambling is hilarious.

When I start to feel bad again, I cut her off and let her know I need to go lie down. She ribs me one last time, and I promise her there is nothing more wrong with me than a stomach virus. For whatever reason, that satisfies her and she lets it go.

But it doesn't satisfy me.

When I hang up, I start wracking my brain. When was the last time I had my period? I thought it was over the Christmas holidays, but for the life of me, I don't remember if I had it or not. We were busy with family and school events and co-op events; I know we were stocked with supplies, but I genuinely don't remember if I used any.

Racing to my bathroom, I fling open the cabinet and sure enough the box is half gone. Because I used them, right? The thought occurs to me maybe Julie ran out in her bathroom so she used mine instead.

"Shit," I say and glance at myself in the mirror. "SHIT!" I yell louder.

So much for that nap. Now I have to go buy a damn pregnancy test!

Chapter Three

Ace

"**G**reer!"

There's no answer when I call out her name, even as I trudge from the front door to the open living room. I happen to turn and catch her out of the corner of my eye. She's sitting at her desk staring at her computer monitor, not moving.

"Babe."

Her whole body jerks when she finally registers I'm here.

"Oh sorry. I didn't hear you come in."

Cocking my head, I assess her mood. Something's not right. Normally when she hears me come in, she meets me halfway for a quick make-out session, maybe even a little groping. But this time, she doesn't notice I'm here?

My heart begins beating fast, and my mind automatically goes to the kids.

"What's wrong?"

"Nothing," she claims, her eyes wide. But I call bullshit.

Even if nothing's wrong, something is definitely not right.

Walking up to her, she swivels her chair to face me and I squat down between her legs. "No seriously, Greer. Is it one of the kids?"

As soon as she realizes I'm starting to feel panicky, she immediately shakes her head. "No! No, the kids are fine. I mean, Julie still isn't turning in her homework, so her grades are falling. It's just…" But then she sighs. "I need to talk to you about something."

So much for my heart going back to normal. Now I'm feeling anxious again. No good conversation ever started with those eight words.

Trying to get some clarification before I freak out on her, I ask, "Is it good or bad?"

"I don't really know yet."

She looks at the ceiling as she tries to decide how to answer. In that split second, I'm pretty sure I stop breathing. Wracking my brain, I frantically try to figure out if I did something wrong. Did I say something offensive? Did I try something she's uncomfortable with in bed? Is she upset I let Oli have a little electronics time the other day at the farm as a reward because it was raining and he was having a particularly hard day?

My thoughts run wild as I try to come up with something, anything that could have gone wrong in the last couple of weeks. I really thought things were going well between us. I'm stumped.

"Greer, you really need to level with me. What is happening? I'm starting to freak out a little."

She stares down in her lap, wringing her fingers together. Another deep sigh before she finally says, "I don't have a virus."

Now I'm really confused.

I look at her, at the monitor she was staring at, and back at her. "On your computer?"

For whatever reason, that breaks the ice and she bursts out laughing. Covering her mouth with her hand, she tries really hard to pull herself back together, but she can't stop.

"No, Ace," she says through even more giggles. "Not on my computer. In my stomach."

"Okay." This isn't clearing things up at all. "You don't have a virus on your computer and you don't have a virus in your stomach—"

I stop when it hits me. My whole body runs cold. Greer holds my gaze, waiting to see how I'm going to react. If she's saying what I think she's saying, I'm not sure how to react because I've never had anyone say this to me before, but since she's not actually saying anything, I'm not one hundred percent sure what we're talking about, but no matter what, I'm thinking in run-on sentences, which means I'm starting to Freak. The Fuck. Out.

"You're…. you're pregnant?"

Her eyes fill up with tears and she nods. That one movement, one small motion of her head turns my world upside down and literally knocks me back on my rear.

"I'm sorry, Ace. I'm so sorry. I don't know what happened. I've been on the shot for a long time. It's always been effective. But maybe it really wasn't effective, and I just didn't know it because I haven't needed it in a while and… I'm so sorry, Ace. I know we're too old for this. I understand if you don't want anything to do with this."

"Whoa." And the world turns right-side-up again in half a second flat, only this time instead of being confused or stunned, I'm downright angry at the insinuation I wouldn't want anything to do with her because she's pregnant. Or with my own child. "Do not ever say I can leave you and my child if I don't feel like being here. That's not the way this works."

"Yeah, but this is not something we planned on—"

"Exactly," I interrupt. "We. *We* didn't plan on this. *We* are in this together. Not you. *We*."

She stops trying to put excuses in my mouth, and her face flushes. I'm not sure if it's from embarrassment or emotion. Or hell, if she needs to throw up again. Either way, before this nonsense continues, she needs to know how I really feel.

Rising off the floor, I kneel in front of her and cup her cheek with my hand, forcing her gaze to mine. "Greer, I want to make sure I'm one hundred percent clear on everything happening because my thoughts are a little tangled up right now." I swallow hard. "You and me—we're having a baby?"

She nods again and whispers, "Yeah."

That's when every single emotion leaves my body and is replaced by the most magical feeling of joy and excitement I have ever felt.

"I'm gonna be a dad," I say quietly, and her eyes fill with tears again, only this time she's smiling.

"Yeah. You're gonna be a dad."

"I think…" I clear my throat when it cracks. "I think this is possibly the best day of my entire life."

That does it. The dam breaks on Greer's tears. She throws her arms around my neck, and she begins sobbing.

"I never thought this would happen," I continue, so overwhelmed I can't think straight. "I wrote it off that I was never going experience those things and… Greer…. I'm gonna be a dad!"

She pulls back and kisses me, brushing her wet cheeks against mine. "And I'm going to be a mom. Again." She stops and her face falls like she's had a realization. "Crap! I'm gonna have a baby when I'm forty!"

I start laughing and pull her to me. "Looks like our lives are just beginning."

"No. No, I don't think that's what this means," she deadpans. "Pretty sure this means we're in for a run for our money."

"What are you talking about? A baby is going to keep us young."

"Or drive us to an early grave."

"You're no fun," I joke. "But I do have something serious I need to say here."

She sits back and my hands rub on her hips. My gaze immediately drops to her stomach, and I can't believe my baby is in there. You can't see it yet. She's obviously not showing. But knowing he's there, I'm in awe.

"Greer, I don't want you to do this by yourself. And I don't want to miss out on anything. Not the dirty diapers and the sleepless nights and the feedings and the colic. I don't want to miss out on all of that."

"You can have as much of it as you want."

"But Greer, I also want you."

"I know you do." She looks at me with such love in her eyes, I know right now this is my forever. *She's* my forever.

"I don't think you do, though." Shifting on my haunches a bit, I settle in for the next most important moment of my life.

"I love you. I love Oli. I love Julie. And you know full well what we have is going to go the extra mile." She sniffs back more tears and nods, so I go on. "Greer, I want to marry you."

Usually I'm the one dumbfounded. Not this time. For the first time since I've known her, I'm pretty sure I made her brain short out.

She blinks at me. Then blinks again. Then a third time and starts laughing hysterically.

That's not how I planned for this to go.

"We can't get married, Ace. We've only known each other for three months. That's like twelve weeks."

"No, it hasn't only been three months, Greer. It may have been only that long since we've been dating, but we've been preparing for this for a long time. We're not in our twenties anymore."

"What does that have to do with anything?"

"It means I'm not being rash. Yes, I'm asking for your hand in marriage right now because you're pregnant. But I was already planning on us getting married at some point. I'm in my forties. I'm not some stupid kid trying to figure out who I am. I already know. I'm a dairy farmer who has a heart for kids and wants to help them succeed." Grabbing her hands, I shift until I'm on one knee. This hasn't exactly been romantic so far, but the least I can do is assume the position. "I'm also madly in love with the most beautiful woman I've ever had the chance to know. Who also isn't a dumb kid. You know you're a reader by hobby and an editor by trade. You're a mom whose goal is to raise your children to be the best, most successful members of society they can be. Don't you see, Greer? We already both revolve our lives around children with special needs. We've done it separately. But our lives already intermesh. I love you, and I want to be with you. You. Are. It for me. And with our baby coming… Greer, I don't want to wait any longer. Will you please marry me?"

Tears run down her face as she considers what I'm asking.

"Twenty years ago, I would have thought this was exciting. Fate and a whirlwind romance, ya know?" She scratches at my scruff, not making eye contact, but I know she's still right here with me this morning. "But Ace, I'm not twenty years old anymore. I don't want to get swept up in a moment. That's not a solid foundation for a marriage, and I don't want to ever be in a position like that again."

Wiping her tears with my thumbs, my heart breaks that she's been hurt before. While I respect the fact that she stayed put in her marriage for the children, the longer she stayed, the more beaten down she was. It's not right. She never deserved that. The only thing I can do is try to be patient with her fears.

"That being said"—she wipes her nose with her sleeve—"I would be lying if I said I didn't want to marry you."

I try very hard not to smile or jump up and down with excitement, but I am so, so excited. "I know this is scary for you. I understand. Do you need a couple days to think about it?"

She shakes her head. "No. I absolutely do not need time to figure out if I want to marry you. I need time to think about how soon to do it. Maybe we can do like my brother and Joie. They've been engaged for a while but don't have any wedding plans set, and it works for them."

My hopes soar, because she's not saying no. In fact, I'm pretty sure she just said yes. "I have my momma's engagement ring at the house. I wish I had it with me right now. I wasn't planning on my proposal going this way. You deserve all the hearts and flowers and stuff."

Tears fill her eyes again, and I make a mental note to pick up a pregnancy book on my way home. I've never seen her cry this much. Hell, I don't know if I've ever seen her cry. And to do it three times since I've been here? That's got to be those elusive hormones Pedro used to bitch about before Nio was born.

"I don't need any of that stuff, Ace. In fact, I don't want any of it. It's all just distractions from the important things anyway." She continues to sniffle, but her tears are finally at bay. "But now that that's worked out, do me a favor."

"Anything."

"Ask me again."

This time when she sniffs, she's smiling too. I stand up, stretch my legs for a second, then get down on one knee for the second time this morning and give her as much romance as I can come up with on a whim.

"Greer Declan, I always thought I was content with being single and running the farm, helping the kids, being Pedro's extended family. Then a boy by the name of Oli came roaring into my life."

She giggles because it's true. If it weren't for Oli, we wouldn't be here.

"That boy brought me you, and I have never for one day not been grateful for that gift. Greer, I love you. I love the kids. I love our baby."

I reach out to gently touch her stomach. She puts her hand over mine like we're holding our child together.

"I would be the most privileged man in the world, if you would do me the honor of being my wife. Someday. Eventually."

She laughs out loud and nods vigorously. "Yes. I will marry you. Someday. Eventually."

I cup her cheeks in my hands and kiss her gently on the lips. And her cheek. And her jawline.

Her neck. Her collarbone. Right over her heart on her chest. And her sternum. And her bellybutton.

And her tummy right below. I kiss it several times, feeling so much love, I swear my heart is going to explode.

"Get ready for the craziness, baby," I say to her stomach, knowing full well my child doesn't have ears yet. "It's gonna be a wild ride. But you are already so, so loved."

Greer runs her fingers through my dark hair. I close my eyes and lay my head on her lap.

"You're going to be a great dad," she whispers. "But I need you to get up."

Hearing the desperation in her voice, I quickly pop up and move out of the way as she takes off running. She makes it as far as the kitchen sink before throwing up.

Looks like I'm going to be picking up more soup tonight too.

Chapter Four

Greer

Ace and I are sitting around on the couch chatting when Oli and Julie get home from school.

We tossed around the idea of hiding our news until I'm farther along in this pregnancy. But then we realized how unfair that is. Everything happening now, every decision Ace and I are making, directly affects them.

Don't misunderstand, I'm the mom. I make the decisions. The children don't run this house. However, I also recognize their entire world is about to be upended.

Again.

Oli came home and nothing abnormal really happened.

He went straight to the pantry for an afternoon snack.

We fought over peanut butter.

Ace helped him out with not using too much.

Oli got all proud of himself.

We fought over him putting his backpack in the mud-room.

He claimed he didn't do it.

I told him I saw him drop it by the door.

He says someone moved it there.

The same opposition we have every single day. But it was nice having Ace navigate through it with me. And as I stood there watching, I noticed something completely different than I had before… Ace really has turned into a member of this family. He's not just some guy I'm dating who comes over and tolerates the things going on around him. He gets in and helps. He loves. He disciplines. He jokes. He pitches in.

It might be his personality, but either way, he fits with us. And we fit with him.

I know I'm going to marry this man. I know it. I just need to figure out when.

The door slams as Julie comes into the house.

"Hey," I greet her when she comes through the archway. "How was school?"

She shrugs. "Fine."

"Did you get all your homework turned in?"

"Yes."

"Julie." The warning in my tone has her looking over at me.

"No really, Mom. I turned it all in. You can email my teachers."

"Okay." She doesn't know it, but I already did. She's getting far enough behind I have to stay on top of her grades. I'd push the issue further with her if I'd heard back from anyone at the school, but I haven't yet, so there's not much I can do except chat with her about other topics. "Still no invitation to the sweetheart dance?"

She plops down on the couch next to me. "I think it's

clear by now no one is going to invite me."

I smack her lightly on the leg. "Then get a group of girl-friends to go together."

She looks at me incredulously. "Mom, that's not the way it works here."

"What do you mean?"

"People don't do that here. If you don't have a date, you don't go," she explains. I know I've been out of high school for a long time, but I really don't understand the teenage social hierarchy. I thought the trend was to go stag. When did that change?

"Well that doesn't sound fair."

She shrugs again. "Like you always say, it is what it is."

"Hi, Julie." Now that he's helped Oli clean up the kitchen, Ace sits next to me and intertwines our fingers.

My daughter looks at our hands and cringes, then looks back at my boyfriend. "Hi. I figured you'd be heading out the door by now."

He gives me a knowing look since we have a lot to discuss with the kids today.

"Nah. I called in and gave Pedro a heads up I wouldn't be back until later."

Julie immediately perks up. She knows that's not normal.

"Why?" She's clearly fishing for information. "Are you guys going on a date?"

"No. We're going to stay around here."

She quirks an eyebrow and leans forward. "Why are you sticking around here? Aren't you usually milking right now?" No one can say my girl's not an astute observer.

I don't bother making excuses, knowing we have to fess up soon enough anyway. "We wanted to talk to you kids about some things."

She bites her lip, and I'm not sure if she's biting back a smile or a frown. I guess we'll find out soon enough.

Ace leans to speak directly into my ear. "You wanna do this now?"

I nod in response. "Don't you think we might as well? Look at Julie. She's already trying to figure out what's happening. Best to not make her wait."

Ace chuckles lightly as Julie continues to track us with her eyes. "Good point. She might pop that vein in her forehead. Hey Oli, can you come in here and sit down?"

"I didn't do anything." Oli immediately goes into defensive mode. My poor boy. Always paranoid someone is out to get him.

"You're not in trouble, buddy," I call out over the couch. "We need to talk to you about a few things."

"Okay." He ambles over and sits on the loveseat perpendicular to us. "What?"

Ace and I look at each other and he nods. "They're your kids so maybe you need to start."

Taking a deep breathe, I look at Oli first and choose my words carefully. "Oli, I'm going to have a baby."

"A baby what?" he immediately asks, and Julie makes a garbled sound, halfway between a gasp and a laugh at Oli's question.

"A real baby," I continue, keeping my eyes focused on my son, making sure he catches the most important parts of this information. "There's a baby growing in my tummy. Do you know what that means?"

He thinks for a second. "It means you're going to have a baby?"

Ace chuckles.

"Right. You know how you always said you wanted a little brother?"

"Yeah, because I already have a sister and sisters are stupid."

I can almost hear Julie rolling her eyes. "Well, I don't know if you're going to get a brother this time, but you're definitely going to get another baby."

"Cool. Can I have my tablet?"

Huh. That went over better than I expected.

"No, Oliver. We're having a conversation right now."

"Yeah but I need my tablet," he argues.

"That's not how it works. You don't get it until seven o'clock. I need you to focus on our conversation."

He throws himself farther into the sofa in frustration while I turn to Julie.

"Besides total and complete shock, what do you think?" I ask her.

She thinks for a second before speaking slowly. "I don't really know." And then she giggles, but I'm not sure if it's from shock or humor. "You're not married, Mom, and you're really old."

Pursing my lips at her, I quirk an eyebrow. "Really? You're going to go there right now?"

"Hey, don't blame me for being shocked by your age," she says snottily. "You're the one who's been trying to convince everyone for the last five years you're still thirty-five."

Ace snorts and I elbow him in the rib. "I can claim whatever age I want."

"But there's more," Ace interjects, and Julie looks between him and me. "I've asked your mom to marry me."

It takes a second for his words to register, but my two kids have two completely different reactions. Julie yells "What?" while Oliver sits up straight and yells, "Does that mean you're going to be my new dad?" I've never seen Ace smile so wide.

"I guess that means I'm going to be your step-dad, yeah."

"That is so. Cool!" Oli continues. "You're gonna be my dad. Ace! Ace, the guy with the farm! Ace, the guy with all the bessies! Ace is gonna be my dad! Did you hear that Julie? Ace is gonna be our dad!"

"Yeah, I heard Oli." She sounds way less enthusiastic than he does.

I nudge her with my elbow. "I haven't said yes yet."

Ace leans forward to talk over me. "That's not true. You said yes to an engagement which is basically the same thing."

"I said yes to an engagement. I didn't say yes to a marriage yet. We've got some time to think about it." I turn back to my daughter who is staring at the blank television, chewing on her lip. "But what I'm really worried about is what you're thinking. I know this is all a shock."

She huffs and says, "Doesn't really matter what I think. You're gonna do it anyway."

I reel back like I've been slapped. "Excuse you. I know this is all a lot to process, but don't disrespect me please."

Julie shakes her head and rolls her eyes. "Whatever."

Leaning forward, I turn my body all the way to face her. "No, not *whatever*. You're being extremely rude right now, young lady."

This entire conversation has me stunned. I thought Julie had it together. I thought she was doing okay. I thought she was rolling with the punches, and as difficult as it was, she was taking it like a champ. But when she bats away a stray tear, I realize how wrong I've been. The homework should have been my first clue, and I overlooked it. And now I feel terrible for missing how hard she's struggling, while be pissed about how she's acting.

"Julie," Ace interjects.

She doesn't answer him, just wipes another stray tear away.

"I love your mother more than anything in this world. And I love this baby we're going to have. But I don't want you to ever think I don't love you and Oli like you're my own, because I do. I worry about you when I'm not here. I ask your mom about you all the time and your swimming and your school stuff."

She doesn't respond, but I hope she's at least listening to what Ace has to say.

"I don't necessarily talk to you guys about it because I don't want you to feel pressured to feel the same way about me. So yeah. I would be honored if you would allow me to step into the role of father figure in your life. But that would require moving out to the farm at some point. That's where the business is. I can't run a farm out of your mom's office, but your mom can run her office from my farm."

"I know." At least she's responding. We haven't lost her completely.

"I know it's not ideal. But you do bring up a good point. None of you have grown up on a farm. And the main house is the hub of all the activity for the farm hands. Once your mom decides when she wants to get married, and when we decide we need to all be together, I think it's a good idea to build a different house on the property."

"What?!" I yell, staring at him like he's lost his damn mind. "You're going to build a house so we feel comfortable?"

He gives me the same look I'm giving him. It's like a silent argument over who the crazy one actually is. "Uh, yes."

"You are out of your mind. I understand we need to get used to some things, but building an entire house?"

"It's not only that, Greer," he argues.

"Then explain it to me, Ace, because that sounds whack-a-doodle."

"Do you know how old my employees are?"

I shake my head, not having any clue why this is relevant information to our conversation.

"My youngest is eighteen years old. When he was fifteen, he started working for me part time because he wants to own a farm someday. He's a farm hand now. Graduated high school, immediately moved into the staff quarters, and is my youngest employee. My next youngest is nineteen. The one after that… twenty. You think I'm going to give those guys an open-door policy with my beautiful sixteen-year-old step-daughter sleeping upstairs in her jammies? I don't think so."

I look at him with shock then look back at Julie who has a blush on her face. I've never seen him have so much passion for one of my kids before. He wasn't kidding when he said he loved them like they're his. Apparently, that means protecting them too.

Julie shrugs at me.

"Okay then," I respond. "I guess we're building a house."

"Thank you," he says with a nod, then pushes to a standing position. "Well, now that that's settled, I need you kids to convince your mom to marry me soon. Also, I need to borrow your computer, so we can pull up some home builders and begin looking at designs. It's already January, and if we want to get in by summer, we need to get this moving."

He stalks out of my room and into my office. We watch as he opens my computer, puts in the password I didn't realize he knew, and starts pulling up floor plans.

I'm stunned by this turn of events. And also, oddly, very turned on. Maybe I need to look at marrying him sooner, rather than later.

Chapter Five

Ace

Over the last month, while I've been antsy and ready to walk down the aisle, I've been giving Greer her space. I know she's struggling with a bunch of things. With whether or not it's too soon to get married, if we're getting married for the right reasons, how getting married is going to affect the kids. Not to mention the questions of where we'll live and what happens to her house if we move to the farm.

She's proud of what she's built and that she can stand on her own two feet, providing for her kids. I don't want to diminish that. She has every right to be proud of herself for pulling them out of a bad marriage and bad situation, only to raise an extremely difficult child by herself. Hell, he's hard when there are two of us.

But on the flip side, I know she loves me as much as I love her. It's clear every time we're together and in every interaction. I know she'll get there. She just needs time to process it all.

I hope she figures it out soon. We both want our child to grow up in a stable, loving home, not split time between two houses. The sooner our family is together and settled, the better off for everyone.

Still, I won't pressure her. She internalizes a lot in every situation. This is no different. Instead, I've stepped back so she can come to her own conclusions. And as much as I'm chomping at the bit to sleep next to her every night, I'm waiting as patiently as I can. Admittedly, it's a struggle. I want to be here to watch my baby grow inside her. It seems to be happening rapidly these days.

Almost immediately after finding out about the baby, there've been some physical changes in her body. Most people wouldn't necessarily notice, but since I'm the one who gets to see her without her clothes, and I'm looking for it, I can tell her belly is a little more rounded. I can see how much darker her areolas are. It's obvious to me a dark line is developing from her belly button all the way down to her pubic bone.

They're all changes other people won't see. But I see them. And they fill me with pride.

I think the biggest thing stopping Greer from moving forward in our relationship has been the kids. How in the world would they adjust? This has been a whirlwind romance. We didn't get to see each other every couple days like a lot of couples do at the beginning. It's a few times a week. So I know she's been afraid of pushing her kids too fast. Oli has finally settled into a routine, and she's worried about messing with that delicate balance. But Julie—Julie hasn't found her place yet. She's always running late and still forgetting to turn in her homework. It's been the subject of more than one argument, and I know Greer is concerned another big transition will be impossible for her teenaged daughter to come back from.

"Mom. Ace."

Greer and I look up from the movie we're watching. I'm trying to get all of us on a Marvel movie kick. With so many movies in the series being made, it's taking lots of time to catch up. Sure, I've seen a couple *Iron Man* flicks, but I wanted to start at the beginning and see them in order. I also thought it would be a good way for the kids and me to have something to do together. Something to bond over besides talking about farm stuff.

My plans went awry though. Some of the movies haven't been holding Oli's attention so he went outside to bounce a basketball. And Julie, despite her love of Webtunes and anime, has been completely uninterested. I guess I'll have to move onto the DC comics next since they're darker and more cartoon like. Maybe Julie will like those more.

I contemplate asking her, since she's staring down at us anyway. But she seems to have something on her mind.

"I'd like to talk to you," she says sternly.

Yep. She definitely has something on her mind.

Greer and I look at each other then back at Julie. "Sounds serious," Greer responds.

"It's very serious. Can we stop the movie for a minute?"

As much as I want to know if Jarvis is really dead, or if he's actually one step ahead of Ultron, I'm more curious about what Julie has to say.

"Do we need to go to my office?" Greer asks as we shift on the couch and I turn the TV off.

"Here is fine." Julie sits on the love seat and turns to face us. Leaning forward, she puts her elbows on her knees and clasps her hands together. Then she says the last thing I was expecting. "Why are you not married yet?"

A garbled noise comes from Greer's throat, that obviously means she wasn't expecting this confrontation either.

Obviously, even though I've been giving her space, I've been curious where Greer's head is at. But I had no idea Julie wanted to know.

Still, her statement reiterates the fact of how much this marriage is going to affect the kids.

"Well," Greer finally begins after taking a moment to pull herself together, "there's a lot of factors to consider when making a decision like this, ya know?"

"No, I really don't know." Julie shakes her head. "Please explain it."

I smirk, because it sounds like Julie is manipulating her mother into processing out loud, so a decision can be made. Little shit.

Greer blows out a breath nervously. "Well, we haven't been dating long."

"Uh huh. But you're having a baby together."

Damn. Julie isn't holding back today.

"Yeah, we are. But I'm not sure having a baby together is reason enough to get married. Marriage is a lifelong commitment."

I crinkle my brow because that makes no sense. Julie rolls her eyes.

"Right. Because having a baby is just a short-term thing," she snips sarcastically. "What's your next reason?"

A laugh bursts out of Greer. "Are you trying to convince me to get married?"

Julie sighs. "Yes, Mom. Yes."

I stand corrected. There was something she could say that would surprise us even more.

"Mom," Julie pleads, "you love him. We love him. Ace is the best thing that has ever come into our family. I know you're scared. But if the reason you aren't married yet is because of Oli and me, you need to stop."

Greer grabs my hand and squeezes tightly. I put my arm around her shoulder, knowing she needs reassurance.

"I know this means we're going to have to move. And as much as I'm tired of moving, I only have a couple more years of school anyway. It's not going to make much of a difference. Look, I can't tell you whether or not to get married. But what I can tell you is stop worrying about me. We need Ace. All of us do. Oli. You. My baby sister."

"Sister, huh?"

She nods. "Me too, Mom. I need Ace too."

Greer wipes at a stray tear, and I'm glad when neither of them notice mine.

"Just get married already."

Greer looks at me. "You still want to marry me?"

"More than anything."

"Looks like we have a wedding to plan."

Chapter Six

Greer

Much to my surprise, my teenaged daughter knocked some sense into me and a wedding was planned.

I still haven't told anyone I'm pregnant. I can't help it. It's not that I don't love Ace with my whole heart. I do. And maybe more importantly, I want to build a life with him. I want us to grow old together and be together as our kids grow up and have lives of their own. I can practically envision us sitting on a porch swing, sipping on lemonade as we watch our grandkids play in the yard. Of course, we'll have to install a porch swing first.

It's not about Ace or even this baby at all. It's about my own experiences. My former therapist mentioned one time there is a small element of PTSD a lot of parents go through when their children have extra issues. It's not full-blown like someone who may have been to war or gone through a traumatic event. I don't have flashbacks or debilitating fear that renders me non-functional. But there still is the lingering anxiety. The nervousness that comes with making any changes that could throw things off balance and back into the depths of conduct disorder hell. I've been there. I don't want to go back.

But when Julie sat us down and forced the issue, I had a moment of clarity: I was the one holding us back. I was the one keeping us from healing. And I needed to snap out of it.

I realized Oli was going to react to major life changes no matter what, and avoiding those changes will never change that fact. I realized Julie is more grown up than I've been giving her credit for, but she also needs a father figure in her life. She only has a couple more years of school, and to keep her and Ace from fully developing a relationship because of my own fears was doing her more harm than good.

I also realized one very big thing… no matter how much I may be in denial, this baby is coming and I have to get prepared. No, he or she won't care where we live or if we move in the first year. But this baby's father is here, waiting to be included. And by holding us back from moving forward, I'm doing him or her a huge injustice.

My ex-husband no longer contacts our kids unless he has something up his sleeve, and it's caused a tremendous amount of hurt for my children. But this baby's father is *right here,* wanting to be a part of every single moment from conception on. And I'm the one denying my child of their father.

Ouch.

That realization hurt.

So, I pushed my own fears aside, thought about things rationally, and even had a pow-wow with Adeline, who knows first-hand about relationship fears. We basically told each other the same thing… stop assuming the worst and trust the integrity of the man.

Now, here I sit, in the bridal room of the courthouse, waiting for our turn to get hitched. I look down at his mother's engagement ring, now mine, and think about how perfect it is. It's a one-carat diamond held to a thin platinum band by a four-pronged setting. It's simple. Like us and our wedding.

At first, Ace wanted a church ceremony, but I nixed the idea. Been there. Done that. It's a waste of money. We've got baby crap to purchase and college to fund in the next couple years. Talk about a double whammy financially.

I much preferred to elope when we had time in jeans and T-shirts, sign the marriage license, and be done with it. I thought Ace's head was going to explode when I threw out that idea.

So, we compromised. Yes, we're at the courthouse, which it turns out he's okay with. But I'm in an actual wedding dress and he's wearing a suit. And lucky him, Valentine's Day fell during the week so here we are, preparing to be married in front of our closest family and friends on the day of love.

"Knock, knock!"

I catch a glimpse of Joie in the mirror as she peeks her head in the door. Her face immediately lights up as she takes in my appearance. I opted for something less traditional. Closer to cream than white for obvious reasons, the scoop neck has a bit of extra material, making it looser at the bust, and the cap sleeves give it less of a summer dress and more elegant on top. But the skirt flairs all the way to my knee, giving it the extra room I need to hide my new baby bump. And because I know Ace loves them, I topped the whole outfit off with my cowgirl boots.

Smoothing down the sides of my skirt, I'm careful not to draw any undue attention to my midsection. We haven't told anyone except the kids about the baby. Partially because I'm having a hard time wrapping my brain around the fact that I'm going to have a newborn shortly after my fortieth birthday. And partially because I didn't want to hear any comments about having a shotgun wedding. I know my brother well, and there's no telling if he'd show up with a Nerf version of the real thing just for shits and giggles.

"Is the coast clear?"

I shrug in response. "Sure. I'm not worried about anyone seeing me before the ceremony."

"Don't say that." Brittany gives me a pointed look as she comes in behind my sister-in-law, carrying baby Nio. "Ace would never recover if you didn't give him this tradition."

I giggle because it's true. While I've been married before and gone through the pomp and circumstance, I have to remind myself Ace hasn't. And by nature, he's a traditional guy so certain things are important to him. This is why Julie is acting as my bridesmaid and Oli as his groomsman. This is why my brother and Joie took the day off work. This is why Pedro made sure his shift was covered. Those six people are the most important people in the world to us so he wanted them here. After thinking about it, I realized he's right. We need to share this moment with our family. It's a new journey, and we're celebrating it.

"Is he sweating bullets yet?" I ask, as Brittany gets comfortable in a chair and yanks the top of her cotton dress down to free her breast and pop it in the baby's mouth. I feel the familiar ache in my own breasts as I watch little Nio latch on. Breastfeeding is one thing that didn't go well with my other two kids. I make a mental note to do some research in the next few months on how to make my milk come in, but not yet.

"Close to it." Brittany leans her head back and makes a face when her milk lets down, then relaxes into the couch.

"Greer, you really do look lovely." Joie fawns all over me, tucking in stray strands of hair and wiping invisible lint off my sleeve. "You look cowgirl chic."

"Good. That's what I was going for. Now that we'll be living in Texas permanently, I'm trying to embrace my new culture."

"You mean nationality?" Brittany jokes, shifting Nio around when he gets a little fussy. "People in Texas seem to think they live in a country all their own."

Joie laughs and plops down next to Brittany. "Ain't that the truth?"

I don't sit next to them, nervous I'll wrinkle my dress. It's odd having this many nerves. It's not like I haven't done this before. Gotten married, I mean. But this time feels much more important. Like it's the beginning of something remarkable.

I realize as my two new friends chat about different traditions you only find in the Lone Star State, this is happy anxiety. What I'm feeling isn't worry the bottom will fall out. It's feeling excitement about what's finally beginning.

Another knock sounds, and we all look to see my brother sticking his head through the door. I appreciate he's being careful not to accidentally flash me to everyone outside.

"Hey. You're up."

The ladies hop to it, so they can take their positions at the front of the court room. In her excitement, Brittany forgets Jack is in the room and he blushes after getting an eyeful of boob.

Once they leave Jack and me alone, the mood turns serious.

"You look beautiful," he says.

Tears form in my eyes. As much my brother and I love to argue and banter, he's still my big brother. His support means everything.

Plus… hormones.

"Thank you. You don't look too bad yourself."

He breaks into a grin but doesn't lose his serious tone. "No really. You know Mom and Dad would be proud of you, right?"

I wave my fingers in front of my eyes, trying to dry the tears that still threaten to fall. "Jack please," I plead, "don't make me cry on my wedding day."

He walks toward me and gently puts his hands on my neck, rubbing his thumbs on my cheeks. "I'm proud of you too, baby sis. Ace is a good man. He loves you and the kids so much. I'm not worried about you anymore. I know he's going to take good care of you."

"You were worried about me before?"

"Always. Why do you think I practically dragged your ass down here?"

I bark a laugh through my sniffles. "You ass. You did not. I drove that damn truck down here all by myself."

"One more year and I would have been up in Kansas throwing your shit in that truck myself, just to get you where you needed to be." He pulls me into a hug. "And if this marriage lasts forever, I'm taking full credit."

I laugh against his chest, trying to be careful not to smear makeup on his shirt as a stray tear or two finally fall free.

"You're such an asshole. Now my mascara is about to run."

He pulls away and looks at me. Taking a handkerchief out

of his suit pocket, I furrow my brow in confusion because I've never seen him carry one before. "Nah. You look amazing. Now are you ready to go make this permanent?"

I nod vigorously, more ready than I thought I'd ever be.

Confident now that Ace isn't going to lose his shit if he sees me, and knowing there's nothing he can do anyway since the wedding is starting, we exit the waiting room. Julie is standing in the hall holding two flower bouquets. One for her and a larger one for me.

They're simple, made of the purple wildflowers found in Ace's field. The same flowers I found beautiful the first time I stepped foot on the farm.

I wasn't planning on having a bouquet during the ceremony, but we had an unseasonably warm week and things bloomed suddenly. When Brittany saw them, she couldn't resist picking as many as she could and making them for today. Just one more of Brittany's many talents I never knew she had.

Julie hands it to me, and I peek through the door to see Oli standing at the front, yanking at the tie around his neck. "I knew he was going to hate that tie." I giggle to myself. Jack looks down at me and smirks, knowing full well what I'm talking about. He loves his nephew fiercely but had to threaten him to get him to put it on.

Brittany and Pedro are standing on the same side as Oli.

Joie is standing on the opposite side to represent me. Once we get to the end of the short aisle, Julie and Jack will stand next to her completing our side of the family.

I take all this in in just a quick second, but what catches my attention and holds it is my husband-to-be.

Ace is in a dark navy suit, tailored to perfection. His tall frame is practically vibrating with excitement as he looks at his watch and shifts his shoulders. His dark hair has been styled. No hat for him today, which I'm almost sad about. We would have been the stereotypical Texas couple if he had a cowboy hat on.

As if he feels my gaze, he looks at me and everything else fades away. My nerves, my fears, my anxieties. Even my denial of what the future holds disappears as he breaks into a smile. I can tell when his shoulders relax, and I know, *I know* this is it. This is perfect.

"Are you ready, Mom?" I hear Julie ask, but I never take my eyes off my man.

"More than you know."

"Ew," she responds. "You don't have to make it gross."

I barely register Jack chuckling next to me at Julie's typical teenage disgust. But I don't care. Now, I'm finally ready to get married. No doubts in my mind.

Julie steps in front of me, momentarily blocking my view and bringing me back to the present. As the standard "Wedding March" begins, she makes the short trek to the front of the courthouse.

It looks just like you'd expect a courtroom to look, with a judge's bench and benches for spectators to sit on. There are standard state and county plaques attached to the walls around the room. Someone tried to make it look nice, though. There are some white flower decorations along the pews creating a makeshift walkway. And there's as small archway of those same white silk flowers where the judge stands.

Once Julie gets about halfway, Jack and I start walking. It takes but a moment to get to my destination, and it feels like that's when things finally begin.

Jack kisses me on the cheek and passes me off to my future husband, completing the exchange with a handshake and a manly pat on the back. Without asking, Julie takes my bouquet out of my hands, leaving me free to clasp onto Ace's.

"Is everyone accounted for?" the judge asks, and we nod, never taking our eyes off each other.

He's so handsome, his eyes sparkling. And he looks at me like, well actually, I'm not sure if he's looking at me like I'm the most precious thing he's ever seen or like he wants to rip my dress off. Either option is fine with me.

There go those hormones again.

"Let's do this quick. I'm ready to be married to my girl."

At Aces' prodding, the judge doesn't waste any time.

"Good afternoon. We are here to witness the union of Grayson Whitman and Greer Declan. As is tradition, if anyone here has a reason why these two should not be joined, let them speak now or forever hold their peace."

I don't expect anyone to say a word, but of course I should know better. Oli immediately opens his mouth and says, "No, because I need my new baby brother and me to have the same dad."

My jaw drops open, Ace's expression mirroring mine.

"Oli, that was a secret!" Julie hisses at the same time Jack bellows, "What?!?!" and everyone else gasps.

A nervous giggle escapes me because what else can I do? We wanted to wait at least until after my first ultrasound, but honestly, I'm surprised Oli hasn't spilled the beans until now. His timing though, is impeccable.

"Can someone please explain what's going on?" Jack demands, Joie quietly murmuring to him to shut up and wait until a different time to do this.

Pedro, of course, starts belly laughing, making Ace turn

around and glare. "What the hell is so funny over there?"

Wiping tears from his eyes, Pedro says, "You're going to get your ass kicked on your wedding day."

Rolling my eyes at the insanity of it all, I realize it's up to me to pull this back together. Tugging on Ace's arm to focus him back on me, I shoot a glare Pedro's way.

"Can we please discuss this later? I'd like to focus on the happiest day of my life."

"Hey!" Julie immediately responds.

"Sorry. Third happiest."

"Hey!" Ace responds.

"Oh good god. You people are a bunch of babies," I mumble. "Top three. It's in the top three happiest days of my life."

"Remind me not to ask that question again," our judge says under his breath. "After thirty years, you would think I would know better by now."

"I'm sorry," I say to him, embarrassed at this turn of events. Not only is my family ridiculous, but I'm an almost forty-year-old bride having a shotgun wedding. I'm not embarrassed by the situation per se, but I know how uncouth this looks. My late prim-and-proper mother would be mortified by this entire conversation. "Can we just skip to the getting married part?"

His amused smirk is my first indication he's not judging me and is honestly finding humor in this whole situation. "Of course," he says kindly, and straightens his posture, going right back into judge mode. "We'll make this quick. Grayson Whitman, do you take Greer Declan to be your lawfully wedded wife, to have and to hold, from this day forward as long as you both shall live?"

"I do," he answers proudly, without hesitation, and my heart swells with emotion.

"Greer Declan, do you take Grayson Whitman to be your lawfully wedded husband, to have and to hold, from this day forward as long as you both shall live?"

"I do."

I didn't think Ace's smile could get any wider, but the words are no more out of my mouth than I'm proven wrong. I've never seen him this happy before.

"Do you have the rings?"

"Oh shit." Ace whips his head around and we watch as Pedro pats down all the pockets in his suit, looking for the rings. A growl comes from low in Ace's throat making Pedro break into a smile. "Ha! Just kidding." Then Pedro turns serious. "Now we're even for you getting me blitzed the night before my wedding."

Ace rolls his eyes and mumbles something like, "We were in Vegas. I couldn't keep you away from free alcohol at the poker table if I tried," while snatching the rings from his best friend's hand and passing them to the judge.

He immediately gives mine back to Ace. "Place this on her left ring finger and repeat after me. Greer, with this ring, I thee wed."

Ace slides the platinum band over my knuckle, giving it a small shove when it almost gets stuck. His eyes flick up to mine in question, but I nod subtly. No surprise to me, my fingers are already a bit swollen since we got them sized.

The judge then hands me Ace's ring. "Greer place this on his left ring finger and repeat after me."

Pushing the black onyx ring on, I repeat, "With this ring, I thee wed."

Clasping hands once again, I can feel Ace's excitement. In fact, I'm just as excited as he is.

"Now, by the power invested in me by the State of Texas, I pronounce you husband and wife. You may kiss your bride."

I ignore the tears that are welling up in Ace's eyes, because if I concentrate on them, I know I'll become a blubbering mess. He reaches for my face, cupping my cheeks in his hands, he leans in and whispers, "I love you so much, Greer Whitman."

"I love you too, husband."

His nostrils flare at my nickname for him, and he licks his lips just before pressing them gently to mine. I thought he was going in for a quick peck in front of this audience.

Oh, how wrong I was.

Very quickly, it becomes obvious how excited he is about our small honeymoon. As I part my lips, his tongue delves in, making sweeping motions as he takes his time pressing all his emotion into this first kiss as husband and wife.

I don't hear the applause around us. I don't hear Pedro yell, "Get a room." The only thing I hear is the sound of my own heart, and the only thing I feel is the love I have for this man, now and forever.

Chapter Seven

Ace

Finally pulling away from kissing my wife—wow, my *wife*… that's surreal—for the first time, I grab her hand and lead her down the aisle and straight out of the courthouse.

"Ace!" Greer giggles. "Slow down. Where are we going?"

Despite her protests, I don't slow my stride. "I'm not sticking around for your brother to kick my ass. We're going to dinner."

She laughs but doesn't try and stop me until we reach the front steps. Somehow Valentine's Day has turned perfect weather-wise. It's in the mid-sixties with just a very slight breeze. The sky is a vibrant blue. A few fluffy clouds are lazily rolling by. Beautiful. And perfect for wedding pictures.

Dammit, I think to myself. Of course, we forgot to hire a photographer. But as fate would have it, another couple has just finished taking their own wedding pictures, and there's a man with a camera who looks like he's tearing down. Changing trajectories, we approach him.

"Hey, excuse me."

He turns to us, taking one look before a smile lights up his face. "Let me guess. Newlyweds and you forgot about the pictures?"

I nod sheepishly. "Obvious, huh?"

He just shrugs off my embarrassment. "It happens a lot. About half my business is last-minute work." Looking at the sky, he remarks, "It's a perfect day, though. If you want to stand right where that last couple was, I'll get a few shots."

Greer thanks him profusely as we situate ourselves where he wants us. Flinton may not be a huge town, but it wasted no expense on the courthouse. It's the perfect backdrop to what is sure to be some amazing pictures.

A few snapshots and poses later and the photographer hands me his card with the instructions to email him in the morning so he can shoot us the information about pricing and packages. Grabbing Greer's hand again, I lead us to my truck. Now that we have pictures out of the way, it's time to hightail it out of here while we can.

"Wait, wait, wait." She tugs on my arm, pulling me to a stop. "Don't you think we should wait for everyone?"

"Nah. They'll be okay."

She quirks an eyebrow at me and crosses her arms.

"I'm serious. It's our wedding day. Let all those Bozos worry about cleaning up and getting our things."

A smile lights up Greer's face as she decides to take advantage of their hospitality. "Okay. But can we make a quick stop first?"

I cock my head, confused by the change of plans. She's

been craving Mexican food every day for the last week. It's why we made plans to have an early dinner at Maldano's after the ceremony.

"Of course we can." Pulling the passenger door open, I usher her in. "Where are we going?"

Snapping her seatbelt into place, she smiles at me, a hint of mischief in her eyes. "There's a secluded spot about a mile in at Flinton State Park. I'd like to have some alone time with my husband, if you catch my drift."

I blink once.

Twice.

A third time.

How this woman continues to make my brain stutter, I will never understand.

Not waiting for me to pull myself together, Greer grabs the handle and pulls the cab door closed herself.

That's my cue.

Racing around the front of the truck, I climb in, crank the engine and gun it to the park. That's the other part of this pregnancy I didn't know was coming—Greer's soaring libido.

Once we decided on a wedding date, it was a natural progression for me to move into Greer's house. The kids didn't seem to have any issue with it so it just sort of happened. I started spending the night, and slowly but surely, all my essential items ended up in Greer's bathroom and in the half of the closet Greer wasn't using.

Living in town doesn't change the responsibilities I have to the farm, though. Things still start rolling at four thirty in the morning and sometimes don't end until nine or later. Adding the drive time makes for some long days and thank fuck for Phillip taking charge when I'm running behind, but it's worth it. I get to hang out with kids I love like they're my own. I get to sleep next to the love of my life every night. And thanks to Greer's hormones, our sex life is off the charts.

Yeah, I'm exhausted, but it's absolutely worth it.

Reaching over, I place my hand over Greer's baby bump and rub it gently. Her hands cover mine, and it occurs to me I have this little thing to thank for how quickly all the good in my life has come to fruition. Sure, I was going to marry Greer at some point. I have no doubt about that. But there's no denying her pregnancy gave us a jump start.

Making our way past the iron barricades into Flinton State Park, Greer begins navigating.

"See that little gravel road right there?" I look at where she's pointing, and sure enough there is a small road. It looks more like a trail, but it's definitely wide enough for a car. "Turn there."

She continues to guide us through the trees until we come to a small clearing. By the way it's been shaped over the years, it's clearly a designated parking space for cars. But it also looks like it's been forgotten recently.

"How did you find this place?" I ask, as I park and roll down the windows, letting the breeze flow through the cab.

"If you know how to use social media, it's easy to find the local make-out place all the kids are using."

Unclicking her seatbelt, she slides over to me and crawls up on her knees, attempting to straddle me. It's not an easy feat with the steering wheel in front of me and her growing midsection between us.

"You wanted to find a local hideout for our wedding day?" I joke, loving that she's desperate to be with me.

Greer huffs a laugh. "By this point in my pregnancy, you

should know there was no way I was going to dinner with my family without making love to my new husband on our wedding day first." With that, her lips crash into mine.

Cupping one of her cheeks with my hand, I reach down between us and grab the lever to move the seat back. With the extra weight on my side, it slides much faster than I anticipated, and she squeals in surprise.

"Sorry about that," I say with a chuckle, as I thrust my other hand into her hair.

"Stop talking," she demands, and her tongue delves into my mouth, searching for its mate.

My hands slide down her back and grip her firm ass, pulling her so she rocks against me.

"You sure you wanna do this out here?" Based on the sounds coming from her since she climbed on top of me, I'm positive I already know the answer, but I want her to verify anyway. Especially since attacking me in the outdoors is pretty out of character for my wife.

I'll never get tired of saying that word. Wife.

"I have never been more positive of anything in my life," she responds, her lips still touching mine. "Now make love to me, Grayson Whitman."

With no more hesitation, I comply. I no longer care we're out in public. I no longer care if we get caught. Because this is my wife, and as far as I'm concerned from here on out, as long as she wants it, I'm game for anything.

***

We finally get to the restaurant and our family is already waiting. When they see us walk in, everyone starts clapping.

Everyone except for Jack.

He pops a chip in his mouth and leans back in his chair, crossing his arms over his broad chest. He never takes his eyes off me, just glares in my direction as we sit.

As luck would have it, Oli is sitting at the end of the table with Jack next to him. Greer sits on the other side of Oli and I sit next to her—catty-corner from my new, very pissed-off, brother-in-law. The one who looks like he wants to kill me.

"Took you guys long enough to get here," Brittany chides.

Greer is still flushed from our romp in the woods, but she smiles like nothing's happened. "Well if it had been a traditional wedding, we would have gotten about thirty minutes of alone time before the reception. We just had ours elsewhere."

Jack grunts. "Do I want to know what that means?"

Greer narrows her eyes at him. "I don't know. Did you tell anyone what you were off doing right after you got married?"

He narrows his eyes right back at her before flipping his gaze to me. On one hand, I appreciate the fact that Jack's trying to look after his sister. I can never repay him for standing by her for all these years. And I can never, ever repay him for helping her move down here after researching and finding my program. But that's where my appreciation ends.

Yes, she is his sister. But she is now my wife. And in my mind, my responsibility to love her, cherish her, protect her, and take care of her always trumps his big brother act.

"So," he finally says, never leaning forward even though the chatter continues around us and it's hard to hear him. Not that I need to. I know what's coming. "You knocked up my baby sister."

Greer slams her hand down on the table in anger while Joie gasps and barks out, "Jack!"

"What?" He looks at his mate and shrugs like his rude comment was no big deal. "That is my baby sister. And she is knocked up by him. Correct?"

"No, I am not knocked up, you jack ass," Greer hisses, the anger dripping from her voice. "I am pregnant with your next niece or nephew. You got a problem with that?"

For just a split second, he looks unsure about his caveman act. But the uncertainty disappears quickly.

"Yeah, I got a problem with that. Remember what happened the last time you had a shotgun wedding?"

The entire table goes silent and Greer tenses next to me. I whip my head over to look at my bride. "You never told me," I say quietly.

"Because it doesn't matter."

I beg to differ because it matters a lot. Not because it makes me look at her any differently. Not because I think there's anything wrong with it. But because now the intensity of her reservations about us getting married under similar circumstances makes more sense. It would have been nice to know before so I could have handled things a little differently.

Then again, I think they turned out perfectly, so maybe I would have done everything the same.

Except inviting Jack. I'm starting to think that was a terrible idea.

"Mom?" Julie's eyes are wide as she watches her mother, taking in all the venom being spewed around her. "Mom, is it true?"

Greer's shoulders fall in defeat, and she covers her eyes with her hands.

Joie finally intervenes. "Can we not talk about this right now? I don't think this is appropriate wedding talk."

Catching Jack's eyes, he's still looking at me like I've done something wrong, even though he's thrown this entire celebration into a tizzy. His nonchalance is starting to piss me off.

Leaning forward in my own chair, I clasp my hands together and direct my stare at him. "Since you've decided to agitate my pregnant wife by bringing up things from her past she's not particularly proud of, I'm going to say this one time. I appreciate you as her support system. I respect you as her big brother. But that's where the line is drawn. Whether you like it or not, she is my wife and this is my child. If you disrespect either of them again, or make either of them feel like this is a mistake, you and I are going to have more than words."

The entire table is silent except for the sound of Pedro munching on chips. If I looked over at him right now, I'm sure he'd resemble that gif of Michael Jackson eating popcorn. The one the kids in the program think is hilarious and post on the co-op's Facebook page regularly. It's not in response to anything and rarely makes sense, but they think it's funny.

It takes about two beats before Jack breaks into a grin. "Okay. That's what I was waiting to see."

"Are. You. Kidding me?" Greer screeches, and I put my hand on her arm, sure she's about to launch herself over the table and scratch his eyes out. "You pull that shit on *my* wedding day in front of *my* kids and my new husband as some kind of a… a test to make sure he's good enough for me?"

"You're damn right I did." He should probably be embarrassed about Greer's beratement, but I'll give it to Jack, when he thinks he's in the right, he holds strong to that belief. Even if everyone else thinks he's being a dick. "I was never tough enough on Neil and look where that got you. Divorced and raising two children alone. I will never let that happen to you again."

Greer sits up straight, tears suddenly in her eyes. I can't tell if it's more hormones or if she's just that angry. Hell, those could be happy tears. I have no idea these days. Turning to Julie, I give her a sympathetic smile. "Julie, why don't you and Oli go outside for a bit. I think I left a present for your mom in the car."

"There's no need," Greer says, putting a hand on my arm. "This conversation is over. Jack, I love you and your desire to keep me safe." Jack's eyes soften as she picks up her napkin and uses it to blot under her eyes. "But if you ever humiliate me in front of my family again in the name of protection, so help me I will cut you out of my life so fast you won't see it coming."

Jack sucks in a breath. "But I *am* your family."

"Not if you keep up this bullshit, you're not."

Greer looks at her menu, making it very clear she is done with this conversation. Jack, on the other hand, looks completely taken aback for the first time since we sat down. Joie leans over and murmurs in his ear, quietly enough no one can understand her, but I have no doubt it's something along the lines of letting it go for now and making amends later.

Pedro, catching my attention and looking me in the eye, finally speaks up, trying to break up the tension. "The enchiladas look good."

The rest of the table, seemingly grateful for a change of subject nod their agreement and begin debating between chili con queso as an appetizer or quesadillas.

Putting my arm on Greer's chair, I kiss her on the temple.

So far, this hasn't been the warm welcome into her family I was hoping for. Moving out to the farm is looking better and better.

Chapter Eight

Greer

The day I have dreaded has finally arrived.

Maybe dreaded is too harsh of a word. Avoided is more accurate.

Usually the first thing women do when they find out they're pregnant is call their doctor to make sure. Not me. I already knew the truth. Why did I need to hand over a co-pay to confirm my life is being flipped upside down?

I'm just having a really hard time wrapping my head around the fact that I'm starting over at the ripe old age of thirty-nine. That instead of having a surprise party or maybe a trip overseas to celebrate my fortieth birthday, I'm going to have a baby shower.

Not exactly the birthday of my dreams.

And I know I should be grateful. There are a lot of women out there who can't have kids and would love to be in my position. But I don't feel that way. I keep trying to force myself to feel something, anything, some sort of attachment, and I just can't.

It's like I was finally wrapping my brain around the life I had. Finally, I was enjoying where I was and BAM! Out of nowhere, once again there's more work I have to do. Another person to be responsible for. Another human whose needs I have to put before my own. I'm already exhausted and stretched thin. How am I going to fit another person into my life and how will it be fair to anyone?

Not to mention my brother throwing the closet door holding in all my skeletons wide open for everyone to see. Not only did it piss me off, I felt like any emotional progress I had made was undone and all the excitement I was beginning to feel unraveled. It was just another reminder things don't always go as planned and sometimes turn out terrible in the long run.

Marrying my kids' father was not exactly the greatest moment of my life. Sure, I got Oli and Julie out of it, but I also got a lot of heartache, a lot of criticism, a lot of judgement, and a lot of extra baggage for me to carry on my shoulders. I don't want that to happen this time.

While I trust that Ace and Neil, my ex, are two completely different people, it still doesn't totally ease my anxieties.

That doesn't mean I'm not good at covering up any insecurities I have. No one knows how much I'm struggling. Ace suspects, but he doesn't know how deep they run. And right now, as we walk into the waiting room, I'm not sure he's focusing on anything except his own excitement.

Walking to the window to check in for our first appointment, you'd think Ace would be headed to Disney World with as big as his smile has been. He hasn't stopped holding my hand or rubbing my stomach since we got in the truck.

"Hi. What's your last name?" a cute, young, *not pregnant* receptionist asks. Why can't they ever have pregnant receptionists at the ob-gyn's office? You know, the kind of women who know exactly what you're going through because they're in the thick of it too?

I suppose that would mean rehiring the staff every nine months, so it's out of the question. Still, the fantasy of being greeted by someone whose ankles are as swollen as mine makes me smile. Maybe she would hand out ginger pops for morning sickness.

"Declan," I answer, pretending not to be disappointed there's nothing in her stomach except lunch. "Greer Declan."

Ace's smile falls, and he gives me a strange look. "Why are you going by Declan?" he asks quietly in my ear.

"Relax." I pat his arm. "I haven't been here since we got married. I still have to change it several places."

"Here you are." The receptionist pulls a pre-made file from the file holder and slaps a giant, bright red sticker on it.

I purse my lips knowing exactly what it's for. Ace, on the other hand, is stumped.

"Um, what does that sticker mean?"

"This one?" She smiles and holds the file up for practically everyone in the tri-county area to see. Awesome. Ace nods, not noticing my agitation at all. "That's just to give the doctor a heads-up of our advanced maternal age patients."

This is going to be a long few months.

I sigh deeply and close my eyes to keep my emotions under control. Ace, on the other hand, takes the information in stride and moves right on to the next question.

"Okay. And how do we change her last name on the file?"

The receptionist gives him a quizzical look. "I'm sorry?"

Ace points at me, like I'm an object up for discussion. "Her last name. It's Whitman now, not Declan. How do we get that changed?"

"Oh!" She snaps her fingers and pulls open a drawer, thumbing through some files. "That's easy. It usually takes a couple days, but it's just a matter of processing. Just fill out this paperwork, and I'll get it entered."

Ace frowns, obviously unhappy with that news. "But won't her last name come up on the ultrasound?"

"Yeah."

"Ace, it's not that big of a deal." I pat his arm, trying in vain to get him to let it go.

"But your last name is gonna be on the ultrasound."

"And?"

"And my baby's last name is Whitman. As is your last name. I don't ever want our baby to wonder why there is a different last name on those pictures."

I look at him, confused. "You do realize children almost never look at their ultrasound pictures. They might find them long after we're dead."

He huffs. "Okay fine. I want my last name on the ultrasound pictures for me."

I roll my eyes, amused he's making such a big deal about this. And grateful as well. I know when this baby is finally born, I will love him or her with my whole self, but right now there seems to be a disconnect between my emotions and this pregnancy. I'm so appreciative Ace can't contain his joy. It makes up for my lack of it. I guess that's what a partnership really is.

The receptionist giggles, finding this whole interaction cute. "Tell you what. Fill this out real fast, and I'll make it a priority to get it done before you get in with the doctor. How does that sound?" She hands Ace a clipboard with paperwork on it and his eyes light up as he takes it from her.

"Yeah, that sounds great."

It doesn't take long for him to fill out his paperwork, for me to fill out my own paperwork, and for us to get called to the back. We go through the regular rigmarole of taking my weight, my vitals, and a urine analysis. It's all very fascinating stuff I've done dozens of times before over the course of two other pregnancies, and Ace seems delighted to be in the middle of it all.

Well, not the peeing in the cup part. I drew the line at him being in the restroom with me.

Surprisingly, my doctor, Dr. Haam, who I've seen once for a well-woman visit last year, is not only running on time, she's quite possibly running a bit early as well.

"Hi Greer," she says with a smile on her face, her spectacles perched on the end of her nose. She immediately heads to the sink and begins washing her hands. "How are we feeling today?"

"*I* am feeling very bloated and old. *He*"—I point at Ace— "is feeling very excited and anxious to make sure his last name is on the ultrasound."

Dr. Haam laughs and grabs the paper towels from the dispenser. "I've already been informed and we have that taken care of." Taking a seat on her rolling chair, she grabs my file off the counter and opens it. "Greer, I know you've had two other pregnancies, both where normal until delivery, and with one there were complications, is that right?"

And here we go. I know these are standard questions, but I can't help the feeling of dread that washes over me. I don't want her to go there today. I can't do it and stay happy for Ace's sake. So, I opt to keep things simple and straight forward.

"Yes. He had a double cord wrapped around his neck. I had an emergency c-section."

She writes something down on my chart, never looking up while she continues with the inquiry. "And did he have any long-term effects that can be linked back to that delivery?"

My heart begins to beat wildly. *Stay calm, Greer. These are normal questions.*

"Not at first. He met all his milestones until around six or seven. That's when he stopped progressing at such a rapid rate. He's still about nine in his head and has a myriad of issues like impulse control and defiance. Most of it seems to indicate brain damage due to oxygen deprivation."

She nods but doesn't say anything. Just continues to scratch on my file with her pen. It's making me nervous. Not only do I have a huge red sticker announcing I'm practically elderly, but if she keeps writing, I'm going to have the thickest file in the office too.

"Grayson"—she still doesn't look up—"it says your brother was born with Down Syndrome, correct?"

"That's right."

I concentrate really hard on my breathing because I know where the conversation is going, and I don't like it.

Dr. Haam puts her pen down and looks at Ace. "Have you ever been tested for any genetic abnormalities."

His face pales as he shakes his head. "No. Should I have been?"

"Not necessarily. Down Syndrome is almost never heredi-tary, but in rare cases it can have a genetic component. At this point, it's not necessary to get you tested, but if you decide to have any more children in the future, it may be worth taking a look. Just to make sure you don't happen to carry the balanced translocation gene."

Before she can even explain what all that means, I snort a laugh. "Oh no. There will be no other children after this. This one right here"—I point at my ever growing belly—"has been surprise enough."

She smiles kindly and stands up, dropping the file on the counter again and guiding me to lie back. "Well, we can definitely discuss birth control options as soon as this one is born. But in the meantime, I'm going to schedule some blood drawn, and I'd like for you to have an amniocentesis." Dr. Haam begins feeling around on my stomach, like tossing out the idea of genetic abnormalities in your child is everyday conversation. I suppose it is for her, but for me, for us, it's much more life-altering.

"Why does she need to get the amnio?" Ace asks. I'm almost positive he already knows the answer and wants confirmation of what Dr. Haam is concerned about.

After helping me sit up, she crosses her arms and explains, "With Greer's age, the chance of genetic abnormalities increases. Granted, you will only be forty when this baby is born, but there is still a higher probability. Combine that with the possibility you could carry a hereditary gene, and I think it would be wise to check."

Ace runs his fingers through his hair and sighs. What was supposed to be an exciting day of seeing our baby for the first time has turned into a somber moment. He looks at me, concern all over his face.

"Babe, I don't want you to have an amnio."

I don't like the idea of a giant needle plunging into my uterus either, but I don't think that's his cause for hesitation. "Why?"

"There's too much risk. I know there's not too much chance of a miscarriage, but if you're already considered high-risk, why take the chance?"

I crinkle my eyes at him. "How do you know that?"

He flashes me a sheepish look. "I've been doing research."

Of course he has been. I'm actually surprised no pregnancy books have magically shown up on our nightstand yet.

"An amnio will tell us if there is anything medically wrong with the baby," Dr Haam explains. "It gives you a chance to weigh your options."

Ace never takes his eyes off of me, despite Dr. Haam's encouragement to go ahead with the procedure. "If something's wrong with the baby, it won't make a difference to me. Will it make a difference to you?" he asks me.

I recognize this is a pivotal moment for us. One that could possibly determine our future. And as much as I hate myself for it, I have to pause and think about my answer. Will it make a difference to me? Not in the sense that it will change my mind about going through with this pregnancy. That is already a done deal in my mind. The real question is, do I want to know the answers to these medical questions yet? Am I emotionally ready to handle them?

I take a deep breath and look up at the ceiling, unwilling to look anyone in the eye as I speak. "I don't think it makes a difference. If something is wrong with this baby, between you and me, we probably already know where the resources are. I'm not worried about that. And I just… I don't want to know yet. I'm having a hard enough time wrapping my brain around all this anyway. I just can't."

A tear runs down my cheek. No surprise there. I cry over everything these days. I hate that the room is still silent. That no one is speaking.

And then I feel it. I feel my husband reach over and grab my hand, squeezing tightly. Right now, I know he gets it. He understands where my head is at and all my fears. He understands that as much as I love my son, no one wishes for their child to have disabilities or limitations. We love them through it, but we don't hope for it.

I blink back the rest of the moisture and turn my head to look at him.

"We're going to do this together. No matter what," he says quietly and kisses me on the forehead gently, fingers running through my hair.

Dr. Haam finally moves, pulling the ultrasound machine closer. "Well then it's settled. We'll skip the amnio and just do the blood test. If you change your mind, it's as easy as getting with our scheduling department. In the meantime, you guys want to see your baby for the first time?"

"Oh yeah," Ace responds, his smile reappearing. I force a similar expression on my face, so she won't know how very anxious I am.

I really am interested and excited to see my baby. That's one of the best parts of pregnancy. But now, with one little conversation, once again, I'm not as excited as I should be.

The ride home is quiet. For the most part, I stare out the window, clutching the ultrasound pictures in my hand.

After fifteen weeks of pregnancy, it finally feels real. This is really happening. It's not just a dream. No alternate reality. It's real. I have the pictures of a little head and a button nose and some little hands to prove it.

Blowing out a breath, I will myself to be happy. For Ace. For our family. But I just… can't. I'm not as unhappy anymore. More of an acceptance. But the biggest emotion I still have is that damn fear.

Even when I think about the possibility of having a perfectly healthy, "normal" child, I'm terrified. I already feel like I'm drowning half the time under the weight of my responsibilities. A healthy newborn means recovery time, sleep deprivation, losing the ability to use my arms that are always full of baby, no time to work, no time to eat, no time to shower…

The list of things that will have to be done is endless. I don't know how I'll be able to do this.

"You okay?"

I look over at Ace who keeps turning to glance at me while navigating through traffic.

Giving him a half-hearted smile, I say what he needs to hear. "I'm okay. Just nervous."

It's way more than nervous, but I don't want to admit that. He's so excited about us having this baby. The last thing I want to do is put a damper on it.

"You don't have to hide how scared you are from me."

Maybe I'm not as good at hiding my feelings as I thought.

Wiping away another tear I didn't know was coming until my husband proved once again how much we're in this together, I take a deep breath. "I'm trying to not be."

"I know. I also know we have more odds stacked against us than most pregnant couples. But I promise you, Greer. You won't be on your own, no matter what."

"I'm sorry, Ace." The guilt overwhelms me and a stray tear escapes. I didn't even know there were any threatening to fall. "I'm trying hard to be excited. I want to look forward to this but I just…"

"You're just stretched really thin." My man is so understanding. "I get it, Greer. I do. You've been a single mom for all of these years and this is one more thing added to your plate. This is the big reason I'm ready for us to move to the farm. I don't think you can wrap your brain around how much support you're going to have once we get there. Yes, I know it's isolated, but babe, I come home every day for breakfast. I come home every day for lunch. I come home every day for dinner. I'm right there if you need to come out to the barn to vent and yell or just get a hug."

"I'm not hugging you when you smell like cow pies," I joke, making him smile at me.

"Noted. But you know the other day Brittany had been up all night long with the baby, so Pedro put him in that backpack carrier thingy, made sure Nio had a floppy hat on his head, and carried him around while doing his basic chores."

I sniff and look at him wide-eyed. "He did?"

"Yeah. I mean, he was probably using it as an excuse to not do all the heavy lifting, but it worked. Brittany got the rest she needed, Pedro got some bonding time with his son, and honestly, it was kind of fun knowing the next generation was already out there learning how to do chores."

I can't help but giggle while I bat away that tear. "You really think it's going to help when we get out there?"

"One hundred percent, babe. Just having Oli outside, wearing himself out is going take a weight off your shoulders."

He pulls into the driveway of the house I was proud of, yet somehow, I'm looking at it differently now. It seems almost claustrophobic.

Maybe he's right. I know the transition is going to be hard, and we absolutely must wait until the school year is over. But maybe being on the same property as so many people who are emotionally invested in our lives is going to take some of the pressure off.

"I need to get back to work." He grabs my hand and kisses my knuckles. "I'm going to try to leave early tonight. No guarantees."

"No! No. The farm is your business. I know Phillip and Pedro have taken up a lot of the slack, but you can't leave them in a lurch because I'm emotional."

He chuckles softly, my fingers still brushing his lips. "Yes, I can. And I will if I feel like it. It's the only perk of being the boss. But I do need to check in at least."

"I'll be okay, Ace. I promise. And I'm glad you went with me today."

"I will always go with you." He holds my gaze and suddenly snatches one of the ultrasound pictures out of my hand. "Especially if it means I can get more of these."

"Hey!"

"You think I'm not going to take my baby's first pictures out with me and show them to everyone? Especially Pedro. I'm going to show him every. Single. Day. Until he is sick of me talking about it."

A laugh bursts out of me. "This is some sort of payback for something he did, isn't it?"

"You damn well better believe it. I couldn't get away from his pregnancy talk. He's going to hear about every ultrasound, every middle of the night craving, all the pregnancy gas…"

"Ohmygod you will not tell him about my pregnancy gas!" I shriek with laughter. "That's it. I'm outta here."

"You know it's true!" he calls after me as I climb out of the cab and drop as gracefully as I can to the ground. "He wouldn't have to take it if he didn't dish it out!"

"See ya later, cowboy!" I slam the door and wave as I walk to the door.

He revs the engine behind me. Probably as some show of masculine testosterone or something.

When I walk into the house, the last thing I expect to see is Julie lounging on the couch.

"Aren't you supposed to be in school?" I ask as I toss my purse onto my desk.

"It was a half day, remember?"

"Oh shit," I mumble under my breath because I don't remember much of anything these days. Damn pregnancy brain. "I completely forgot. Is your brother back yet?"

"No. It's his day at the farm."

My eyes shoot up as an idea crosses my mind. Ace says being on the farm will help relieve some of my stress. Today seems like a good day to test that out. I shoot out a quick text to my husband.

Me: *It's a half day at school. If I call Mrs. Johnson, can Oli stay with you for the rest of the day and you bring him home after dinner?*

His response is quick.

Ace: *Absolutely. Between me and Pedro we can keep him entertained.*

Me: *Thank you. I love you. And quit texting while driving.*

Ace: *It's voice to text, Greer.*

Me: *Liar. If it was voice to text, my name wouldn't be spelled right.*

Before I can put my phone down, it dings with an email. Opening it, I see it's from the school.

"Shit," I say under my breath. I have certainly upped the potty mouth talk since my hormones started fluctuating. However, I'm right to be ticked off. Julie is now officially failing two classes.

"Uh, Julie?"

She doesn't even look up from the TV where she's watching some random movie targeted to teens. If I was a better mom, I would be making sure it's appropriate. Just another thing to feel guilty about these days.

"Uh huh."

"You wanna tell me why you're failing two classes?"

"I don't know." She still doesn't look at me.

"Well I'm about to find out, so I hope you can come up with a reasonable excuse quick. Like you were hospitalized or had amnesia and forgot all your test answers."

She doesn't bother responding while I click on the link taking me to her grades. As I scroll, I feel myself getting angrier and angrier the more I see.

Slamming my phone on the desk, I stalk into the living room, grab the remote, and turn it off. She looks at me like I'm the one who's lost her marbles, which makes me even more upset.

"You are failing two classes," I grit out, my mom voice coming out full force.

"But I did good on my tests."

"Oh you did fine on your tests, child. But you still have not turned in your homework." I can feel my nostrils flaring, and I wouldn't be surprised if there is fire coming out of my eyes. Julie has always been my studious kid. She's always liked learning. And now suddenly she's going to fail high school out of laziness? Unacceptable.

"But I did, Mom," she argues.

"No. You didn't."

"They probably lost my homework," she justifies, refusing to take responsibility for her actions. What the hell is happening here?

"Really? Every time? You're telling me more than one teacher has lost all your homework?"

She looks at me like I'm stupid and says, "Yes."

"I. Call. Bullshit. Hand me your phone." I hold out my hand and flick my fingers, just in case she doesn't know where to put it.

She shoots up off the couch, shrieking. "What? Why do you need my phone?"

"Because you're grounded from it."

Julie crosses her arms and it feels like my body is vibrating from the sheer willpower it's taking not to launch myself at her to shake some sense into her. "Uh, how do you expect me to reach you when I'm in school?" she pops off.

I cross my arms back. "You don't need to be communicating with me when you're in school. You are there to learn, remember? Until further notice, you are grounded from your phone. You are grounded from the television. And if you're not careful and keep sassing me, you'll be grounded from your books too."

She throws her fists to her sides and stomps her foot. "You can't do that!"

"Oh, I damn sure can do anything I want. Get in your room. Go find the homework you need to finish. And it better be turned in tomorrow."

"But it's too late!" she yells. "I can't get more than a fifty now!"

"I don't care if you can only get a zero!" I yell back, knowing this tension isn't good for the baby and doing it anyway. "You will keep up with your responsibilities whether you like it or not! And I'll be emailing the school to make sure, so don't you dare lie to me about this shit again!"

She stomps to her room yelling, "I hate you! I HATE YOU!" and slams her bedroom door.

"If you hate me, I'm doing my job!" I yell back.

Plopping down on the couch, I rub my belly and say, "Sorry baby. You didn't need to hear all that. It's not usually like that around here." Which is a lie, because there's always someone yelling around here. That doesn't mean I don't feel bad about it, though.

Maybe we need to get out to the farm for more reasons than I thought.

Chapter Nine

Ace

When I got home last night around eight, it felt like all hell had broken loose. Considering Oli was with me and having a great time at the farm, it was surprising to say the least.

Julie was locked in her room, music turned up and refusing to open her door. Greer was at her desk trying to work but not being able to focus on anything.

It took about thirty minutes of Greer venting to me to finally figure out how bad their fight really was. And no matter how much Greer can say she's angry at Julie, I know she's partially blaming herself. She always does. Rational or not, she takes any situation and tries to see if there is anything she could have done differently.

Honestly, there are a lot of things Greer has done that have led to the situation, but none that she could have avoided doing at all. A move, a new step-dad, and a new sibling are a lot for any teenager to adjust to, but what part could Greer have done differently?

None of them.

But the thing is, I'm responsible for two of those things, and I'm about to be responsible for another move. I need to do what I can to help Julie navigate through all this.

That's why we're here, wearing coats while sitting on the dock over the lake. Because right now, she needs the quiet and calm that only come with fishing.

Once we get our hooks in the water, we settle in, relaxing and enjoying listening to the sound of the wild. Julie's dark hair blows in the wind, since she forgot a hair band. She really is having a hard time remembering just about anything these days.

We sit in silence for a while, just enjoying. We don't have anywhere we need to be. I already finished my morning chores, and it won't kill me to take the day off again. Eventually, I'll have to get back on track, but this is more important. There are things Julie and I have to discuss. And she's not talking yet, so I'm not moving. All too often it seems like hard conversations are happening on our time. This one needs to be on *her* time.

It takes a while, but she finally breaks the silence. "How's the house coming?"

I look to my left and point several hundred yards away. "See for yourself."

She squints. "That's the house? It looks small. I thought it was a new barn or something."

"The framing always seems smaller to me," I say in agreement. "Once the walls go up, I can visualize it better. I promise, it won't be small."

Julie gives me a pointed look. "Mom's gonna kill you if

it's too big. She's always complaining about how hard it is to keep the house clean."

A laugh rumbles out of me because it's true. Greer hates cleaning. I already plan to get her one of those Roomba vacuum things for her birthday. I know people say that's not romantic, but I'm willing to bet the thought of never having to vacuum again will get me laid.

"It's not huge, I promise. Big enough for the five of us and your mom's office. That's it."

"No formal living and dining room?"

I shrug. "Why do we need those? If we want to entertain a huge crowd, we'll just use the farm house."

Julie nods in agreement and turns back to the water. Now that the door is open, though, I keep going.

"Speaking of your mom, how are you feeling about the baby coming?"

"Fine," she quips. It's the answer she thinks I want to hear.

"Julie," I plead, hoping she'll give me more than that.

"What?"

"I don't want to hear what you tell everyone. I want to know what you *really* feel."

She breathes a heavy sigh before finally giving me what I want. The truth. "I'm excited about the baby because who doesn't love babies, ya know? But I don't want to have to raise it."

"Wait," I shake my head, confused. "Why would you have to raise the baby?"

"Oh come on, Ace." She gives me an incredulous look. "Do you even understand how much time my mom spends supervising Oli? If she has to feed the baby, but Oli is having a meltdown, who do you think she has to deal with first? And who do you think has to pick up the slack?" She points to her chest and gives me a pointed look.

I pause, absorbing her words because I've never thought of it that way before. She's right. If Oli is in the middle of a crisis, he takes precedence. Not because he's more important, but because the more agitated he gets, the harder he is to control, and for everyone's safety, the sooner de-escalation happens, the better.

"And I know nothing is going to happen to you guys," she continues, looking back at the water. "But what if something does? Do I have to take care of two kids then?"

"Wait, wait, wait." I hold my hands up to stop her because nothing about this conversation sounds rational. "Why are you planning for our deaths? Don't you think that's premature?"

"Oh come on, Ace. I'm not stupid. I know Oli will never be on his own. Mom already has a lawyer, so she can keep guardianship of him when he's eighteen. I know I'll 'inherit' him at some point. I just hope I have a job where I make enough money to pay for both of us because I don't want to live with him forever. He's exhausting."

I open my mouth, then close it. Open again. Close again. I know I look like a fish out of water, but her words have struck a nerve. I had no idea she carried this much emotional weight around her. Her grades suddenly make sense. She's trying to be prepared for the very adult problems she will probably someday face.

Securing my fishing pole between the boards of wood on the dock, I take hers out of her hand and do the same.

"What are you doing?" Confusion is written all over her

face.

I gesture for her to stand up. "Come on. I wanna show you something."

We begin walking toward the new house, talking as we go.

"You know my brother had Down Syndrome?" I ask her, unsure if she heard the story.

She shrugs. "I heard, but I don't really know much about it."

"He was born when my parents were in their forties. I was a little younger than you then. He was the cutest little baby, and I loved him so much."

"Did he grow up to annoy you as much as Oli annoys me?"

I laugh. "No. I went off to college before that happened. I came home when my dad died and took over the farm."

"I didn't know that."

"Yeah. My mom couldn't do it by herself, especially with my brother still here. Then she got sick."

"She did?"

"Yep. Lung cancer from smoking. By the way, don't smoke. It's bad for you."

She rolls her eyes, making me chuckle before I continue.

"When Mom got sick we talked a lot about what would happen to my brother. Who would take care of him and how would that work. I've been there, Julie. I understand your fear and your worry about taking care of Oli. But I want you to know, that's part of the reason we started the co-op."

"What do you mean?"

"I doubt you know this because most people don't, but all my farm hands have to agree to take a basic training course about working with people with disabilities."

Julie's eyes widen. "They do?"

"Yep. That was one of the agreements we made with the state education agency when we decided to start the program with the school. Everyone who works on site is trained in de-escalation techniques and has some sensitivity training. We do it on purpose because we want everyone here to be able to work together."

I stop walking as we approach the house so I can get to my point.

"Julie, All Hands Farm isn't just my business. My goal was to have a place for my brother to live out his golden years in the event he outlived me. Pedro is actually in my will to inherit the farm, so he can take over and continue with that mission should something happen to me."

Putting a hand on her shoulder, I urge her to look me in the eyes. "This farm is already set up for Oli. You don't have to feel stuck or locked into taking care of him. If something happens to me or your mom, sure, you can maintain custody. But Pedro loves this farm. It's his home and his mission as much as mine. Oli will most likely live here as an adult, even if you decide to live halfway around the world."

She huffs out a breath, and I'm not sure if it's a laugh or a sob. "You already have him taken care of."

I nod. "I already have him taken care of. And I have you taken care of too."

"What do you mean?"

"Follow me."

We walk through the door frame that has yet to hold an actual door. I walk her around the cement foundation, pointing out the various rooms of the floor plan before stopping at a small enclosed area.

"See this right here?" I point to the marked out portion of the walls.

"It looks like a closet."

"Not quite. That's the beginnings of a staircase."

"It's two stories?"

I shake my head. "Not really. It's considered one story and a bonus room. Julie"—I turn to her so she knows how serious I am—"I know how hard this move is for you. I know you left everything behind and just as you're starting to rebuild, you have to leave everything behind again. I don't want you to leave again until you want to. I want you to have options and choices."

She crinkles her eyebrows. "And how is a staircase to a bonus room going to help?"

"The bonus room has a walk-in closet and a full bathroom attached," I explain. "And it's for you."

Her eyes widen as I continue to explain.

"The architect put the staircase over here because it's right next to the kitchen. The mud room is right there," I point behind me. "That means you don't have to go through the entire house to get to your space. You can just walk through the kitchen and out the back door, avoiding the living room or bedrooms. If you decide to stay while you're in college, you have a quiet, private area to be where neither of your siblings will bother you."

"Are you serious?" she whispers, tears in her eyes.

"I want you to feel like this is your home too. Not that you're living in our home and your job is to be the third adult. That's not fair. You've done an amazing job helping your mother out for a long time. But it's almost your turn. In just a couple years you'll be graduating, and I want you to have choices. Whether it be to go off to college knowing we've got everything covered here, or to stay here and join the family business because you're tired of transitioning. You deserve to have more say in how your life is going to go."

She slams into me, hugging me and sobbing into my chest. "Thank you, Ace. Thank you so much."

I kiss the top of her head and hold her tight.

There's a lot to still work out, but she's going to be all right.

Chapter Ten

Greer

They say pregnancy takes forever, and it also goes by in a flash.

The fact that I can't see my feet is proof both parts of that statement are accurate. Somehow life went on fast forward and my last trimester showed up out of nowhere. Yet, this pregnancy is dragging along at a snail's pace, and I'm pretty sure it's never going to end.

At least I can see my toes if I lean over far enough. Which reminds me, I need to get a pedicure since I can't get to those scraggly things to fix the chipped paint. Maybe Julie and I can go this weekend. Jack can come over and hang out with Oli now that football season is over, and we can invite Joie so she can drive. Right now, when I'm this huge, it takes a village.

Over the weeks, things have gotten less strained with both my brother and my child.

Jack began his campaign to get back in my good graces almost immediately after his faux pas at my wedding dinner. It started with an apology phone call where I told him he was forgiven, but apparently, it didn't alleviate his guilt. Since then, I've been the recipient of regular phone calls checking in, invitations for us to come have dinner, and offers to babysit. I'm not sure when Jack will be able to forgive himself, but that's not my concern. He really is the best big brother a girl could ever ask for, but sometimes he doesn't think it through before spouting off hurtful words. Sometimes I wonder if Hank is rubbing off on him too much. From what I understand, a similar issue almost ended he and Joie's relationship before it even began, so I have no problem with him taking some time to work through his own guilt.

Plus, it means I might get that pedicure this weekend. Julie and I could use the time together. Since she and Ace went fishing a while back, things have gotten so much better. I don't know what happened while they were out there, and no matter how much I ask, neither of them will tell me. But Julie seemed to settle somehow. She started smiling more. She started turning in her homework. It wasn't every time, but it was a definite improvement.

She still has her teenage moments, but she's not failing anymore. I feel like I'm breathing better because she's breathing better.

A knock at the door has me looking away from my toes and around the house. Picking up has gone on the wayside for the last oh, dozen weeks or so. Whoever it is better not expect to be invited in.

"Oli!" I yell, hoping he'll answer for me. Of course, he doesn't respond. I have no idea what he's doing, but my guess is he fell asleep sprawled out on his bed. Today was his farm day, and he's always zonked when he gets home.

Grumbling to myself as I waddle to the front of the house, I swear if it's someone asking if I know Jesus, I'm going to be cursing them to hell for making me walk all that way. Thirty weeks pregnant is no joke.

I don't remember being this big when I was pregnant before. Maybe it's my age. Maybe it's the tacos. Maybe everything really is bigger in Texas, including pregnant women.

Case in point, the other day I was walking around the grocery store when a lovely older woman who happened by said, "Don't worry, Mama. You're almost there."

I looked at her, exhaustion written all over my face and said, "I have ten weeks to go."

Her eyes immediately got wide and she responded with, "Bless you. I'll be praying for you."

If it wasn't so damn funny, I might have been offended, but that's the reaction when people find out how much longer I have to go.

My mumbles are replaced by confusion when I open the door and see Ace and Pedro standing on my stoop. "What? Did you forget your key?"

"Hello, ma'am," Pedro says politely. "We're here to speak to Oli. Is he available?"

My heart drops. "Oh god. What happened."

Ace's face morphs into one of compassion, realizing why I'm starting to breath heavy. Anyone coming to my front door asking about Oli in an official capacity is my worst nightmare.

"Nothing is wrong, babe. This is a good thing. Just humor us, okay? Is Oli available?"

I furrow my brow. "Yeeeeees," I respond slowly, thoroughly confused by what's happening, but now settled in the knowledge I need to just play along for whatever reason.

The two men walk through the door and I close it behind them. That's when I realize they both smell good. Not like they just finished milking, but like they showered and put on cologne. And they're wearing fresh clothes in the middle of the day. Now I'm really confused. "Listen. I don't know what's going on here, but I'm willing to roll with it except for one thing."

Ace takes that moment to give me a quick kiss hello. "What's that?"

"Oli is asleep on his bed, and I'm not waddling my way back there. You guys are going to have to break out of character for a few seconds to get him yourself."

They both laugh as I do my best impression of a Weeble on my way back to the couch. I weeble and wobble, but I don't fall down.

Not until I sit down anyway. I get about halfway before my legs give out and I plop onto the couch. It takes me a few seconds to get situated and put my feet up. Seriously. I have ten more weeks of this? How big can my stomach get? I'm already defying all sorts of scientific laws with my ability to stay standing without falling over.

By the time I'm somewhat comfortable, because who is honestly ever comfortable at six months pregnant, the guys are already back in the room with me. Oli is rubbing his face like he just woke up, hair sticking up every which way. He sits next to me while Ace and Pedro take the love seat together. I can tell Ace really wants to sit next to me so he can touch my stomach. He loves rubbing my baby bump. Maybe it's more like a baby mountain at this point.

I know most pregnant women hate it when people touch their stomach, but I love it. My skin itches too bad and that part of my body aches non-stop, so it's like getting belly rubs. I may as well be a cat with how I practically purr when someone touches me there. It's not strange at all when I moan my appreciation in public. Nope. Not at all.

Getting down to business, Pedro sits on the edge of the couch to begin. "Oliver, we're here because we want to talk about the work you do on the farm."

"Don't call me Oliver," he says quickly, startling Pedro. "What?"

"I don't like Oliver. I like Oli."

I bite my lip to stifle a giggle. Obviously, no one told Oli he needed to play along with whatever charade the guys have going. Pedro, though, takes it like a champ.

"I'm sorry. I knew that and called you by the wrong name anyway. I'll make sure to call you Oli from now on."

Putting my hand over my mouth, I'm still trying not to laugh. I have no idea why that was funny to me, but it was. Probably because the two men are trying so hard not to break character and leave it to Oli to throw the whole thing off.

"Anyway, we're here to talk about your work."

"We've been very impressed with you, Oli," Ace jumps in. "You're good with the animals and you've been a huge help in the milking parlor."

Oli's face lights up. "Cause I like the bessies. And they like me. They always lick me when I hook them up."

I love seeing my son animated like this. Who knew after so many years of worrying about finding him a place in the world, it would end up being on a farm milking cows.

"Well, you do a fine job with them," Pedro adds. "And since you're graduating from high school next month, we'd like to offer you a paying job."

My jaw drops. They want to hire Oli? To be a real employee?

My eyes snap over to Ace's and he's got a huge smile on his face. He nods at me, and I know that's his way of saying this is real. It's really happening. My boy has shown he has value to the business and his bosses want to continue building on those skills. Knowing they don't offer jobs to everyone makes me so proud I honestly think I could burst.

Tears well up in my eyes. This is like a dream come true. I open my mouth to respond, but Oli beats me to it.

"Like I'll get money?"

Pedro sniggers while Ace answers. "Yes. But there's more to it than that. One of the requirements is you have to stay in the school program to keep this job."

Oli crinkles his nose and drops his head on the back of the couch. "But I'm almost done with school," he whines.

"I know," Ace continues. "But it's not the same kind of classes, Oli. Instead of going to school every day and coming out to the farm two days a week, you'll be at the farm every day and go to school two days a week."

"Do I have to read books at school? I hate reading books. They're boring," he grumbles.

"Not as far as I know. The classes you'll be taking are for adults, which is what you'll be. Mrs. Johnson will teach you things like grocery shopping and how to pay all your bills. It's not at all like the classes you take now."

I bat away a stray tear that rolls down my cheek. Ace glances over briefly, but when he realizes I'm happy, he smiles and returns his focus on Oli.

"There's more, Oli."

How could there possibly be more? This time, Pedro answers my silent question.

"One of the perks of being one of our farm hands is you get to live in the bunk house."

I gasp, while Oli says, "Really? I get to live with the other ranch hands?"

Pedro nods. "Yep. Not right away. You need to get a good six months of work under your belt before we'll move you in, so you can prove what a good worker you are. But if you do a good job, right after Christmas, we'll have a bunk just for you."

"And since your mom and Julie and I will be living in the new house, we'll be really close if you need us."

So much for that lone tear. Now a bunch of them are cascading down my face. Not only is my son going to have a real job, he's going to have a place to live that's close enough for me to still guide him, but far enough away I won't be doing it alone anymore.

A sob breaks free and Ace is immediately next to me, arms wrapped around me, charade forgotten.

"These are happy tears, right?" he whispers in my ear, one arm wrapped around my shoulders while the other hand rubs my stomach.

I nod vigorously while getting my breathing under control. "Am I dreaming?"

I feel the deep rumble of his chuckle. "Nope. You are wide awake, my love."

"Thank you," I say, because I can't think of anything else. "Thank you for loving me. For loving us. For giving us everything we never dreamed of."

"Don't do that," he responds. "Don't thank me. Oli did this all on his own. The rest, that's just me taking care of my family."

I nod again and sink into his chest. I didn't realize until this exact moment how much tension I was still holding on to. But finally, finally I feel like I can relax. We're going to be okay. All of us are going to be okay.

Chapter Eleven

Ace

My alarm has got to be the most annoying sound ever. Worse than the gears grinding in my favorite truck. Worse than that damn heavy metal stuff my office manager listens to. Worse than when Pedro whines about chaffing in the summer.

It probably wouldn't be bad if it didn't go off at four fifteen every morning.

Rolling over, I smack the clock, shutting off the noise, then reach for my wife. Unfortunately, she's already sitting up.

"What are you doing?" I whisper and rub the sleep out of my eyes.

She sighs and rubs her back. "I haven't been asleep in hours. I might as well do some work."

"Legs again?"

She nods.

This pregnancy has been rough on Greer. She's been suffering from horrible restless leg syndrome from the beginning.

At first, she could get up and do a few jumping jacks to calm it down. But as her belly and boobs grew, it became more painful to jump than it did to suffer through. I feel terrible for her. She hasn't had a full night's sleep in several weeks.

Add onto it, she's in a lot of pain in general. Somehow the baby is sitting low, which you would never know by how huge she is. She's so big, we keep asking the doctor if there's a hidden twin. Because of it, Greer complains of pain in her entire abdominal and genital areas constantly. Well, she doesn't complain constantly, but I know her pain is non-stop. It's to the point where sex isn't enjoyable to her anymore.

Too bad. I would love nothing more than to help get this baby born sooner rather than later. I hate seeing Greer miserable, even if she's a good sport about it all.

I brush my teeth, swipe on some deodorant, and throw on my work clothes before waking Oli up for his shift. He typically works mornings with me, which helps get him back in bed at an earlier time. That helps all of us. It's all about balance these days.

Once I know he's rolling, I make my way into the living area, passing by Greer's new office space.

We moved in to the new house about a month ago, and it's proving to be everything we needed. That includes the dedicated office area I made a priority when drawing up the floor plans. While the layout is very different in this house than in hers, I knew she loved her office with the custom book shelves and big window. I made sure it was almost identical here. The biggest difference is her window overlooks the lake.

I'm glad I put so much though into it. When the house was finally done, and I brought Greer out to see it for the first time, she squealed at this room. She loves being able to look out her window to the water and yet still be able to keep an eye on everything happening in the living room. Oli won't always live here, but the new baby won't always be sitting still either.

I couldn't care less what direction the windows face. I'm thrilled to be back on the farm, so I can get an extra forty-five minutes of sleep at night. Living in town was a hardship I was willing to deal with so I could be with my family, but I'm grateful to be back.

"Here ya go, cowboy." Greer holds up a travel mug of hot coffee, knowing I was headed for the coffee pot.

"You already made coffee?"

She shrugs and takes a sip of some juice she has in a mug. I think it's weird she doesn't use a glass, but she claims sometimes she can trick herself into believing it's a cup of her highly-coveted joe. "I was wide awake."

Leaning against her desk, I reach down and rub her belly. She groans at my touch and leans back, closing her eyes. I know that's my cue to keep rubbing. "Are you feeling okay?"

"I just hurt like always. I'm ready for this baby to get here."

"Just two more weeks, babe. Two more weeks."

"Yeah. And then my breasts will hurt from feedings. I'll get even less sleep than I get now. And I'll lose my arms from holding a baby all the time."

I laugh softly through my nose. She's trying hard to be excited about the baby, and I know once he or she gets here, Greer will be okay. She'll love our child no matter what. The anticipation of what life will be like is making her terribly anxious. And hormones have made her seriously grumpy. But at least she's relaxed a bit about our chances of genetic abnormalities. No, we don't have all information yet. Hell, we don't even know the gender. But nothing on the ultrasounds or in the blood tests have indicated any problems so far. For that, we're grateful.

Oli ambles through the room, also headed for the coffee maker, if I had to guess. He's been doing a great job of going to work every day. He's still supervised closely, and he likely always will be. But with the exception of troubleshooting, he does a pretty good job as a dairy farm hand. When he's not working, he gets his fill playing with the animals and feeding them all their favorite treats. Plus, he gets along with the other farm hands who are really good to him.

It's been nice seeing him blossom, and I can only imagine he'll do even better once he gets used to living in the bunk house.

"Don't forget your medicine," I call out to him. He holds up the medication bottle and flashes it at me in response.

Looking at Greer, who might be dozing off while I make circles on her stomach, I can't help but think how beautiful she is like this. I can't believe a year ago we were getting ready to meet for the first time. Talk about a whirlwind romance.

I wouldn't do anything differently, though. Not one single thing.

Leaning over, I whisper, "Gotta go, baby. Why don't you get back in bed?"

She shakes her head and opens her eyes. "You know I won't sleep. Afternoon naps seem to work best these days."

"Okay. But promise me you'll rest today." She nods, and I kiss her gently on the lips before leaving for the day.

Several hours go by, and it's turning out to be a normal day. Milk cows, muck stalls, fix fences. It's all fairly redundant.

The most interesting part is the phone call I got from Mrs. Johnson regarding the new school year which starts next week and how many students we can expect. We only have three so far. I'm surprised by how few will be coming out, but it seems to come in waves. We had a few kids roll out of the program last year, so I'm not shocked.

The other fun has been watching the temperature gauge hit one hundred seven for the fourth day. We've been taking bets on how many days in a row it'll be this hot before a "cool front" knocks it back to ninety.

I'm glad to be going home for lunch just to get out of this heat. I'm also glad to be checking on my wife. The closer we get to "go time" the more worried I get. And for some reason, this morning didn't sit well with me.

Closing the door behind me when I walk in, I take a split second to stop and enjoy the air conditioning. It's this moment that I hear her on the phone.

"I can't really tell if they're consistent or not," Greer says. "I'll have a mild pain for about a minute, then another one three minutes later, then I'll have a big one three minutes after that. That cycle has been going on for several hours."

She's been timing contractions for hours?

Racing into her office, I find her sitting straight up in her chair, rubbing her back while she talks. She looks up briefly when she sees me walk in but doesn't address me.

"Uh huh. How soon do you want to see me?" Her eyes widen, I assume at the answer she's given. "Oh. Okay. Well it's going to be a little bit. I need my sister-in-law to come out to stay with the kids."

That's my cue to start texting people, starting with Pedro.

Me: *Baby time. Take over.*

Pedro: *What? Right now? She's not due for two weeks!*

Me: *You think babies care about that? Take over! And watch Oli for me!*

"Julie!" I yell and race to the staircase leading to her room. "Julie! I have to take your mom to the hospital!"

The only response I hear is her racing down the stairs. "Is it time?" Her eyes are wide, and I can tell she's trying to balance excitement with fear.

"I think so. Pedro is going to watch after Oli, but can you hang out until your aunt and uncle get here? I could drop you at the main house and you can stay with Brittany for a while."

"Yeah sure," she says quietly, then adds, "She's gonna be okay, right?"

I tamper down my desire to race back to Greer and throw her in the car, instead focusing on my step-daughter who is battling her own emotions. "She's going to be fine. She's probably calmer than I am right now. In fact, maybe we should be worried about me passing out. I've never done this before. At least she knows what to expect."

That rewards me with a smile, and I know I said exactly what she needed to hear.

"Well before you go, you may want to shower," Julie advises. "You stink like cows, and I doubt the first thing my new sibling wants to smell when he or she is born is farm crud."

Taking a whiff of myself, I realize she's right. If we're going to be at the hospital for the rest of the day and all night, I need to clean up.

Racing to the shower, I refuse to stop and enjoy the three shower heads I had installed as an over-the-top luxury for myself. It does wonders to help relieve my muscles after a fourteen-hour day, but this time, I take the world's fastest shower instead. We have somewhere to be.

Faster than I clean up, I throw clean clothes on and race out the bedroom door, still pulling my T-shirt over my head. Somehow, in the thirty seconds it took to shower, my house has become a hub of activity.

Julie is eyeing Greer curiously, while Oli is asking all kinds of questions about what's going to happen at the hospital. And Pedro is tracking dirt on my floor, pacing the room.

I try to ignore all of them, instead going straight to my wife. "You ready to go or do you need to do anything first?"

Surprise is written all over her face. "Oh. I didn't realize you knew they said to come in."

"I overheard you on the phone. Three minutes apart, right?"

She smiles at me and grabs my hand. "Yeah, but it's weird. It's definitely a pattern, but it's not the kind of pattern they tell you to watch for. I'd honestly think it was Braxton-Hicks except for the fact that it's been going on for so long. Maybe we should wait."

I shake my head vehemently. "No. No way. Babe, you are pale and something feels different. I can't put my finger on it, but I really think they're right."

She sighs heavily. "Okay. Let's get checked out. But Ace"—she looks me dead in the eye as I pull her to a stand— "if Pedro even thinks he's coming with us, I will drive a stake through his heart. I'm not doing another delivery with him there."

A hearty laugh breaks free from my chest. "I'll get rid of him. Why don't you start waddling to the car?"

"Har, har, very funny." But she complies and once again, I'm glad this is almost over. One hand is under her belly, holding it up to alleviate some of the pressure from her back. The other is running against the wall, like she can hardly stand up. I gesture for Julie to walk with her while I approach the men standing around doing nothing.

"Pedro."

He rushes to me. "What do you need. Water? Towels? A car seat?"

I roll my eyes. "Yeah, we're not doing this again. What I need is for you to head back to the barn with Oli and run things."

"Are you sure? I'm here to support you, brother, just like you did me."

I clap my hand on his shoulder. "I know. And I appreciate it. But after last time, I'm pretty sure my wife wants nothing to do with you. Oli, however, really needs you to stay calm and help him finish up all his work. Besides, the hospital might send us home."

I know deep down in my gut there's no way we're coming home without a baby, but I'm not about to share that information with the two guys that are likely to freak out. Shuffling them out the front door with a wave goodbye, I watch until they safely drive away, then clamor into my own vehicle.

Greer's eyes are closed and she's breathing deeply, obviously in the middle of a contraction. Grabbing her hand, I encourage her to squeeze as tight as she can.

"I got you, babe. I got you."

Within seconds, her eyes are open and she's smiling at me. "It's painful, but not as painful as labor should be. I'm telling you, it would not surprise me at all if they send us home."

I disagree, but I'm not going to tell her that. I may not have a ton of experience with this kind of thing, but I'd also be a fool to have any form of opinion at all right now. She's already threatened Pedro's life. I'm sure mine is next.

We drop Julie off at the main house where Brittany is doing all her daily cooking for the staff, then head straight to the hospital. Fortunately, the drive is only about twenty minutes, but I swear Greer's pain level increases ten-fold in that time. By the time we park and get to triage, she's stopping every few minutes to grip my hand. All I can do is rub her back and not scream out in my own pain when it feels like my fingers are breaking.

And this is only the beginning.

"Name?" a bubbly nurse asks. She's too bubbly in my opinion. Can't she see my wife is in pain?

"Greer Whitman." Greer leans against the counter, not actually looking at the nurse. "I think my doctor's office called and gave you a heads-up."

"Oh yes. They did. You know Dr. Haam is on vacation, right?"

Greer nods, while I bellow, "What?"

She blows out a breath, still shifting around from discomfort. "I didn't tell you?"

"Uh, no."

"They told me a couple weeks ago when I made my last appointment. We actually joked that baby would come this week because, isn't that always the way?"

"What do we do now?" Honestly, I have no idea. Any time our vet has been on vacation when one of the bessies give birth, we just do our best and hope for a good outcome. Somewhere in my brain, I know that's not what's going to happen here, but it still doesn't keep me from wondering what the hell we're going to do instead.

"Don't worry," the nurse says, as she lays some paperwork on the counter for us to fill out. "Dr. Ruiz is here today. He's covering all of Dr. Haam's patients. Now fill this out please."

The good news is, we have a doctor. The bad news is, they won't give us a room until all the paperwork is filled out and processed, because of course our due date isn't for a couple weeks so we haven't pre-registered yet.

So we wait. And wait. And wait some more.

Some of the time, Greer is pacing, holding her hand on her back. Some of the time, she's standing, leaning on my shoulders for support as I encourage her to breathe. Just when I think we're about to have this baby on the floor of the hallway, they shuffle us into a room. I don't know if it's to triage her or for delivery. Hell, it could be both. Either way, I'm grateful she finally has a bed to lie down on, even if the first thing they do is check her cervix and declare her officially in labor, which doesn't help her pain levels at all.

"You okay?" I ask, when everyone finally leaves the room, satisfied they have a few minutes to get ready. I hold her hand and kiss her knuckles. She looks tired, and I wish more than anything I could trade places with her. I feel helpless.

She runs her fingers through my hair and closes her eyes. "It's weird because it hurts, but it doesn't hurt much more than it has for the last two months. Just more localized, maybe?

You know, I'm still not sure about getting an epidural because I don't think the drugs are the best for the baby, and if this is as bad as it's going to get, I think I'll be okay without it."

"Whatever you want, baby. Whatever you need."

We rest like this for a while, me holding her hand, only knowing contractions are happening when she squeezes my hand tightly. Finally, the door opens and a couple people, including the first nurse we spoke to come in.

"There's our patient!" A tall man with dark, curly hair swaggers forward. He's got a slight accent and a big smile on his face. "I'm Dr. Ruiz, and if these contractions keep happening, I'm going to be delivering your baby today." He shakes both our hands then washes them and grabs gloves. "I know the nurse checked you when you first got here and you were dilated to about a three."

Sitting down, he situates the blankets around Greer's legs and pushes his hand between them. She grimaces but doesn't make a sound.

"Oh wow. You're already at a six in what, about thirty minutes? If you want an epidural, we need to get one right now before it's too late."

Greer's eyes widen, and I can tell she's bewildered by how fast this is happening. "I was thinking about going without it. Especially if I'm already a six. Is there any reason I need one? Since I'm having a vbac?"

"That's totally up to you." Dr. Ruiz snaps off the gloves and tosses them into the trash. "There really is no medical reason why an epidural would make it safer to delivery vaginally after a cesarean. Especially since it was so many years ago. Really, the epidural is up to you."

"I, um." She looks at me but I don't have any answers for

her. It's her body. I can't decide this. I can only support her. "I really am afraid it's going to get worse, and I'll be stuck without it."

Tucking her hair behind her ears I give her the only answer I can think of. "Babe, it's fine if you want the epidural. If you'll be able to get a couple hours of sleep, it might be worth it."

She relaxes, like a load has been lifted off her shoulders. Then turning to Dr. Ruiz she says, "I haven't slept in weeks. I think I need the epidural."

He nods and the nurse immediately picks up a phone and makes a call. I assume to have the anesthesiologist paged.

"Well, Mr. and Mrs. Whitman, settle in," he says, as he turns toward the door. "Looks like you're about to add a new member to your family."

His words hit me harder than I anticipated they would. I've had months to prepare for this. Months to get used to it. But suddenly the crib set up in the little nursery and the swing in her office have new meaning. The high chair in the corner of the kitchen has a real purpose. The car seat still in the box in the back seat of my truck is about to be installed.

August nineteenth is about to be the best day of my life.

Well, second best.

Okay fine. Top two.

I look at my wife, my beautiful, exhausted wife, and whisper, "We're gonna have a baby."

She laughs and then grimaces, squeezing my hand tightly.

Chapter Twelve

Greer

"**I** TOLD THEM IT WASN'T WORKING!"

I don't mean to scream at my nurse, but seriously. I told the anesthesiologist the epidural shot too far to the left. He said in his hoity-toity-I'm-the-doc-so-I-know-more-than-you voice it looked straight from his angle. Never mind that I *felt* the medicine run to the left side. Oh no. I was wrong, even when my left side numbed, leaving my right side to feel everything. All the contractions. All the pain. All of it.

It probably wouldn't be as bad if it was everywhere, but it is the strangest feeling to have one side of your body numb and the other side clearly embroiled in some sort of wrestling match with all my insides being used as a giant pincushion.

I tried to explain that to my fucking nurse. All she did was roll me to my right side because "Sometimes gravity will make the medicine work better."

Snotty little bitch. Not only did it not work, now it's too late to fix it because I'm nine-and-a-half centimeters dilated.

"I'm sorry, Greer," my new, not so snotty, nurse says. "If I had known the epidural was only working on one side, I would have paged him hours ago."

"I know you would have. Because you're a good nurse." I situate myself as I wait for the next contraction. They're coming frequently now. "And you aren't texting your fucking boyfriend while I'm dying!" I bellow as another contraction hits.

Ace grabs my hand again and tries to remind me to breathe. At least he does until I give him the dirtiest look I can muster. I must look like a cross between Beelzebub and Charles Manson because he shuts the hell up.

"She was texting?" my nurse asks in horror.

As soon as I can relax I respond. "Oh yeah. I was hoping it was a hospital app or something to keep track of patient information, but I'm going to say by the look on your face it wasn't."

She clears her throat and looks away. I didn't mean to put her on the spot. I'm sure there's nothing worse than hospital politics, and I don't want to put her in the position of having to decide if she needs to turn her co-worker in or just ignore it. Well she doesn't have to worry. I'll be calling the patient advocate after this shit-show and letting them know all about it.

Assuming I still give a shit after the baby is born. Once the pain goes away, I might be on cloud nine and not care. Who knows. Right now, I'm going to use my anger to fuel this delivery.

The door flies open and Dr. Ruiz swaggers in again, still smiling, making me want to punch his lights out. "Greer! I hear it's about time to push. Are you ready to meet your baby?"

"No," I snip. "But if you could get both sides of my body

working together that would be great."

He looks over at my nurse, who's name I never bothered to get because I don't. fucking. care right now, and all she says is: "The epidural is only working on the left side."

Understanding crosses his face and he nods as he finishes washing his hands and whatever the hell else he does while I'm writhing in pain *again*.

The really great part of the epidural experience, and by great, I mean shitty, is on top of still feeling the contractions, labor slowed down significantly, with almost no pain relief at all. I went from three centimeters dilated to six in thirty minutes. *Five hours* after they gave me half an epidural, I still haven't slept a wink because of pain, but I'm finally ready to push.

I bet they're going to charge me for the whole thing too. Bastards. I'll never get another epidural in my life. Ever.

"Okay, let's have a baby," Dr. Ruiz says. Ace situates himself next to my head because who wants to see *that?* "Push, Greer."

I bear down as hard as I can and push with all my might. When I finally stop, I look down at Dr. Ruiz who has the strangest expression on his face.

"Um, were you pushing?"

I cock my head. "Yeah."

"Huh," he responds, truly perplexed. "Well sometimes when an epidural only works partially it makes it hard for the muscles to work together."

Fuck my life. Of course, this would happen to me.

"Let's try it again. Here."

The nurse rolls a huge mirror down to the edge of the bed and now Ace and I both can see me in all my glory.

Oh joy.

I'm never getting sex again after this. I just know it.

"Sometimes when you can see what you're doing, the brain catches on better," Dr. Ruiz explains. "Let's push again, only this time watch the mirror, okay?"

"Don't you dare look in that mirror," I growl to my husband, who starts laughing.

"And miss watching my baby being born? Not on your life."

Asshole.

Oddly, watching in the mirror seems to work and within minutes, I'm seeing hair between my legs. And not my own, thank goodness. No, this is my baby's hair. *How weird is that?*

"There's the baby!" Dr. Ruiz exclaims. "Would you like to touch your baby? Just reach right down there and feel your baby's hair." He shows me exactly what he's talking about by doing it himself, which is possibly the weirdest thing I've ever seen in my life. Who ever expects to see some man reaching between your naked legs to pet your baby as it comes out?

And yet, I'm fascinated. So, I follow his advice and do exactly as he did. "Ace. Ace that's our baby's hair! It's soft. Oh wow."

The words are no more out of my mouth than another contraction happens and I have to bear down. This one feels different though.

"Oh shit!" I yell, eyes closed tightly. "There's that ring of fire thing they always talk about!"

The room erupts in laughter, because my privates burning is *so funny*. But when I look down again, there is a head.

I think.

It's so squished it actually looks more like a brain. My

heart beats faster and my breathing catches.

"Oh god, is that my baby's brain? Where is her head?"

Dr. Ruiz chuckles again and for a split second, I consider taking my leg out of the stirrups to kick him in the face. But that would squish my baby even more, so I don't.

"It's a very tight squeeze," he reassures. "But I promise that's the baby's head right there."

I relax at his words, although I'm still agitated for many, many other reasons. "Oh. Okay. As long as she's okay."

"You still think it's a girl?" Ace asks, a chuckle in his voice.

I turn my head to look him right in the eyes. "A mother always knows."

The next few minutes go so fast, I can barely keep up. One second, I feel like I have for the last several months and the next, all this pressure I didn't realize was there is released from my lower half, and I'm pulling a baby to my chest.

"It's a girl!" Dr. Ruiz shouts and continues doing whatever it is he does down there in my nether regions.

I look at my husband who has tears cascading down his face. "It's a girl, Greer. We have a daughter." He kisses me softly, then turns all his attention to her and rubbing his finger down her soft cheek.

I take this moment to look at her for the first time and really observe. Her face is squinched and she's making the same scowl Oli makes when he's mad. Her nose is a little too big for her face, and if I didn't know better, I'd think she was an old man.

Kissing the top of her head, I coo, "You are so stinking ugly. And I love you so, so much."

At that exact moment, just as I predicted all those months

ago, my heart explodes with the love I have for my little old woman baby.

"Hey, look at this!" Dr. Ruiz suddenly exclaims. "No wonder you looked like you were having twins. This is the best looking placenta I've ever seen!"

He holds it up to show us and sure enough it's the same size as the baby I'm holding.

Looking back down at her, I add, "And I'm never, ever doing this again."

***

There were a few scary moments after the baby was first born. Her APGAR scores seemed fine, but she wasn't making any noise. I didn't realize, until the NICU pediatrician walked in, how serious the situation was. But the second he put a stethoscope to her chest, she let out a wail to rival all the other babies on the floor.

It appears she got the same stubborn gene as my other kids, refusing to do what she's supposed to until the last second.

Other than that, she was quickly deemed in good health. No distinct features of Down Syndrome or any other genetic abnormalities, and I reminded them multiple times to not write anything off. But nope. Despite my fears, it seems we're in the clear, much to my relief.

Finally having a baby out of my body instead of inside it, is also a sweet victory. Seriously. Pregnancy at forty is not for the weak-minded.

"How are you feeling?" Ace asks, although I'm not sure he can really hear anything beyond the beating of his own heart. He's been holding our daughter since the nurses cleaned her up and handed her over. He's wrapped around her little finger already.

"Honestly, like I could run a marathon."

He looks over at me from his perch at the edge of my bed and furrows his brow.

Well, lookie there. He actually is paying attention.

"What do you mean?"

I lean back on my bed slowly, trying to be mindful of the three stitches I have down below. I make a mental note to ask Brittany to make some of those icy maxi pads. I'd bet money she has a recipe for them.

"I knew I felt bad for the last few months, but I must have gotten used to it. Except for this whole thing," I gesture to the lower half of my body, "I feel good. It's almost like I had a low-grade fever and it's finally gone. I really should take advantage of this energy and work a bit."

Ace nixes that idea quickly. "Uh, no. You haven't slept in weeks. You need to rest while you can."

I open my mouth to argue, but a knock at the door stops me.

"Can we come in?" Brittany pops her head in the door, making sure the coast is clear.

I wave her in. "Did you bring the kids with you?"

She pushes the door open wider and sure enough, there is the rest of my family.

Wow. That's surreal to say. In just a year's time, our little family of three has increased to five, plus more extended family. I never ever saw that coming when I was packing the moving van in Kansas.

"Mom!" Oli yells and barrels toward the bed to give me a

hug. I have to hand it to my boy—as defiant as he can be, the thing he hates more than anything is to see someone he loves in pain. I'm sure knowing I was in the hospital but not knowing if I was okay was hard on him.

"Hey buddy." I kiss him on the top of the head. "Ooh. You smell good. Did Pedro let you borrow his Axe spray?"

Oli smiles up at me. "No. Phillip did. He said I needed to smell my best for the baby. Is it a boy or a girl?"

I chuckle at his candor. "It's a girl. You have a sister."

"Aw man."

A look of disappointment crosses his face but is replaced by curiosity when he sees Ace sit down on the couch, still holding the tiny bundle. Julie sits on one side of him, stroking the baby's cheek, staring at her new sister in awe.

Brittany approaches and hands me a bag. "Pedro wanted to come but I made him stay home. I convinced him Nio couldn't be here, but really I was saving him from imminent death if he did something stupid."

I can't help but laugh. Brittany loves Pedro with everything in her, but she's also no fool. She knows he's a handful. Frankly, I think he plays it up sometimes because he likes getting her agitated. It's their "thing."

"Also, I found this recipe before Nio was born and swear by these things."

Peeking my head in the bag, I squeal in delight. Sure enough, she brought me frozen maxi pads. "Yay! I was just thinking about needing these! Thank you! You really know how to please a girl."

She laughs and gives me a hug. "If we're going to live on this farm and survive with all these men, we've gotta have each other's back."

"Don't I know it."

"Hey, Mom," Oli calls, now sitting on the other side of Ace, touching the baby's foot. I've never seen a look of amazement on his face quite like the one he's sporting now. "What's the baby's name?"

Ace looks up at me and shrugs. We've been debating, but still haven't come up with something that sounds right. We have a lot of names we like, but they don't seem to fit.

"I don't know, buddy. We haven't decided yet."

He looks back down at her and smiles. "I think you should call her Grace."

My lips quirk up in a smile. "Yeah? How come?"

"My mom's name is Greer and my dad's name is Ace," he explains. "When you put them together, it's Grace."

My eyes snap up to Ace's.

Grace.

It seems to be the running theme in our family. Grace for our mistakes. Grace for our insecurities. Grace for our failures. Grace is what I give my brother when he's a jerk. Grace is what Ace gives me when I shut down. Grace is what Julie gives Oli when he has a meltdown.

Grace is what keeps our family together.

And this little bundle is what cemented us together permanently.

Ace blinks a few times as he wraps his brain around this idea.

"Grace Whitman," he breathes. "I think that's just about right."

I agree wholeheartedly.

She's our little saving Grace. And she's amazing.

Epilogue

Greer

"Run, Grace, run!" Ace yells over shouts of all the other parents. "No not that way! Run to second base. No not back to first base, run over there!"

Pedro stands next to second base, waving Grace to him, but she's having none of it. There is a dandelion in the middle of the infield and she is running straight to it.

Brittany and I are laughing so hard, we're trying not to pee in our seats. Because seriously, there is nothing funnier than watching three-year-olds play t-ball. Expect maybe watching our husbands try to coach it. It's like children leading children.

Grace finally gets her flower and walks calmly over to Pedro who has his hands on his hips and is shaking his head. I'm not sure how the men didn't anticipate her distraction. She loves the wild flowers on the farm as much as her mama does, so it should be no surprise she had to pick it before playing ball.

Wiping our eyes of tears, Brittany and I refocus our attention on the field.

"Let's go, Nio," she yells happily, rubbing her swollen belly. Baby number two will be here any day and she looks fantastic. No swollen ankles or pain. She's one of those "happy" pregnant women who has the glow that's not made from sweat. I would roll my eyes about how much she enjoys being pregnant, but my shop is closed so she can do it all she wants.

We watch as Nio struts up to the plate, using the same swagger I've seen on his dad before. The kid is the spitting image of his father, except with blond hair and blue eyes. The contrast is striking, and we've had more than one conversation between the four of us that these two toddlers are never allowed to date.

Nope. The second hormones kick in, we're all going to sit down for a long, honest conversation.

Not that it'll do any good. Nio already has a huge crush on Grace, who doesn't give him the time of day. We all know that means he'll be eating out of her hand by the time they're in high school. Heaven help us all.

As Ace balances the ball on the tee, Nio gets in position.

"Okay, bud. Go for it," my husband says, and Nio takes a swing.

He misses and spins around a few times before falling over in the dirt.

Brittany and I start laughing again, trying to muffle it behind our hands but it's just so hard.

Once Ace helps him wipe the dirt off his pants, Nio gets in position again and swings.

"THWAK!" The ball ricochets off the bat and flies through the air, surprising all of us, including several tiny kids in the outfield who are startled when it lands in the grass.

Then the race is on.

Nio runs for third base while Ace tries to get his attention, four kids clamor for the ball, three of them end up crying when one of them gets it. That kid throws as hard as he can and the ball nails another kid on the back of the head, knocking him to the ground as his too big helmet falls off.

I look over and thankfully, Julie has her phone up, recording the whole thing. No doubt it will end up on social media later, and I'm glad. This debacle needs to be seen by the masses.

Finally, and unfortunately for us, the official umpire (some kid Julie graduated with who works for the YMCA part time) calls time and the game is over.

Parents collect their chairs and their kids, heading for their cars, all praising their kiddos for a job well done.

Or to post their own videos. Who knows? I just hope I get tagged in anything that ends up on social media. I may hate that Brittany loves being pregnant, but I'm thrilled we'll get to do this again in three more years.

"Great game, babe." I flash a smile at my man and give him a big smooch.

"Uh huh," he deadpans. "You're biased because you have a thing for the coach."

I gasp. "I would never flirt with Pedro!"

He slaps me on the ass, making me squeal, then picks up the chair, now safely in its carry case, and throws it over his shoulder.

"I did good, Mama!" Grace announces, grabbing my hand with the one not holding the now wilted dandelion.

"You did, baby girl. And Julie has it all on video!"

Grace's eyes widen, and she lets go of my hand to race toward her sister. Those two are thick as thieves. It's a good thing too. I don't see Julie moving out any time soon.

I sigh. Julie has had a rough go of it. She's getting herself on track, but it's taking time. I'm grateful to the guys on the farm for giving her a safe place to land. They look out for her and take care of her like a bunch of big brothers. I know it's helped.

But I also know the struggles she has are temporary, and because of it, I need to let the chips fall where they may. I'm grateful she has such a huge support system. Just like I'm grateful for the fact that Grace is a perfectly normal, healthy baby girl.

Don't get me wrong, the relief I have felt over the years isn't in having a perfect baby. Because she isn't any more perfect than either of the other kids. She's a tiny little human who will grow up to present her own flaws, have her own ideas, have her own opinions. She will make her own choices, like picking flowers in the middle of t-ball. Because that's what babies are—little humans. We can't figure out what most of their opinions are until they're older.

And I know full well what it's like to love a child with a disability. So does Ace. If any couple had been equipped to handle it, should Grace have had issues, it's us. We understand there is perfection in imperfection.

No, the relief was in the fact that at that moment in time, we didn't have any additional stress beyond normal newborn stuff. Even three years later, we are acutely aware that things could change in an instant, though. Illnesses happens. Accidents happen. Crimes even happen. There are absolutely no guarantees.

But knowing that firsthand is what makes the small victories, like perfect APGAR scores and testing negative for genetic abnormalities, a little sweeter.

It's what makes days like today when all three of my kids, my husband, and our closest friends are celebrating the milestones of our children, that much more special.

It's what makes the drive to the nearest Culver's for frozen yogurt because my husband is a sucker for making his little girl happy, that much more fun.

Life has no guarantees. But if you can look beyond that to find the joy, even through the difficulties, well… it can be pretty sweet. Some might even call it amazing.

I know I do.

The End

Interested in learning more about Julie?
Her story is coming soon in a #MyNewLife
Young Adult Romantic Comedy!

Acknowledgements

It takes a village to raise a book baby from the ground up. Probably more for me than for most! While I have learned to embrace my hotmessness, it still means other people have to help me out. I'm so, so grateful to them for always helping me at the last minute and never complaining about what a pain in the ass I am. You guys are way better people than me.

Andrea Johnston for talking out plot twists and dialogue, and for putting up with my general moodiness when I got close to the end. It's a wonder you stick with me.

Kate Spitzer for picking up all kinds of slack and cheering me on. Who knew a random night at a bar would turn into a long-lasting friendship and fun!

Marisol Scott for making me laugh every day with her sarcasm, and for running my group when I'm freaking out of over deadlines. Which is basically always. Oh! And also for the farming compliance information! And let's not forget Debra Winger. HA! That was classic.

Amber Higbie for reminding me that not everyone has lived "in the bubble" for way too long. And for not being afraid to tell me what she hates so we can figure out how to fix it. The stockholders of Kleenex also thank you. I'M KIDDING! Maybe.

Erin Noelle for always pushing me to be a better technical writer. You "get" me and my writing. None of these books would be half as good if you hadn't come along.

Karen Lawson for cleaning up my errors, but maybe more importantly, for cheering me on from the beginning. I'm so grateful there are women like you in this community… who see the good in authors and push us to be the best we can be. You're a role model and I think I wanna be you when I grow up.

Amelié Vahle for those last-minute eagle eyes before the finishing touches are put on. Finally getting to hug you in person has been one of the highlights of this year. You are more dynamic in person than you are online. And that's saying a lot.

Alyssa Garcia for this amazing cover. Isn't it beautiful? But even more than that, your advice and guidance as I venture into other areas of publishing has been priceless. There are no words of thanks that will ever be enough.

Julie Titus for multiple things. 1) Formatting. 2) Keeping an accurate calendar for those of us who get it wrong frequently. 3) Never being upset when certain people freak out about deadlines. 4) Always responding even when certain people ask about dates. Again. 5) Changing dates and flexing and just generally being a compassionate and understanding person full of grace while some of us freak the fuck out regularly. 6) Not firing me as your client yet.

Allison because if I don't put her name in the back of a book, she'll stop letting my kid spend the night. Please don't make me go to the beach again.

Dad for being the expert on dairy farming. He grew up on a dairy farm and was able to give me the ins and outs of certain aspects. Ace's farmhouse is actually reminiscent of the farmhouse he grew up in. I still miss that place. But at least it's now immortalized in a book for my kids to enjoy someday.

Carter's Cheerleaders for being the best group on Facebook. You all have become true friends to me. Not everyone can say that. So thank you for all the entertainment you provide! Even when you're sarcastic and making fun of me. Assholes.

The Walk for breathing life into my soul every single day. I cannot even express what you all mean to me. And yes, I will continue to cry every time I hug one of you. Every. Time.

Thank you, Lord, for loving me even in my hotmessness.

About the Author

Mother, reader, storyteller—ME Carter never set out to write books. But when a friend practically forced a copy of Twilight into her hands, the love of the written word she had lost as a child was rekindled. With a story always rolling around in her head, it should come as no surprise that she finally started putting them on paper. She lives in Texas with her four children, Mary, Elizabeth, Carter and Bug, who sadly was born long after her pen name was created, and will probably need extensive therapy because of it.

You can follow her on Facebook at
https://www.facebook.com/authorMECarter,
on Twitter at https://twitter.com/AuthorMECarter,
Instagram at
https://www.instagram.com/authormecarter/?hl=en
or email her at AuthorMECarter@gmail.com

Other Titles by M.E. Carter

Hart Series

Change of Hart
Hart to Heart
Matters of the Hart

Texas Mutiny Series

Juked
Groupie
Goalie
Megged

#MyNewLife Series

Getting a Grip
Balance Check
Pride & Joie
Amazing Grayson

9 781948 852104